RISKS AND WHISKEY

DANI MCLEAN

SET THE MOOD PUBLISHING

RISKS
&
WHISKEY

DANI MCLEAN

RISKS & WHISKEY

Book 3 of The Cocktail Series

Copyright © 2022 by Dani McLean

First edition: March 2022

Ebook ISBN: 9780645162448

Print ISBN: 9780645162455

www.danimclean.com

Cover Design by Bailey Designs Books

Edited by Beth Lawson at VB Edits

Author photo by Rachael Munro Photography

ALSO BY DANI MCLEAN

The Movie Magic Novella Series:

Midnight, Repeated

Not My Love Story

A Missing Connection

It Has To Be You

The Forces of Love - Out July 2023

***

The Cocktail Series:

Love & Rum

Sex & Sours

Risks & Whiskey

To my family.
Related or found.
Future & past.

PROLOGUE
WES

Eighteen Months Ago

"NOW, fake left, grab my arm, and use the momentum to throw me over your shoulder." Chanel tapped my right knee with her staff. "Remember to lift your heel before you twist." She stepped back, resumed the attack position, and smiled. "And this time, stop holding back."

I laughed. "I'm respecting my elders."

"I'm only your elder because you look like you should be in kindergarten."

I twirled my matching weapon, moving my weight to my front foot. "Well, this kindergartener is about to kick your ass."

Chanel had been a stunt performer for years, and as stunt coordinator, had the unenviable job of making it look like I *could* kick someone's ass. At six foot two, I towered over my co-stars, but keeping up with Chanel's fancy footwork meant pushing myself harder than most.

We moved through the actions, faster this time, our

footsteps light on the tactical mat. When she rushed forward to strike, I grabbed her arm and twisted. To the camera, it would look like I had thrown her over my shoulder, but in reality, we worked in conjunction, Chanel jumping into the lift, rolling, and landing safely on the mat as I thrust a false blade at her throat.

She smiled up at me. "Perfect!"

I pulled my prop staff back and stood, returning her smile. There were a few different fight choreographers working on the show, but Chanel was one of my favorites. She was precise, and occasionally stern, but also extremely knowledgeable and, thankfully for me, patient.

"You're a good teacher."

She swung her long dark braid back over her shoulder. "We'll see." With a quick nod to the two stunt men watching on the sidelines, she took her original position. "Ready for the full sequence?"

I stepped back with my right foot, keeping the weight in my left, as Toby and Marcus picked up their staffs and took their spots behind me, ready to strike. My blood raced like electricity in my veins. I lived for this shit.

Goddamn. There were exactly two things I loved in life, and this job was one of them.

Leading off my back foot, I stepped, ducked, swung—moving in time with all three of them as we traded blows. I twisted Chanel over my shoulder, then Toby knocked my knees out with a kick. Block, twist, lunge.

It ended with my favorite move of the sequence—a one-two stab to my right to take down Marcus before spinning the staff around my neck to skewer Toby on my left.

I'd practiced the neck wrap probably a hundred times,

and it never stopped looking cool. Especially now that I was in full costume, ready to film it.

Some actors thought it was ridiculous to dress up and fight bad guys for a living, but I didn't.

Bryson, the showrunner and our fearless leader here on *The Guild*, called out soon after, and then it was showtime. Chanel gave me a thumbs-up, and I felt my adrenaline rising again.

I sidled up alongside my co-star and buddy, Jackson, who was getting a last minute once-over by makeup. One of the costuming assistants was on me in seconds, straightening my collar and brushing off dust.

People weaved around each other, adjusting lights, calling out instructions, moving cameras into place. If it took a village to raise a kid, it took an army to film a TV show.

"Looking good, J."

Jackson smiled as best as he could while not disturbing the hand reapplying foundation. He'd already spent the last hour shooting a scene with the show's resident damsel and the bright star of our little trio, Olivia.

"How did this morning go?"

It wasn't the question I wanted to ask. I wanted to know Liv was okay. Today marked two years without her mom, and I knew it wouldn't be easy for her.

Freed from his touch-up, Jackson nodded. "Good, I think. Bryson wants to go over his notes for this afternoon with you and Liv."

The ladies swapped, and now I was the one unable to speak while setting powder was reapplied. Between the harsh lighting and sweating through stunt work, this would be a regular part of the next few hours.

I didn't answer, and Jackson didn't follow up. We stood in silence until Bryson called us over. Back to it.

As we worked, I focused on lines and action, all thoughts of Liv pushed to the back of my mind.

Not gone, though. Never gone.

———

"You've got an hour for lunch, then I need you back on Lot C. That should give the crew enough time to dress the church set for your confrontation scene," Bryson said, and I knew better than to be late. He was an okay guy. Figured himself a genius and took every opportunity to remind us he was in charge, but I'd worked with worse.

Recently, he'd taken to treating me like a kid, always repeating things like I needed the reminder. I kept my expression still when he turned to me.

"Don't be late."

I winked at him. He wasn't impressed.

Bryson wasn't that much older than me—forty-two to my twenty-seven—so I didn't know what his problem was.

Yeah, he was an accomplished director and the showrunner for the most popular urban fantasy show for the teen to twenty-five audience, but it was also the show in which I played Ares, the Greek war god, Liv played a witch with premonitions and untapped power, and Jackson played an immortal detective who was tasked with keeping humans safe as part of the aforementioned "Guild." It wasn't exactly high art.

Hell, last week we'd filmed a sequence where the dream god, Morpheus, had twisted reality so that our characters thought they were pirates on the run from Blackbeard.

It was a weird show. It was also awesome.

And sue me, I get paid to look hot and play a god. Who wouldn't want that?

As soon as Bryson disappeared, Jackson was face deep in his phone, no doubt texting the woman he'd started seeing recently, Auburn or Ali or something.

I was only 80 percent jealous.

An hour wasn't enough time to leave the lot, so I stopped by craft services and shoved a BLT down. It was semi-stale, but I was starving, so I didn't care. Practicing a fight sequence for three hours would do that to a guy.

I was swallowing the last dry mouthful when Liv's melodic voice sounded behind me, and I fought to contain the way my body shivered in response.

"Wow, Wes, you look like shit."

A black cotton robe fell to her mid-thigh, covering her costume and her curves. She smiled as she tucked a piece of honey-blond hair behind her ear, the rest brushing her collarbone. Perfectly put together and as heart-stoppingly beautiful as ever.

My heart thudded. "You should see Jackson." It was barely a joke. Poor guy would need an ice bath later.

"No, I'm pretty sure you always look like that," she teased.

"Says you. I have the numbers of at least four Victoria's Secret Angels who feel differently."

"Please tell me you aren't keeping count."

When I opened my mouth, she put her hand up to stop me.

"No, don't tell me. It'll ruin dating for me."

"If you want me to ruin you, doll, you just need to ask," I said, using the endearment my character called hers. It had become something of a catchphrase, and I liked it.

"Which lucky lady was it this time?"

Someone who could never compare to you.

Liv huffed a laugh to herself. "Let me guess, you DM'd her something flirty, and she couldn't resist."

"Wouldn't you like to know?" I teased.

"Some things never change. You know, at some point, you might think about keeping them around for longer than a night. Or at least slowing down. Don't you want to find *the one*?"

I already have.

I averted my eyes. She had no idea how I felt about her, and I didn't see that changing any time soon. I had been harboring this crush for years now, and no matter what I did, no matter who warmed my bed, I still wanted her.

"Jealous, Liv?" I joked, but the joke was on me. Funny, right? That this heavenly creature would ever see me as anything more?

Liv rolled her eyes, as she always did when we joked like this, but it was half-hearted at best, and now that I was really looking, I could see the strain in her eyes, the sag of her smile.

"Hey," I started, going for casual. "I finally found *The Burbs* online. I thought I'd come by later—PJs, popcorn, and ice cream. Since today is …" I trailed off. "Maybe watching one of her favorites would help."

Her warm brown eyes disappeared behind closed lids, and I internally kicked myself. *Great work, Wes.*

"Thanks, but," Liv whispered, "I can't tonight."

I felt awful. Had it already been two years since Rebekah's death? Two years of Olivia putting on a brave face and giving her all to the show, then crying on my shoulder afterward.

Stepping closer, I reached for her hand, linking our fingers together. "How are you holding up?"

She squeezed. "Not good, but I'll keep it together until we're done."

"Liv, if you're upset, say something. If you can't do this, I'm sure Bryson can rearrange the schedule."

"I can handle it." Her words were firm, but her eyes were glassy.

It killed me to see her like this.

"I just …" Liv's voice wavered.

I couldn't stand it. I moved closer. Close enough to feel her breath ghost my cheek. When her eyes darted to my mouth, my breath hitched.

I'd only have to lean down …

Around us was a cacophony of sound. Coordinators called out directions. Production assistants loudly discussed problems that had them losing sleep this week. The pterodactyl laugh of a camera operator.

No one told you about this when you were starting out. That you'd never be alone. That the only quiet on a set was when the camera was rolling.

Under the overhead lights, Liv's eyes sparkled. Show makeup accentuated their depth and the pillow of her lips. I desperately wanted to cup her face in my hands and feel the softness of her cheeks. Everything I wanted was standing here in front of me.

All I had to do was take a risk.

The sound of my breathing was lost to the noise around us, but I felt how shaky it was. Stuttering like an engine on its last legs. My own weren't doing so well, either. They were bolted in place, and yet I knew if I made the slightest movement, I would tumble over.

My phone rang, breaking the spell. It was my mother. I barely spared a second before I sent it to voicemail.

By the time I looked up, Liv had stretched the gap between us, looking anywhere but at me.

"I better go. Bryson said he needed to tell me something about the next scene." She was gone before I could reply.

Shit. *Shit.*

I needed to fix this. I'd almost kissed her. What the hell had I been thinking?

I hadn't been thinking, obviously, and it had shocked her enough to send her running.

But I wouldn't risk our friendship on something as ridiculous as my crush. I had to talk to her.

The set was bustling when I got there, grips, set dressers, and production assistants. But no Liv.

I checked hair and makeup. Nothing.

Wardrobe—even though she'd already been in costume. Not there either.

She couldn't have gone that far.

I was ready to give up, then it hit me. *The office.* Of course.

There was every possibility I would walk in on our script supervisor pretending not to vape, but it was worth a shot. I opened the door without knocking. But it wasn't Jasper.

It was Olivia and Bryson. Kissing.

My lunch lurched as I mumbled an apology and slammed the door. I wanted to run, but my feet were stuck. Liv came out a second later, closing the door behind her. Good. I didn't think I could handle looking at Bryson's face right now.

Not when my heart was sinking to the floor. Maybe it would keep going. Just pass right on through my body, like a cement block in water, until it reached the center of the earth and could be crushed under its gravity.

"Wes, shit. What you just saw, it's ..."

"What?"

Her eyes pleaded with me, and dammit, I could feel my resolve buckling. "You can't tell anyone. It's only been a few months, and ..." Liv continued, but I'd stopped listening. *Months?*

"Wes?"

I forced a smile. I should win a damn Oscar for this performance. "Hey, of course. Not a word, I promise."

"Thank you," she said, rushing to hug me. "You're a good friend."

Strange, the way a heart could break and keep on beating.

1

LIV

New Couple Alert! Forty-two-year-old director Bryson Green was spotted tongue deep in twenty-five-year-old actress Olivia Davis. Sugar daddy inspiration or abuse of power? You tell us.

SO THIS WAS what it felt like when shit hit the fan.

I stared at the images on my tablet, blurry from the telephoto lens all paparazzi shots had, yet clear enough for me to recognize myself and the yellowish shirt Bryson had worn yesterday. It was a series, enough shots to capture the kiss I'd given him by his car, plus a few of our faces to ensure no one could deny it was us.

Two years of keeping our relationship a secret, and now it was here for the world to see. The gossips were celebrating. *Showrunner and TV star outed!*

My phone was blowing up. For sanity's sake, I'd only opened the messages from my manager, Jen. Short, panicked texts promising she was on it and to *please call me*. I breathed in. My chest fought it. What a disaster.

I wanted to talk to Wes.

But first I had to deal with my angry boyfriend.

Bryson cut an imposing figure as he slammed his fist into the wall again. I'd warn him against brutalizing my drywall, but he had the upper body strength of a toddler.

"I can't believe it. What the hell happened? The whole point of being careful was to avoid the publicity. I never wanted this. Two years, Olivia. And what? Some asshole just happens to get lucky? I call bullshit."

"What do we do?"

He let out a harsh breath. "I need to call the studio. Mike and Alicia are going to be pissed."

And like Wiley Coyote realizing one second too late that the ground had fallen out from beneath him, my stomach dropped. Shit. If Bryson was worried about the producers, we really were in trouble.

"You really think they'll be mad?"

"Of course they will!" Like it was obvious.

I hated it when he treated me like a child.

"Why did you think I wanted to keep it quiet?"

I watched from the couch as he paced, caught between wanting to stop him and wanting him to walk out the door. Wes would crack a joke and wink as he kicked Bryson to the curb, but I was holding on to the decreasing sliver of hope that we could work through this.

I just needed Bryson to calm down and listen for a minute.

"Can you stop and talk to me?"

He kept going. "This is a nightmare. How the fuck did this happen?"

I shrank farther into the couch, hoping it would swallow me up.

"It'll be okay," I ventured. Maybe if I said it out loud, it would be true. "We're two consenting adults. Mike and Alicia know that. So there's a small fire to put out. Tomorrow it'll be something else, and we'll move on."

His condescending laugh cut through me, and I blinked back tears.

"Jesus, Liv, you can't be that naïve. This is my career we're talking about."

I nodded, not mentioning that my career would also be affected by this.

Bryson huffed, a bull preparing to charge. "They'll probably say I took advantage of you."

"But you didn't."

"Tell that to TMZ!"

"Bryson—"

"Don't."

A cold snap rushed through me. This was bad. Really bad. The plane is going down and there's only one 'chute, *bad*.

He pounded on the wall again, the sound echoing. "Fuck. I can't do this right now. I have to figure out how utterly screwed I am."

I, I, I. Yesterday it had been we and us.

"Bryson, let's talk about this."

But I might as well have been invisible as Bryson continued.

"I bet it was that shit, Owens. He's been hanging on to you like a lovesick puppy since day one. Probably expecting to swoop in and save the day."

Thankfully, Bryson couldn't see the flip my heart did in

my chest. Wes wasn't lovesick for me. I waved the idea away, even as I felt my skin flush.

"That's ridiculous. Wes is my friend. I think I'd know if he felt that way."

"Then you're more blind than I've been. Fuck. I knew I should have ended this when we got sloppy." Bryson picked up his pacing again while I remained frozen in place. This was all spiraling out of control.

Our relationship hadn't been good for a while. Keeping us quiet from everyone in my life had been slowly eating away at me, but I had assumed, hoped, that if anything happened, we'd weather it.

Now I felt like Sylvester Stallone struggling to save his girlfriend at the beginning of *Cliffhanger*.

That was my relationship. One loose glove away from catapulting itself into a gorge.

I was only surprised he hadn't said, "I told you so."

"What are you saying?" I already knew his answer, but I needed to hear him say it. I'd made my bed, and if my relationship with Bryson was over, I didn't want any doubt.

"I'm saying that this mistake has lasted too long. I mean, Liv, come on." He was using the condescending "I'm older and know better" voice I hated. "Let's face it, we've been going through the motions for a while now. You see your buddy Wes more than you do me. Maybe you chose the wrong co-worker."

With that, he stormed out. I searched the area of the wall he'd been hitting, but there weren't any marks. No evidence that he'd been here at all, except for the echoes of his voice. It didn't shock me that we were over. He'd been right about us drifting apart. It was why I'd been pushing lately, dropping hints for weeks about going public. To see if we had a future.

He'd always said no. Now I knew why.

My phone buzzed, loud in the silence. I jumped, the phone call sending my heart into a frenzy. *Please be Wes.* I needed his crass jokes and irreverent grin. One reminder that I hadn't completely blown up my life.

It wasn't. "Hi, Jen."

"Finally. I've been worried. Where were you?"

Here. Facing the consequences of my actions.

I caught sight of my reflection in the television. The apartment was the epitome of sleek and modern. Aside from the gray couch, everything was white and black, polished and pristine. A study in expensive cool. Even the magazines had been carefully placed. Then there was me, ruffled hair and yesterday's shirt, looking like a piece of driftwood added to a show home to make it look rustic.

Jen, with her expertly cut bob and piercing blue eyes, had personally picked everything here. It made sense. She had impeccable taste. She'd said it was "A promise to your future success. One day, it'll be photographed." And it had been. Twice.

Most days it felt like I was squatting in someone else's house. What would it look like if it were mine?

My braid was a mess. I tugged at a strand that had escaped, twirling it around one finger. "Bryson was here. He saw the photos." He and everyone else on the internet. "We broke up." I placed the call on speaker, then opened Twitter and started doom-scrolling through the comments.

This had to qualify as a form of torture. People were *brutal.*

"I'm sorry to hear that, Liv. But I'll be honest, that's probably for the best," Jen said. "It'll hopefully minimize the impact. This isn't how I wanted to wake up this morning, but what's life without a little excitement? How are you doing?"

She barely stopped for a breath. "I've already got my assistant looking into the source, seeing if we can't buy the exclusive rights before they get too far. While she's doing that, we'll start on damage control."

I was only half listening, too caught up in the comment section. How were there so many already? Didn't people have jobs?

"How long has this been going on?"

"Can someone say daddy issues?"

"I thought he was married?"

"Guess that's one way to secure your career."

I flopped back onto the couch. Like the Wicked Witch of the East, I'd been flattened. I expected my toes to curl back and shrivel up. I wanted to talk to Wes.

"Olivia?"

"Sorry, I'm here."

Guilt twisted inside me, but the groan my stomach made was all hunger. Bryson had seen the photos before we could have breakfast, and after that, I'd lost my appetite. Now I was craving a stack of pancakes. Maybe a hot chocolate. With extra marshmallows.

Five years ago, Jen had taken on a wide-eyed nineteen-year-old with dreams of being an actress. She must be regretting it now.

Jen had been the reason I'd gotten the role of Meira all those years ago. It had been my first official acting job and her first big break as a talent manager. When my mom's cancer diagnosis arrived midway through season one of the show, I'd gone straight to Jen to ask for her help.

She'd been great. I didn't know what a typical talent manager would do in that situation, but Jen had gotten the producers to agree to film around my visits home, allowing me to spend as much time with my mom as I could.

She'd passed a few short weeks before the finale. If Jen hadn't fought for me, I wouldn't have seen mom at all before she died.

I owed her. She deserved better than this.

"Sorry, I'm here. What should I do?"

"Don't go outside."

I almost laughed. That was the last thing I wanted to do.

Jen didn't wait for my response. "I'm on my way to the office. It'll be easier for me to work from there. I'll call the network. Try to get ahead of this. Keep your phone close but stay off the internet."

Embarrassed, I closed the Twitter app.

"And don't answer any calls that aren't me. I'll write up a statement and send it out on your behalf." The call ended, abruptly throwing me back into silence.

I pulled a pillow out of the careful arrangement and hugged it to my chest. The foam was stiff. Everything in the apartment was built for style over substance. But Wes had rested on it the other night when *Titanic* had passed the three-hour mark, and the crisp smell of his shampoo was comforting.

My heart jumped as a key turned in the lock. *Please be him.* There was only one person I wanted to see right now. Even if Bryson had turned around to apologize, I didn't want to hear it. He could take his smug, self-satisfied face and ugly leprechaun tattoo and find someone else to feed his ego.

I shouldn't have worried. Footsteps approached, light and familiar. I took a deep breath and dropped my shoulders. You know that moment in *The Wedding Singer* when Julia hears Robbie singing to her on the plane, and she can't see him yet, but she knows it's him? I recognized Wes' light, dancing tread. I didn't need to see the mop of loose, dark curls in the TV's reflection to know he was here.

"Hey, doll," he drawled, a line and a habit he'd picked up from his character. "I come bearing gifts."

He could have brought the apocalypse for all I cared. He was here. "Extra marshmallows?" I asked, eagerly taking the takeaway cup of hot chocolate.

"Is that even a question?"

Wearing a loose T-shirt and jeans, he looked every bit the too-cool heartthrob. It was the jawline. Sharp enough to cut glass.

"Nice shirt," I said. Lavender suited him. Unsurprisingly, everything suited Wes. It made him the perfect chameleon, able to sell every outlandish costume thrown at him.

But if asked, I'd say he looked best in blue. Navy. His eyes popped in navy.

He took up his usual spot next to me, throwing an arm behind me and propping his feet on the coffee table. The couch was big enough to seat both of us three times over, a giant gray modular beast that matched everything in the apartment but me.

There was no holding back my moan at the first sugary sip. Wes groaned, clearly not understanding the pure love that could exist between a person and a drink. Well, he was missing out.

Without taking my lips off the cup, I rearranged myself until I was tucked into his side.

"You look about as good as that time Hades dragged you to the Underworld," he said, but his tone was too careful to make the joke land.

"I feel worse. Did you come to see the train wreck happen in real time?"

"What can I say? I'm a sucker for dramatics."

From this angle, I could see the lingering black liner from yesterday's shoot. It suited him, accentuating his whole devil-may-care vibe. I was tempted to take a photo.

A weak laugh bubbled out, quickly turning into a sniffle. Yesterday, I'd been sure of myself. My life wasn't perfect, but I was taking steps in the right direction. Now, I wasn't sure I was on the right path anymore.

Immediately, his arms wrapped around me, and I sank into him, overwhelmingly thankful that he was here.

With that simple act, Wes had dashed a fear I hadn't realized I'd had until just this moment; that I'd lose him. True friends were hard to come by in this business, and we were taught to distance ourselves from scandal.

I could handle losing Bryson. There was no way I'd let Wes go.

"Have you eaten? I can order something." His hands were playing a slow rhythm along my spine.

"Jen doesn't like me eating takeout."

I didn't need to see his face to know he'd rolled his eyes. "I think you get a pass today."

————

A bowl of green curry and a Disney film later—*The Little Mermaid*, of course. Ariel was a hashtag girlboss, and the songs were beyond compare—I finally felt ready to believe things would be okay.

"Of course they'll be okay," Wes reiterated, clearing the containers. I used the opportunity to swap the cushion I'd been holding with the one he'd been resting on.

"I think your OJ is out of date," Wes called from the kitchen.

I caught him sniffing the carton. "Then don't drink it."

He shrugged and ignored me. Whatever he tasted must have been worse than I'd expected, and I laughed as his face contorted. Served him right.

"I told you."

His smile was the nicest thing I'd seen all day.

He let out a final cough and threw the juice away. "What did Jen say?"

I turned so he couldn't read my expression. Jen had called during the movie, but I'd chosen to rewatch the "Kiss the Girl" scene rather than talk to her.

"They found the source of the photos," I lied, my gut twisting. They hadn't really found the source. They'd found the photographer. The source was *me*.

"But they can't stop them from being shared," Wes finished for me.

"Exactly." To try would make it worse. My plan had already backfired. Now all I could do was wait and hope I hadn't messed up too badly.

Wes returned to the couch, his presence doing more to calm me than his words. "It'll be okay, you know. We'll figure this out together."

Somehow it was easier to believe coming from him.

2

LIV

Has Olivia already found a new man? Nope. This is a photo taken from when the blond starlet (harlot?) briefly dated co-star Jackson Ward. Is she only interested in co-workers, or are we still eligible?

"HI SWEETIE, *Mom here. I saw your comment on Twitter this morning—yes, I'm on Twitter now, don't you dare laugh. Your father's already given me enough grief."*

"She's hip now, darling."

"Shut up, Joe," Mom laughed. "Anyway, I just wanted to remind you of how proud your father and I are. You're the strongest person I've ever met. So you just go into that audition and give them hell, you hear? Love you."

I blinked back tears as the voicemail ended. My phone background stared back at me. I'd auditioned to play Meira, and Dad had taken the picture when I'd gotten the call that the part was mine. The image showed Mom wrapping me in a tight hug, swinging me around as we both laughed.

I missed her more than I could put into words. It had been four years since she passed away, and I hadn't gone a day without wishing I could talk to her. All I had left were her voicemails.

"I wish you were here, Mom. I don't know how I'll get through this without you," I whispered so low my driver couldn't hear.

As he parked, I rested my forehead against the cool glass of the window, glad that the dark tint would hide me from any onlookers.

All I wanted to do was cry, but I had interviews to get through today, and makeup could only hide so much. Walking in with bloodshot eyes was the worst thing I could do. So I counted to ten, breathed in slowly and held it, then breathed out.

The car idled, and Jon, my driver, said nothing.

It had been two weeks since the photos had surfaced. I'd asked Jen if there was any way I could get out of today— what better time was there to have a "scheduling conflict"? —but she'd told me to be here, so here I was.

As if knowing I needed him, my phone buzzed. Just seeing Wes' name on the notification was enough. My smile came easily; it was the only thing that had felt that way so far this morning. Getting through this would be much harder without him.

The video showed a cat in a tiny hat running around, angrily trying to remove it. It looked like he was frantically nodding.

Wes had added: *Darth Meowl RN*

I laughed. *Sorry Jen.*

Two sharp taps on my window practically restarted my

heart. I hid the phone, expecting Jen, but thankfully it was Jackson.

"Jen is probably five seconds from calling the national guard," he said when I finally got out of the car.

It wouldn't be the first time. At nineteen, I'd appreciated Jen's enthusiastic management style. What had I known about the entertainment business? Now, she had a team beneath her: someone to run my social media, someone to drive me to and from the set, hair, makeup, styling … she even had someone buy my groceries and deliver them.

She managed almost every aspect of my life. "One of these days, she's going to fix me with a homing beacon."

"Don't give her any ideas," he joked.

He slipped an arm around my shoulders as we walked, and I leaned into the hug. I'd never had siblings growing up, and maybe it should feel weird since we'd once dated, but he was as close to an older brother as I'd ever get. "If all else fails, throw it to Wes."

Wes was flirting with a cute brunette wearing bike shorts and a blazer as Jackson and I were led into the room. She had one hand on his bicep and looked about half a second away from climbing him like a tree.

My mouth screwed up as I watched them. Everyone flirted with Wes. Or, really, Wes flirted with everyone. Why should this girl be any different?

An upbeat young girl with rainbow roots welcomed me to a makeup chair, and I tried not to watch Wes in the reflection.

Wes scampered over when he spotted Jackson and me, and I ignored the excited swoop I felt. The woman looked disappointed, and I didn't blame her. "You made it! I swear, Jen was about to go batshit. I thought for sure she'd have you chipped by now." Was it ridiculous for his joke to make me happy? Most people didn't get my humor. But Wes did, just like my mom had, and that had always made him extra special.

Jackson stood, released from his own touch-up, and gave me a private smile that I couldn't interpret. Wes clapped him on the shoulder before slipping into the seat he'd vacated. I liked him on interview days. Full of energy and dressed cozier than normal. Today he wore skinny jeans and a deep-blue bomber jacket. It reminded me of the old movies, where high school jocks would drape their coats over their girls' shoulders. Wes' shoulders were much broader than mine. I'd probably get lost in a jacket like that.

I didn't understand Bryson's comment about Wes and me. We had always gravitated toward each other. He was the only person I knew when I joined the show, so why wouldn't we? I'd been far from home and my parents. I knew nothing and no one. Wes was a little piece of LA, here with me on this new adventure. I'd taken solace in that. I couldn't imagine not having him next to me. In a few months, we'd film the last season of the show, say goodbye to Jackson, and hopefully hello to a new start. The network was as excited for the spin-off as Wes and I were. Knowing I'd get to keep working with my friend was more than I could ask for.

When the makeup artist moved to work on his other side, he caught me staring and winked. I hid my smile with a turn of my head. He was ridiculous.

I stamped down on the flutter in my chest. Those butterflies had taken up residence the day we met, and they'd gone nowhere since, despite how many times I'd told them that Wes was like this with everyone. He'd never once indicated that he wanted more than friendship in the six years we'd known each other, and considering how many times I'd seen a girl wrapped around him, I knew it wasn't shyness stopping him.

No, this flutter was all me. A silly crush that I'd hoped would have disappeared by now. This was what Bryson had seen. Not Wes' feelings, but my own.

Once we'd been given the all clear, a tall guy in a floral shirt fit our mic packs and told us we had five minutes. In the mirror, I eyed the series of hairpins lined up like little toy soldiers around my ear, keeping two twists in place. I was itching to grab at a lock and twirl it around my finger. Mom said it was something I'd done since I was born. When I was two, I refused to fall asleep anywhere but in her arms, her hair wrapped around one chubby claw.

She used to joke that she'd likely go bald because of it. Continued to say it even when chemo had taken her hair. Only my mother could make a joke like that and still make me laugh.

Wes stepped close, concerned. "You okay? If you don't want to do this, we can say you're sick."

He was the first person to ask me that today. I nodded, not sure that I really was but determined to go on. Wes was always saying things would be all right, so maybe I could put my faith in that. Maybe it wouldn't be so bad.

Slender fingers curled around mine, giving a soft squeeze of support. "I'm serious, Liv."

His jacket was half zipped, the hint of a familiar image poking out from underneath. I pulled at the zipper to expose it, catching Wes off guard, but he didn't pull away. Ursula stared back at me. I had the inexplicable urge to touch her.

"Little on the nose, isn't it?" It came out quiet. So little of my life was quiet these days. When we were shooting, the days were long and the nights were longer. Hundreds of crew members. Any breaks we got were filled with promotion, and Jen had been organizing more and more brand deals lately. I felt like I was always "on." *Be here, say this, do that.*

About the only time I could be myself was when I was with Wes.

"Don't you know I'm the bad guy?" It wasn't until Wes touched my wrist that I realized my finger was still hooked in his zipper. I released it, looking down to avoid his gaze.

"You're not a bad guy."

Wes ran his fingers over the necklace I was wearing, brushing my collarbone in the process. "This is nice." It was handmade, a series of beads and letters spelling out my name. The room tilted at his touch. He lingered over the last *A*. "It suits you."

You suit me. A silly wish. I wanted to laugh. An hour ago, I was anxious, countless comments about my dating life circling in my head. Words thrown around with all the grace of a dog pile. Now, I wouldn't say I was calm, but I felt grounded. Tethered. Wes was here, and he would look out for me.

"There you are," Jen said, appearing out of nowhere. Maybe she did have me bugged.

Wes and I pulled apart, and I stood up a little straighter. Today she wore an immaculate white suit and a confidence that I didn't feel. "Everything's set up and ready to go."

"Any word from the network about the spin-off?" I asked as we walked.

"Not yet. I thought I'd hear from them today, but with everything happening ..." She sighed, resigned. It was a bad sign. "They might not like the added attention on the project, and since they haven't announced your involvement yet … Let's see what the fallout is first, then we can assess."

Who knew my world would shift so dramatically because of a few photos? I'd hoped it would mean Bryson and I could stop pretending and actually be together. Instead, it had thrown my life into a cyclone.

What happened next would be handled by Jen and a flurry of PR assistants. There was nothing for me to do but sit back and wait. And hope.

"Thank you for trying. I'm sorry you have to deal with this."

As I made a move toward the interviewer, Jen stopped me. "Wait. You can't wear that." She stared pointedly at my throat.

I felt the instinct to fight back. I liked how the bright pink band of the necklace looked against the bold orange of my top, but more than that, I wanted to wear it.

"I like it. It's from a fan. Everything else I'm wearing is from a designer. I think this is a good way to show support for all the fans that keep the show running."

But it was no use. Jen was already replacing it with a much more "flattering" gold chain.

"It's from the newest Tiffany collection. I arranged with them that you'd wear it for today's appearances, and in exchange, they'll let you keep it."

Thanks, I hate it. Admittedly, the necklace was beautiful. But I was always surrounded by beautiful. It would be nice to have something meaningful for a change.

I frowned as the cold links weighed heavily on my collarbone. One look at Wes' expression, and I could hear the sarcastic comment he wasn't making. For once, I wanted to agree. But I shouldn't be ungrateful. "Thank you, Jen."

———

A PR assistant led me to the interview room. The walls had been padded for soundproofing, but it looked temporary. Three folding chairs sat facing a bank of equipment: two cameras, directional lighting, and an overhead microphone. All feeding into a laptop that was perched on top of a milk crate. A guy with an impressive mustache and the biggest headphones I'd ever seen was sitting on the floor in front of it, nodding wordlessly to the producer.

Interviews always made me nervous. Four years on *The Guild* hadn't changed that. Years of practice, and I never knew what to do. I wasn't funny like Wes, or sweet like Jackson. I was just *me*. *Eyes too big and no clue what I was doing.*

But this was part of the job. Press and celebrity. A constant split between being authentic and baring too much of yourself. What was shared was never forgotten.

I'd never met anyone more suited for this job than Wes. And not just the acting side of things, but all of it. Somehow, he knew how to separate himself from his public persona, always ready with a joke in case things got tedious.

I liked acting, but what I really loved was telling stories. I wanted to direct.

The interviewer who had been flirting with Wes earlier introduced herself as Gemma and motioned for me to sit. I took the empty seat between Wes and Jackson. Wes playfully nudged my foot and threw a wink over his shoulder in a way that wouldn't be caught by the cameras.

"Okay, I think we're ready to start," Gemma said, flashing a wide smile at Wes. It was silly to be jealous. *What kind of name was Gemma, anyway?*

But it was hard to stay mad at her once the interview started. Gemma was bright and engaging, keeping the questions lighthearted. Relief unfurled in my neck. This was easy. I'd been worried for nothing.

"What is your favorite movie?"

We'd been asked this so many times, I could recite the answers in my sleep. I answered for everybody.

"*Wall-E*," I said, pointing to Jackson (his actual answer, because he was the human embodiment of a teddy bear). For myself, "*Practical Magic*." One of many movies I loved, but the "on brand" answer that Jen felt was best. And Wes, "*Catch Me If You Can*." Only I knew that Wes' real answer was *The Princess Bride*, and that he'd spent hours practicing the Westley/Inigo fight with his brother when they were kids.

Even easier to answer was, "If the three of you were stuck on a desert island, who would be the most likely to survive?"

Jackson and I answered simultaneously. "Wes."

Gemma smiled, positively giddy, and used the excuse to focus all her attention on Wes. "Really?"

I wasn't possessive or anything. Really. *I wasn't.* But I liked proving how well I knew him. "Leave him alone in a room for fifteen minutes, and he'll find a phone charger and the Wi-Fi code."

"And at least one person's phone number," Jackson added.

"It's a unique skill." Wes laughed, and Gemma blushed down to her shirt.

If Bryson was here, I would have pointed at them. *See how wrong you were?*

———

Tyler Connors was a familiar face, having interviewed us a few times before. As far as I could tell, he freelanced for lots of different publications. Buzzfeed, Jezebel, Access. He was nice enough, but he had a sleazy offishness about him. Like he would sell his own grandmother for a story.

Which reminded me, I should really watch *High Society* again this weekend.

"Are you sure you can't give us a hint about the spin-off? We're all on the edge of our seats!"

"If we knew anything, we'd tell you," Wes said.

Tyler laughed, not knowing it wasn't a joke. Who would believe that the two leads of a show—one that was only a year away from filming—wouldn't have a single clue what the show was about? We didn't even have contracts yet. The studio might scrap the whole project tomorrow, and we'd all be out of work.

Another point Jen had raised when I'd asked her about today.

"You've certainly been busy lately, haven't you, Olivia?" From anyone else, the question could have been casual, but Tyler looked too pleased with himself to be asking me something innocuous.

I liked to think I was a kind person. I tried to be. It made me physically sick to think badly of anyone, no matter how much they needled me. But it had been hours. I wanted to be home. In my pajamas.

"Absolutely," I said brightly, while my stomach turned. This was it. I cast a look at Jen, who simply nodded for me to continue. "The whole team has been working really hard to make this season as exciting as possible, and we can't wait for everyone to see the epic finale."

"There's been a lot of talk," Tyler started, and I prepared myself for the worst. No one had asked about

Bryson yet, but if anyone would, it would be Tyler. It wasn't the most original angle, but I guess my dating history was more interesting than the show. "Season four ends next week, and there's a lot of excitement about the kiss in the finale. Is this a sign that we can expect Ares and Meira to get back together?"

The relief was palpable.

"I don't know. Ares has had a lot of fun being single this season," Wes joked. "Maybe it's time for Meira to realize what she's missing out on."

He leaned forward in his chair, brushing his elbow against my arm. What I wouldn't give to hold his hand right about now.

"Ares has been going on as many dates as possible," I said, playing into Wes' banter. "See if Meira takes him back after she finds that out."

Wes grabbed my hand and kissed my knuckles. "You'll always be my first love, you know that."

I laughed and pulled my hand back, hoping the makeup covered my flushed cheeks.

Tyler was undeterred. "It must be a little awkward— kissing your co-worker while your boyfriend is directing." There it was. And jeez, he looked so proud of himself.

On either side of me, Jackson and Wes straightened in their chairs. *Keep smiling.* What else was I supposed to do?

I couldn't wait for the day I could step behind the camera. Get out of the spotlight and redirect people's attention to something more meaningful. I couldn't imagine taking pleasure in making people feel this way and knew it was something I wouldn't allow when I called the shots.

"I think I can answer this," Wes said. His voice was light, but I could see how tightly he gripped the water bottle in his lap. "My boyfriends are always pretty understanding."

A few of the crew laughed, but Tyler didn't crack. His attention laser focused on me. I was really starting to dislike the guy. "It's true as well, Olivia, that you and Jackson dated during the first season, isn't it? Did that make things difficult when you started seeing Bryson?"

There was a crunch of plastic beside me.

Jackson cut in. "Olivia is always a joy to work with. Definitely more than Wes and me. She has to remind us what our lines are half the time." It was a lie, but a sweet one, and the smile I gave him in thanks was 100 percent genuine.

Wes leaned over, aligning our arms until they touched from elbow to wrist. "I keep telling you, I can't remember the lyrics to 'Shake It Off' as well as my lines. Pick one or the other, man." As subtly as I could, I nudged against his arm in thanks. He nudged back.

Tyler opened his mouth to speak again, but Jackson beat him to it. "And I keep telling you, you're not singing that at my wedding."

"We'll see, J. We'll see."

"Back to the kiss."

I wanted to scream "Read the room!" but there was no way to do that without giving Tyler exactly what he'd come for.

"Who would you say is the better kisser? Jackson, Wes, or—"

A crash sounded, Wes' water bottle falling from his lap and spilling water out toward the equipment. Mustache man jumped up quickly, and a number of other people rushed in to pull cables out of the way.

"Sorry guys, my hand slipped," Wes said, not looking sorry at all. I could have kissed him.

"We'll have to film that last question again," the cameraman said, but Jen finally, *finally!* stepped in.

"Actually, our time is up, so I'm afraid we'll have to cut it there. I'm sure you've got everything you need." Her tone left no room for argument.

Jackson's wedding duties meant he couldn't stick around for the inevitable aftermath, which I could tell he felt guilty about. It was sweet how conflicted he looked waving goodbye to us, but this wasn't his scandal.

Jen was in Wes' face the minute we were alone. "That was reckless and stupid. You're lucky you didn't damage anything." Her gaze cut to me, rooting me in place. "Olivia, I'll have the driver take you home."

My heart was racing so fast it was making me dizzy. Maybe that was why I put my foot down. "Actually, I'm going home with Wes."

I watched her eyes flicker back and forth between us, assessing. But I knew Jen. She could be a shark, but she'd also stood by me through one of the toughest times of my life.

In the end, she relented, even if she didn't look happy about it. "Fine." The click of her heels echoed down the hallway as she walked away.

Feeling stifled, I reached to undo the Tiffany chain around my neck. In my haste, the latch caught in my hair, but I was determined to get it off, almost ripping my hair out in the process. Wes waited all of zero seconds while I struggled, then took over, wrapping his arms around me and extracting the offending piece of jewelry from my fingers.

Ursula's white hair was winking at me beneath his

jacket. She was right. I was a poor, unfortunate soul. Problem was, finding a sea witch to help with my troubles would be difficult this far inland.

We were standing so close I only had to lean forward an inch or two to rest my head on his chest. One of my favorite things was how tall Wes was. He was at least half a foot taller than me. Warm, too. Practically radiated heat. It made him the perfect resting spot in winter.

I listened to his steady breathing as he worked to untangle my hair, light brushes of his fingertips soothing the last of Tyler's questions away. When the necklace was freed, I sighed my pleasure into Wes' chest, pressing farther into him.

"Thank you. You're always looking out for me. What would I do without you?"

His chin came to rest on my head, the familiar feeling the last puzzle piece slotting into place.

"Good thing you never have to find out."

3

WES

LIV SWUNG her door open like it had personally offended her. It had only been a few days since that dick over at Jezebel had tried to get a scoop by exploiting her situation with Bryson. I'd been checking his tweets since then, but he hadn't posted anything about Liv. Only a handful of humorless political takes.

Damn, she looked cute when she got worked up—all pursed lips and righteous fury under a halo of golden hair —like a vengeful angel.

Before I could comment on that, her eyes widened, and I knew I hadn't done a great job of hiding the dark circles under my eyes. She pulled me inside for further inspection.

"Wow," she said. "Bad night? You look wrecked."

I suppressed a yawn and shrugged. Yes, I was tired, but like hell was I telling Liv that. She'd tell me to go home or, I don't know, force me to take a nap or something. And there was no way I was leaving her while she was going through this. My tired-ass body could wait.

Truth was, I never slept well. Not since I'd moved to

Chicago. I used to think it was work stress, the long shoots, even adrenaline, but I wasn't so sure anymore. On the worst nights, I'd lie in bed and stare at the ceiling for hours, all too aware of the emptiness in my bed, my life, and my heart.

I'd often thought about talking to Liv about it. Or Jackson. Or anyone.

But I never did. It was easier assuming no one would reach back than knowing it for a fact.

True to form, I sidestepped her concern, walking swiftly into her soulless kitchen in hopes that today would be the day human food would appear. "Why does it have to be a bad night? How do you know I wasn't kept awake for other reasons? Good ones."

The fridge was a bust, filled with the same pre-packaged health meals that Jen insisted Liv eat. The kinds that were 100 percent viral marketing, with none of those pesky things called calories, or flavor.

I turned around in time to see Liv's eye roll. "Spare me the details." Adorable.

What she didn't know was there were no details to share. Hadn't been for a long time. Probably two years.

I'd tried to date, but my heart wasn't in it. Frankly, it needed to get over itself. Ever since I'd walked in on that kiss between her and Bryson two years ago, I'd known Liv would never see me as anything more than a friend. Even if parts of me wished otherwise.

"What about you? You looked ready to murder somebody when you opened the door."

"Have you been on Twitter today?"

I sighed. "No, and you shouldn't be either." I thought she was done torturing herself, but apparently not.

"I was trending. It was hard to avoid." She wagged a

finger at me. "Don't look at me like that. I remember a time when you were the one obsessively checking your mentions. Interacting with everyone until fans started showing up at your favorite café every morning."

Ugh, I didn't need the reminder. Best damn espresso in blocks, and I couldn't order one without getting hounded.

"I'd be nice to me if I were you," I teased when we sat down, Liv fitting herself to my side and making me crazy in the process.

Sit, wriggle, sigh. Every damn time. I couldn't decide what was worse, the way she rubbed against me, stirring up my senses until I was half hard, or the soft sound she made afterward. That perfect little sigh haunted me.

"Why's that?" she asked as she wriggled.

I held my breath, willing my body to, just this once, not react. I failed. Miserably.

It wasn't until after the sigh that I could speak again. My entire body felt pulled tight. "Because it's my turn to pick the movie." It was easier to focus on the screen than on the urge to pull Liv closer, so I scrolled through the list, stopping on one I knew Liv wouldn't enjoy. "Ready to have your mind blown for two and a half hours?"

Nope. Definitely shouldn't use the word "blown" when Liv's inches away from my dick and groaning.

"Don't you dare," she said and wrestled the remote out of my hands. I was so gone for her I didn't even put up a fight.

Since Lord of the Assholes Bryson split, movie nights had gone from once a week to almost every night. I'd seen more of Liv in the last month than I had in the last year, not counting all the time we spent together at work. But that was work. I loved it, but I never got to hold her the way I wanted to when we were filming.

I knew it was reckless. Stupid. One day she'd get a job that took her home to LA, and I wouldn't get this anymore. Until then, I'd stockpile those damn sighs so I'd have the memories to keep me company when she inevitably left.

I was being selfish, but shit, I was sick of being alone. And Liv made me feel needed. If I wasn't careful, I'd get addicted to this. Hell, I already was. I soaked up every sliver of sunshine she bestowed upon me.

I wanted to be wanted. Even if it was only as a friend.

About the time Baby was being heroically saved from a corner, my mother called. I told Liv to keep watching and waited until I was in her spare room before I picked up.

"Hi, Mom. How are you?"

"Terrible. You know I don't sleep well." And just like that, it'd started. "Penny, dear, make sure you pick up my magnesium pills today." I heard her assistant agree in the background. "Have you spoken to your brother yet?"

"Not recently." Lucas and I didn't speak unless absolutely necessary.

She hummed in that way she always did when she was disappointed, and the ghost of a million other conversations waved at me. "Wes, we need your help with the anniversary party. You know how busy your father and I are, and it doesn't seem fair that your brother is doing it all simply because you don't live here."

And wasn't that a blessing? Best decision I'd ever made, and I could have thanked her for reminding me of that. Why would I ever doubt my decision when the alternative had been to stay in LA and deal with this on a regular basis?

What a tough choice. Kickass job with my friends or a brother who hated me and parents who couldn't care less? *Let me think.*

Okay, that was harsh. They weren't completely neglectful. Lucas and I had always had a roof over our heads, plenty of food, clothes, games, good schooling. Blah, blah, blah.

But the rest? The big, squishy, warm feelings of love and home and family? That didn't exist in our house. The closest I'd had to that was my relationship with Lucas, and eventually, he'd decided I wasn't worth it.

"Have you booked your flights yet?"

No, I'd rather livestream an enema than come home. Score one for avoidance.

"Not yet. I've been busy with press for the show. In fact, I'm being interviewed by—" I didn't get to finish my sentence.

"Oh, right. Is that still going? You know I'd watch it if I wasn't so busy, but it's not exactly my kind of entertainment. All those computer effects are more for kids."

"Sure."

"If it upsets you that much, I'll watch it."

"I'm not upset. I'm fine." I was definitely upset. But I absolutely didn't want to talk about it.

"Okay, okay. I'll leave it alone. You don't need to be so sensitive."

There were no words. Not any nice ones, anyway. Thankfully, Penny reminded her of whatever was next on her list, and I was dismissed.

I grumbled all the way back to the living room, where I immediately forgot all my frustrations in favor of watching Liv pace a groove on her ugly, beige rug. No offense to anyone who liked neutrals, but I really hoped the shop had upsold the shit out of it because Jen deserved to pay for making Liv's apartment so devoid of life.

There was that look again. God, I wanted to kiss her.

"I'm worn out just watching you."

Liv stopped, caught. "That's rich coming from someone I've witnessed skip down the street." Quickly, she hid her phone behind her back, but I knew exactly what she'd been doing. Typical. I hadn't been gone five minutes, and she was back online. She needed a better distraction.

"Most women find that adorable."

She snorted. "Most women where?"

"In my DMs."

"In your dreams, maybe."

I loved this playful side of her. It rarely came out, and never when Jen was around. The mad tyrant wanted Liv on her best behavior at all times. Liv might argue she was a good manager, but she also was a shoo-in for "Most Demanding." See also, "Eternal Opportunist."

"If you're lucky." I winked, then grabbed Liv's hand and pulled her onto the couch. "Sit. I told you not to look at that shit."

She didn't fight me as I took her phone and tossed it to the no-man's-land on the other end of the couch.

"It's only going to make you upset."

"Jen said I should *mfph*."

I cut her off, covering her mouth with my hand.

"Nope. No mention of she-who-shall-not-be-named. This is a work-free zone tonight, and 'work' includes doom-scrolling through your mentions."

Liv twisted her face away but couldn't dislodge my hand. She licked across my palm, and my dick hardened so fast I ripped my hand away.

"Fine, but just for that, I'm putting *Inkheart* on again."

It was her guilty pleasure. We'd already watched it twice this month. I liked Brendan Fraser as much as the next guy, but there was a limit. Unfortunately, I was too busy trying to mentally cold shower myself to protest.

The truth was, I'd watch anything she wanted, even if it was a fifteen-hour documentary on bee farms. I just liked being with her.

My phone buzzed.

Mom: Penny will help you if you can't do it yourself.

I groaned. If I didn't book my flights soon, she'd do it for me, and then I'd be stuck there all summer.

"What's wrong?" Liv asked.

I showed her the message, and her face fell in recognition.

"Oh. Is everything okay?"

"It's fine."

Liv looked so concerned it made me want to crack myself open and lay every last ugly part of me at her feet. I ran my hand through my hair. Ripping it out wouldn't help. I'd have to get to the gym later. Hitting a bag for forty minutes would probably do it.

"It's their anniversary next month. Thirty years. They're throwing a big party to renew their vows, and anyone who is anyone will be there."

"And she's guilting you into coming back for it?"

"You guessed it."

"I'm sorry. I know it's hard on you."

I'd spent years perfecting my "stage face"—the one I'd always needed as a kid—and, usually, this is when I'd use it, but I hated lying to Liv. There were already too many secrets here. I didn't want to add one more ... but I couldn't bring myself to tell the truth, either.

"It's complicated." Forcing a smile, I added, "But what family isn't, am I right?"

It was the wrong thing to say to someone who'd lost a parent, and like a fucking moron, I remembered too late. Shit. "Sorry, that was a dick thing to say."

Liv managed a reassuring smile. I didn't deserve it. "It's okay. I'm used to you thinking with your other brain by now."

"Well, when it's this big, I can't help it."

She laughed. An open, joyous sound that bounced off the ceiling. My whole body lit up. Shit, I would say anything if it meant hearing that sound. Would make a fool of myself a million times over. As if I hadn't already. As if I didn't on a daily basis.

"Yeah, yeah. I've heard that before."

"I can always provide you with *hard* proof if you need."

She groaned, then turned serious. "As long as you're okay."

"As good as I can be," I said, brushing a strand of hair out of her eyes. Being with her, even in this bland apartment, was as close to happiness as I could get.

"Are you sure?"

"I'm fine." The words were second nature now. I'd had years of practice packing my feelings away.

Not like Liv. After everything she'd been through, she never seemed afraid of opening her heart again. Trusting people.

I wish I knew how.

"I mean, apart from all the heavy lifting I'm doing on a daily basis," I said, laying a hand over my crotch.

Liv slapped me on the shoulder. "You're ridiculous." And all the accolades in the world didn't mean as much as her laughter.

"Thank you," she said after a moment. "I really appreciate you being here."

Sometimes, when I was with Liv, I felt like a fraud, always hiding my true intentions. Other times, being honest was the easiest thing in the world.

"Trust me, there's nowhere else I'd rather be."

4

LIV

Trouble in paradise? Bryson Green seen shopping alone as rumors of a replacement start to make the rounds.

IF YOU'D ASKED me what day it was, I couldn't have told you. Summer breaks always effectively ruined my concept of time, but it was worse this time around. How had it been three weeks since Bryson had left? The final episode of season four had aired last night, and already the conversation had switched to the next—and last—season of the show. Who would stay? Who would leave?

Wes' apartment was less than a ten-minute walk from my place, but it might as well have been Narnia. A magical place far from reality. Being here meant not wallowing on my couch, even if it was the land of misfit furniture.

Seriously. I couldn't imagine Wes' place looking any less like my own. That's what I liked about it.

An oversized fluffy armchair in bright blue sat in the

corner and made me wonder if we should send our regards to a grieving Muppet family. It was as uncomfortable as it looked, and no one ever sat on it without having immediate regrets.

Next to it was a faded couch in a color I could only describe as moldy avocado. We'd debated many times about whether that was intentional. I still maintained that he'd gotten scammed, but Wes loved the thing.

I smiled, tracing a pattern that looked worryingly like a stain. I wouldn't think about it. This was as close to perfect as I could ask for. I might not have gone very far, but the change of scenery was exactly what I needed. It helped that Wes was here.

"I can't believe you haven't been forced to throw this couch out yet."

"What are you talking about? This is a great couch."

It was pretty great. Soft and a little lumpy, like an old pillow. One that always smelled like Wes—woodsy, with a hint of fabric softener. Not quite big enough to stretch out on, so anytime we watched a movie here, I was practically in his lap. I hoped he never got rid of it.

"Jen would never let me keep something like this."

"Yeah, well, I don't really put much stock in what Jen thinks. That apartment is depressing."

I didn't want to have this argument again, so I changed the subject. "You don't like the way my place looks?" Two point three million likes would say he was in the minority.

"It's not you."

"You say that like it's a bad thing. If I decorated, my place wouldn't look any better." It would look dull.

"Like hell it would."

Shit, had I said that last part out loud?

"Come on, I know you. You've definitely thought about it. What would you do?"

What would I do? Suddenly, the idea of choice, of spreading my wings, thrilled me. My eyes lingered on Wes. What would I do if I could do anything?

I smiled, pulling out the ideas like trinkets from a jewelry box. "Something colorful," I said, eyeing the furry chair. "But nothing too modern. I'd love a window with a bench seat, and I'd get fake sheepskin rugs to throw over it. I'd keep fresh thyme and rosemary in the kitchen because mom always had some. A big TV, obviously."

"Obviously."

"And, um." I felt my face heat. "The perfect couch for cuddling."

"See," Wes said. "Now *that's* more like you." His hand brushed my cheek. Warmth radiated from my chest and spread like wildfire through the rest of my body. "And you could never be dull."

When he spoke like this, it fanned the embers of that long held crush into something dangerous.

As a distraction, I reached into the large box of PR mail that sat open on the floor. We received gifts all the time, from brands we worked with or ones that hoped we'd be seen wearing their stuff. I'd spent the last twenty minutes eyeing a black hooded sweatshirt. It was thick and soft, and I wanted one. "You're so lucky. The freebies you get are so much better than mine. Just once, I want a leisurewear brand deal that isn't a crop top and bike shorts."

"Take that," he said, gesturing to the hoodie.

"Really?" I asked, already trying it on, even though it was too warm to wear. As soon as the fluffy inner lining blanketed me, I knew I wouldn't give it up for anything. If I had one complaint, it was that it smelled like packaging and storage. I should ask Wes to spritz it with his Maison Margiela. The Barber one.

"What do you think?" The hem hid my shorts. I must have looked like a kid playing dress-up. One giant hood, bare legs, black socks. I fell in love immediately.

Wes was quiet for so long I started to worry. He better not want this back.

"Good," he finally pushed out, his voice thick.

A large print on the mantle caught my eye. "That's new." I walked over, mesmerized by the big, bright brushstrokes of teal and green. Hills hugged by blue sky and sea. When I was standing directly in front of it, I could make out the couple at the peak, caught in a passionate kiss. "It's beautiful. Where is this?"

"Thrace. Or the mythological version of it. A fan sent it to me."

"Sometimes I think you get into the show more than they do," I said, trailing a finger lightly over the golden dome of a helmet on the mantle next to it.

The fans adored Wes. Who wouldn't? He was natural on screen. A natural in life. He had a quick wit and an eagerness to jump feet first into any situation—something I envied.

"It's a great show. Yeah, it's never gonna win any awards, but it's a cool concept. And I like Ares. Belittled by his famous father, never quite living up to his expectations. He's not always a good guy, but he's his own man. No one can say that he didn't make it off his own back."

It was obvious how much Wes cared about Ares when he spoke about him. As if he were speaking about a friend or a brother rather than the fictional character he played.

Jackson and I enjoyed our jobs, but we both had ambitions that went beyond the roles we played. Wes came to work invested in making the show the best it could be. It didn't matter if he was fighting demons or spewing monologues. It was what I loved about working with him.

The first year of the show had been overwhelming. I kept waiting for someone to realize they'd made a mistake in hiring me. But no matter how crazy life was, I knew I could look over and say, "Can you believe this?" And Wes would usually wink and respond, "Better get used to it, doll."

———

When I was eight years old, my boyfriend Brad broke up with me after he discovered me drawing in the margins of his favorite book. I couldn't tell you what the book had been about. Probably sports. Anyway, it wasn't even the drawing that had bothered him, but the fact that when he'd asked me if I'd done it, I'd lied. Which had been pointless because he'd seen me do it.

Maybe karma was repaying me for that lie.

Jen cut to the chase. "I just got off the phone with them. Bryson is out. Come July, you'll be filming the last season with a new showrunner."

Shit. Somewhere out there, Bryson was muttering "I told you so." I was sure of it.

"This isn't necessarily a bad thing," she said.

I bet Bryson would feel differently.

"I think we can swing this in your favor. The network chose you over him, so we can lean on the age factor, say you were innocent and Bryson overstepped."

"I don't want to say that. I'm as much at fault as Bryson is." More than, truthfully. "It's been weeks. I want to move on. I don't want to make it worse by throwing Bryson under the bus."

I owed him that. Maybe if I'd known my relationship with Bryson would end like this, I wouldn't have started dating him. It certainly would have saved us both this headache.

A knock on my door surprised me. I wasn't expecting anyone.

"I'll have to call you back. Someone's here."

"No need. I'll be on calls for the next few hours. I'll be in touch."

I opened the door to find a delivery guy holding two small plants. The smell hit me first, stinging my eyes with tears. Thyme and rosemary. I rushed to sign for them before I embarrassed myself, taking them into the kitchen and ripping open the card.

Time to add some flavor to your place. Wes.

I steadied myself against the counter. In two years, Bryson hadn't managed a birthday card.

At first glance, you'd think Wes was an overgrown child. Baby face, perfect pout, unruly hair. But there was an unexpected power underneath which came alive when he moved, and ever since I'd seen it, I'd been low-key aware of it. The way he might use it to crowd someone into a dark corner, his height forcing them to look up at him, his eyes full of intent. Or the way he would feel curled around you, limbs heavy with sleep, protective and comforting, like a giant octopus.

You know, the totally normal thoughts you might have about your best friend—someone you're meant to have nothing but platonic feelings for.

Sighing, I closed my eyes. Wes had done something nice, really nice, and I needed to find the box I'd kept these feelings in and pack them away again. It was probably only loneliness, anyway. Bryson had left, and I missed ... okay I didn't miss Bryson, but I missed the idea of him. Of someone who inspired me.

So that's all this was. Bryson had gotten into my head, and now I was reading into my friendship with Wes.

Except ... I'd liked Wes long before this.

When we'd first met six years ago at film school in LA, I'd seen what everyone else did—the overeager wisecracker. I hadn't even known it was possible to make so many double entendres until I met him. Confidence was part of Wes' charm, and I'd been drawn to him like everyone else. There wasn't a single girl in our class who hadn't had a crush on him. Myself included.

Over the years, I'd seen glimpses at what hid beneath. The depth and generosity. Under miles of flirtation and dick jokes, he had a surprisingly deep heart. He simply refused to let anyone see it. But I wanted to. Desperately.

I cradled the pots in my hands, each inhale bringing another memory. He'd done this for me. Because he'd known how much it meant. For as long as I'd known him, I had stamped out any attraction to Wes. It had never been easy, but life had distracted me enough to move past it.

But it didn't feel avoidable anymore.

5

WES

"NERVOUS YET?"

I leaned against the wall by the window, staring at the
fire escape of the next building. Liv was probably curled up
on her couch, deep in a movie, hair coiled around her index
finger. It was probably best I wasn't there. I'd had the theme
song to *My Best Friend's Wedding* stuck in my head since
yesterday. Liv's idea of a joke.

"Less than a month until you're a husband. Are you
nervous?"

Jackson's chuckle mingled with the clink of glasses as he
mixed the drink he'd used to lure me here. Technically, I'd
come so we could talk about my duties as a groomsman,
but they boiled down to "show up and wear a tux." Not
exactly difficult to mess up.

"I'd like to say no, but I'd be lying."

I liked Jackson. Never had a bad word to say about
anyone, and he was one of the most genuine guys I'd ever
met. Agreeing to be his groomsman had been easy. But as
I'd learned the hard way, being close to someone didn't stop

them from forgetting you. After next season, Jackson was leaving the show, and I was pretty sure our friendship was gonna go with him.

I turned to face him, the wall solid against my shoulder blades. "If you need wedding night tips, I'd be happy to help."

"I definitely don't," he said. "But I do need to know where you'll be tomorrow so you can sign for your suit. Will you be at your place or at Liv's?"

He was aiming for casual, busying himself with pouring the drinks before walking over with them. But he was smiling too much to sell it, as if he'd discovered a secret and was fishing for a confession. He was wearing his "big brother" face.

As a big brother myself, I was immune. "My place is fine."

He nodded, passing over the glass. I hoped he'd let it go, but I should have known better.

"It's good to see you. I know you've been spending a lot of time with Liv lately, but it's nice to have some one-on-one time."

Funny. He'd have to do better than that to get me to spill. He must be rusty. Back when I used this trick on Lucas …

Shit. I let the whiskey burn on its way down.

Jackson wasn't my brother.

He was still watching me. "I remembered something this morning. A conversation we had a couple years ago about someone you liked but couldn't be with. I didn't put it together at the time, but …" He paused, and I knew it was fruitless to hope he wouldn't say it. That conversation was the closest I'd come to telling anyone.

"It's Liv, isn't it?"

I could have lied. Told him I didn't feel the same way anymore. But I was tired. I nodded. Years of keeping this to myself made talking about it difficult. Where would I even begin?

"Why didn't you say anything?"

The million-dollar question.

I couldn't resist a small laugh. I used to be better at this. Hell, I was a damn decent actor when I wanted to be, in front of the camera or not.

But it was getting harder and harder to hide the ache I felt being close to Liv but never quite close enough. She'd never seen me that way, and she never would.

I should have gotten over it. Hell knows I'd tried. Repeatedly. Flirting with every eligible woman in the city, dating as often as possible. But it never worked. Knowing she was happy with Bryson had stopped me from hoping. I'd been happy for her, even though it killed me that she was with someone else.

But I was an asshole, so I hadn't gotten over it. I'd only buried it, bringing it out on special occasions to make my misery a little more festive. I definitely hadn't told anyone about it.

"What was the point? She was with Bryson."

"And now?"

I took up the seat across from Jackson. "I can't do that. Liv means too much to me. I'd rather be her friend than some rebound lay. If anything was going to happen between us, it would have already."

"Maybe," he said, questioning it. Whatever. He might believe there was a possibility, but I knew better. Except saying that to him meant opening this can of worms for real, and I was happy to keep that shit sealed. So I said nothing. Not that it stopped Jackson.

"Wes, man, I've never been in that position. But I do know what it's like to be with someone who loves you, all of you—the good, bad, all of it—it's something else. When I was dating around, it was fun for a while, but in the end, there was something missing. And I think you already know that."

I resisted the urge to squirm under his scrutiny. I wanted that. All of it. And if it could be with Liv, then I wouldn't ask for another thing my entire life. But it wasn't meant to be.

I shrugged. "I don't know what to tell you, J."

"I think you like pretending you don't so you can't get hurt."

Little Klaxons sounded in my head. *Warning. Abort. Abort.* Why was emoting so much easier when I was playing someone else? Doing it as myself sucked major ass.

Regardless of what Jackson thought, he wasn't being helpful. It was one thing to invite me over for a drink, and I had no problems standing next to him on his big day. But digging into my personal life was where I drew the line. As close as we were right now, even the friendships I had with Jackson and Liv would disappear when we stopped working together. It was just how life went.

Everything good ended eventually.

"You, too?" The whiskey gently rolled around the glass in my hands, easier to focus on than Jackson's watchful gaze. "Normally, I have to go to the bar to be psychoanalyzed." I took a slow sip, dragging it out. "And the last thing I need right now is Tiffany and her all-seeing eye," I said, referring to his fiancée's best friend. Tiff might be one of Chicago's more acclaimed bartenders, but she also had the unnerving knack of seeing through all my bullshit.

"Yeah, well, Tiffany could probably see right through the devil, but that's beside the point. Why bother keeping up the act if it's not what you really want?"

I finally looked up. If he thought I hadn't already considered that a million times over, he was wrong. "Seriously? Maybe 'cause I got no chance of getting what I want, and Liv has been through enough to deal with me on top of it."

Did secretly being in love with her break my heart a little more every day? Yes. But the universe had conspired to make me fall for the one damn person I couldn't have, so I'd enjoy what I could get, no matter the pain.

"Look. What Liv needs right now is a friend. So that's what I'll be. Probably all I'll *ever* be."

"And what about what you need?"

"I'm fine."

"Bullshit."

I dared myself to look over at him. The challenge in my eyes met with a raised brow and a look I figured he'd perfected from years of big bro-ing. *Yeah, well, I had a lot of practice behind this wall, so good luck.*

"Leave it alone, J."

It was clear he wanted to say something, but he nodded slowly. I was a real asshole.

"If you change your mind and want to talk, you can. Anytime."

"I'm fine."

———

My tux arrived when Jackson said it would, and I opened my door expecting round two of his questions.

But Jackson turned out to be a sneaky son of a bitch.

He hadn't brought the suit himself. No. He'd sent the one person I didn't want to see.

Suit bag thrown over her shoulder, Tiff wiggled the hook with a finger. "Jackson said this was for you." Her smile was self-satisfied. I should have known they'd conspire against me.

"That doesn't explain why you're here. Don't you have a bar to tend?"

"No, I don't. And you know that." Her long blond hair was piled high in a bun, showing off a gold ear cuff and side shave. "You haven't been by the bar lately, and Jackson told me what happened with Liv. I figured you'd be brooding, so here I am." A likely story.

"Thanks, but I'm fine."

I started to close the door. Tiff's hand shot out, pushing until I released it. Damn, she was strong. I had a frightening image of what she must be like with her boyfriend, then stopped. Better to scrub that thought from my brain immediately and forever.

"Nuh-uh, not gonna work today, hotshot."

This was ridiculous. I let out a hot breath but didn't budge. No way would I admit it, but keeping a hold of the door was taking it out of me. "Fine. If I admit I'm not okay, will you go?" Not quite an admission, but it was all I'd give her.

Her cool hazel eyes examined me for so long I squirmed. She was too observant for my taste.

"I'll go," she finally said, and I felt relieved.

"No matter how much you push us away, we'll still give a shit about you, so you better get used to it." She held out the tux. "You deserve to be happy, Wes."

I took it, and she crushed me into a hug. I let her but didn't return it, swallowing past the lump in my throat.

After a moment, Tiff pulled back, and just when I thought she was going to push, she smiled. "I wanted to tell you. I found the perfect spot for our second bar. You'll like it. It's almost as dramatic as you are."

She pulled the door closed, and I sagged against it, old memories aching like bruises. I didn't need them to care about me. I kept telling them that. Being alone suited me.

I thumped my head against the door, listening to the echo. Boundaries. Distance. That's all I needed. I didn't want to be left with a hole where a friend should be when they inevitably disappeared. The last hole hadn't healed yet.

Crossing that line with anyone was asking for trouble. Liv most of all. No matter how much I wanted to.

6

WES

LIV: *Why did they let Joel Schumacher make two Batman movies?*

Me: It was the 90s

Liv: I'm aware of how it happened. I'm asking WHY

I laughed as I dialed, calling her while I ordered a large frappe in a separate app. My body was desperate for caffeine after another restless night. Four hours of sleep seemed to be the norm these days.

"Are you trying to fulfill some 'hundred terrible movies' challenge? Or do you just like torturing yourself?" Stretched out on the couch, I had one hand behind my head and what felt like a stupid grin on my face. "Please tell me Rebekah wasn't a Schumacher fan." If I thought Liv had eclectic taste in movies, her mom was borderline eccentric for hers.

"Only the formula one driver." Her laughter was heavenly. "I started a Val Kilmer rewatch and thought it would be better to get the lesser ones out of the way early."

"You better be ending it with *The Saint*."

"Wes, come on. Of course we'll end it with *The Saint*."

We. I liked the sound of that too much. I wanted to kick myself.

I canceled my frappe. "Hey, let's have lunch today. That Argentinian grill finally opened, and I think I've ordered from every single restaurant in a ten-mile radius. I need something new."

"Um …"

She was looking for a way to say no. Jen had told her to stay in after the photos had surfaced online, and I hated that Liv felt like she couldn't leave her apartment now. Of all the bullshit Jen had ordered Liv to do—and there was a lot—this took the cake.

But I wouldn't take no for an answer.

"It's been weeks. Unless Jen has you trapped in a tower, defended by a dragon, there's no reason you can't come."

"Are you saying you're my knight in shining armor?"

"I'd rather be your partner in crime," I joked, a little too close to the truth. "Come on, go out with me."

"Like properly out?"

"Unless you have a different definition." She was close to caving. I knew it. "You know you want to."

She laughed, and I closed my eyes to savor the sound. "Fine, but I need to change."

"Why? You look great."

"You can't even see me right now."

"Don't need to. You always look great." This time I didn't need to joke. No matter what she wore, she'd still be the most stunning woman I'd ever seen.

"I'm still changing. Pick me up in fifteen."

———

The restaurant wasn't what I expected. It was an unassuming little spot with bare walls and none of the usual filter-ready trimmings. The rich smell of flame and charcoal wafted from the kitchen. My mouth had been steadily watering since we'd walked in. Oh, and did I mention it was empty? I'd already confirmed twice with the hostess that yes, they were open, and no, she wasn't joking. Typical. My first opportunity to give Liv some excitement, and we'd ended up in an abandoned restaurant.

"Relax," she said, sliding into the booth across from me. "It's better this way. No onlookers."

This was why I'd wanted to get her out of the apartment. Jen, for all that Liv was paying her, kept her hidden away like a shameful relative you tried to forget. If they couldn't see you, they couldn't talk about you. *Yeah, sure.* That was definitely the way the internet worked.

People talked. Gossip would always exist. We couldn't stop it, so why stop living?

Liv had nothing to apologize for. She was allowed to have a personal life, dammit. Although at the rate Jen was going, Liv would have hardly any life at all soon.

But maybe Liv was right. I didn't want to add to her stress, so lunch alone it was.

———

"Thanks for pushing me to get out of the house. I needed this." Liv's frequent sighs of pleasure during the appetizers had slowly driven me crazy, but at least the food was good.

One smile from her, and my heart turned clumsy, tripping over itself and likely shortening my lifespan. "Don't mention it."

"I mean it. This meant a lot to me. I know I've been around a lot. I must be cramping your style."

"My style is just fine."

"Liar," she chided. "It's been weeks since you've mentioned booty calling anyone." Liv cast a look at the waitress. "I know at least one woman who'd let you."

Not the right woman, though.

————

While Liv was in the bathroom, the waitress returned with my drink, leaning a little too close to be casual. "Here you go. Sorry for the wait."

I smiled politely. "I don't mind waiting." For six years, apparently.

"I should let you know I like a big tip." She laid a napkin down beside the cocktail, and I could tell without looking that it had her number on it.

She was bold. I'd give her that. And in another life, I would have gone for it. But it would be a lie, so I smiled and let her walk away.

Liv noticed the napkin as soon as she returned, stealing it out of my grasp. "Oh my god, I leave you alone for thirty seconds."

"I didn't even want it."

"Yes, you did, don't lie."

"People just want to give me their number. I can't help it."

She laughed. "Yeah, okay, stud."

And the smile she shot me was worth all the heartache in the world. This was why my heart hadn't been able to let go. Why it had never moved on. Because a little bit of Liv was worth more than a thousand random encounters.

Angling my phone camera at our cocktails, I posted the photo and tagged us both, happy that we'd gotten this time together. This was her when she was allowed the freedom to be herself. Away from the speculation and comments. Away from Jen.

I knew what it was like to bear the weight of someone else's expectations. To be constrained by it. Liv didn't deserve that life. Movie nights and lunches helped, but maybe I could do more. Maybe I could help her be free.

———

My mother always had fantastic timing. I let my phone ring until Liv's mouth twisted. Fine. I signed for the bill and answered.

"Hi mo—"

"Have you booked it? I still don't have your flight details, and the party is in ten days."

"I—"

"Penny, hun, can you make sure the dog's scheduled for his retreat? I can't have him running around while the marquee gets set up." I heard shuffling before she addressed me again. "If you don't send me your details by tonight, I'm booking them for you."

Actually, I was pretty sure Penny would be the one booking them, but I didn't bother to correct her. "Fine. I'll book it today and text you."

"Send them to Penny. She'll arrange the pickup at the airport." And then she was gone, no doubt dealing with one of the million other things that were more important than her eldest son.

I gritted my teeth. "Everything okay?" Liv asked.

"I better book this trip before my mother has a coronary."

"Oh. When will you leave?" Was it wrong to hope that I heard disappointment in Liv's voice? If I had a choice in the matter, I'd want to be here with Liv. It was foolish to hope she felt the same way.

"Soon. It's less than two weeks away."

"Will you be gone long?"

"Not if I can help it. A few days. Maybe a week."

Her smile didn't reach her eyes. "That'll be nice."

It wouldn't.

———

Any hope of getting one normal day had already been shot thanks to my mother, but even without that looming nightmare, the universe had decided today was the day for testing my patience. *Why make it rain when it can pour?*

The photographer pounced as soon as we stepped out of the restaurant, the incessant clicking of his camera only slightly less annoying than shit he kept saying while he tried to capture our reaction.

"Where have you been, Olivia? No one has seen you lately. Heard the network is about to make a big announcement. Does this mean you're off the show?"

I got Liv into the passenger seat first, keeping myself between her and the paparazzo, a litany of clicks going off from his camera.

He followed behind me, hovering so closely I could smell the tuna he'd had for lunch. "You two look cozy. Have you moved on already, Liv? Going through the cast one by one?"

I spun around and shoved him back, careful of the camera. "Was it you?"

He looked delighted at my reaction.

"Huh?" Another shove. "Did you wait outside her apartment like a pervert? How does it feel to have no morals, asshole?"

He had about a hundred pounds on me, so my pushing did nothing to move him away from the car. He just kept laughing and clicking away.

Liv called through the window, "Wes, leave it. Get in the car."

Tuna guy was loving it. Punching him wouldn't help anyone, but I bet it would feel good.

Instead, I jumped into the driver's seat, my knuckles white as I gripped the wheel.

He continued to yell through the window, undeterred. "Come on, guys, give us a kiss. Don't be shy."

I called back, "Move, or I'll run you over," which finally did the trick, and his sick laughter rang in my ears as we drove off.

Liv didn't utter a word the entire way home. I was seething with rage. Had he followed us to the restaurant? Waited outside until he could accost us? And why wasn't Liv more upset?

"You shouldn't have pushed him," Liv said once we'd made it into her apartment.

"That asshole was a vulture. What did you want me to do? Stand back while he said all that disgusting shit about you?"

I watched as she collapsed onto the couch, all the tension draining out of her. Anguished, she clutched her head in both hands, bowed over her knees. Seeing her like this fucking hurt.

"He was just doing his job." Her voice was so quiet, I almost missed it.

"Harassing people isn't a job."

She scoffed. "Tell that to Fox News."

"I should have broken his camera," I mumbled.

Liv finally looked up. "Wes, stop. You've already done enough."

My heart sank. She was right. I'd suggested lunch. I'd practically forced her to go. This was my fault. I dropped onto the couch beside her, exhaling my anger in one long breath. "Liv, you don't have to be so nice about it. They broke you and Bryson up, remember?"

The sadness in her eyes felt like a physical weight over my chest. "No, they didn't. I did."

"What?"

"The photographer who took the original photos knew exactly where to find us because I arranged it."

I fumbled for something to say, my mouth hanging open. "Does Bryson know?"

"I can't tell him. He's already pissed. Jesus, Wes, he just lost his job. How can I tell him that it was my fault?"

"He also forced you to hide your relationship and led you on for two years."

She placed a hand on mine. "Wes, don't. This isn't Bryson's fault, it's mine. I should never have gone behind his back like that. It's better that we're over. We weren't … It wasn't meant to last. I just wish it hadn't blown up like this."

"You had no idea this would happen. But what choice did he give you? If he'd listened to what you wanted, it might have changed things."

"You don't know that."

I pulled her close, settling us back onto the couch, Liv's

head on my shoulder. Her hair smelled like a spring garden. "I know that he's an asshole who doesn't deserve you."

I could hear the smile in her voice. "You're just saying that to make me feel better."

No, I wasn't. "Is it working?"

"A little."

7
———
LIV

Is Meres real? On-screen couple Olivia Davis & Wesley Owens were caught at the newly opened Hylin, today, exciting fans of the show and posing the question, Bryson who?

IT NEVER CEASED to amaze me how fast insignificant information traveled. Barely an hour ago we'd been harassed outside that restaurant, and now we were trending. The photographer hadn't wasted any time.

And neither had fans. Already, "Meres," the portmanteau of our on-screen characters, Meira and Ares, was trending.

Great. I looked across at Wes. It was one of the rare occasions when we weren't fitted together on the couch like nesting dolls. Instead, we faced each other, legs outstretched, our feet tangled between us. Wes' attention was on his phone. He wouldn't be checking the comments.

Wes never bothered with them. He was probably booking his flights.

This time next week, he'd be on the other side of the country. And I'd still be on this couch.

I knocked Wes' foot with mine. His bottom lip was tugged between his teeth, ruby red from chewing on it as he concentrated. Our eyes met, and I couldn't hold back my smile. A strand of his hair had gone rogue, arched over his part in the wrong direction. Artfully tousled and absolutely gorgeous.

He winked, and my stomach flipped. Three weeks ago, I would have laughed it off. My knees would still be weak, but I could have convinced myself I was unaffected. I was an actress. Pretending was what I did.

I needed to get a grip on these feelings. We were friends. He was here to support me because that's what good friends did. So why couldn't I stop thinking about him?

Having a crush on him now was a bad idea. A terrible idea, probably. Definitely.

"Do you remember the time your mom surprised you on set for your birthday only to walk in on us filming that scene where Ares was interrogating Meira?" Wes asked out of nowhere.

The memory sprang forth with a laugh. How could I forget? My costume had been carefully designed to be torn and falling off in all the right places, and the staging had me held in place against the wall while Wes, as Ares, was monologuing in an attempt to seduce me over to his side.

When Bryson had called cut, I'd noticed my mom standing beside him. I'd immediately frozen, feeling like she'd caught me in bed with a man. From her wide-eyed look, it was clear she'd felt the same way. It remained the one joke she couldn't make without blushing.

I swallowed around the nostalgia thick in my throat. There were so few people I shared memories of her with. "I can't believe you remember that."

He set his phone to the side, holding my gaze. "I'll never forget it," he said. "Rebekah cornered me between takes. Told me if I even thought about taking advantage of you, on or off set, I could count on this being my first and last job."

"She didn't! Wait, seriously?"

"Oh yeah. Said that if my hands went anywhere they weren't supposed to, I'd be down three limbs. I asked her, why not four? And she told me that she was only planning on taking both arms and the one between my legs."

Caught between pride and embarrassment, I covered my growing blush with one hand. "Oh my god." My mom was not a violent person. There was no way she meant any of what she said, but I could picture her, finger in his chest, putting the fear of the Almighty into him.

"No offense, but Rebekah was kind of terrifying."

I laughed. "She would have taken that as a compliment."

In reality, she was a teddy bear. Heart as big as anything, but also fearless. Protective. I cast a glance at Wes. Like someone else I knew.

"There was no way she could have liked me after that." I detected a disappointed note in his voice, and my muscles tensed, ready to launch myself across the couch to comfort him.

"Mom liked you, even though she thought you acted too big for your britches."

His head tipped back as he laughed, the sound tripping off a domino effect of tingles along my skin. My ponytail brushed against my neck as I tugged the end around my finger, desperate to give my hands something to do.

"She was convinced you had a crush on me," I added, all too aware of his toes gently brushing my calf through my jeans.

Wes sobered. "Oh?" His dark brown eyes met mine.

I was hyperaware of where our bodies were connected, suddenly too nervous to move. What was he thinking? Shit. Now I'd made it awkward.

"She wouldn't let it go, no matter how often I told her that you were dating someone. Multiple someones." Nervously, I laughed, hoping to make him smile, but he was still watching me, eyes intent. Searching for something.

I wanted to kick myself for even bringing this up.

Another stroke of his foot. Supportive. Comforting. "I always liked your mom. She was a smart lady."

Between heartbeats, I blinked, unable to let myself believe. Did he mean? He couldn't. The air stuck in my throat, my breathing slowing even as my pulse raced. My gaze fell to Wes' lips.

Two thundering knocks shook my door. I jumped. Shit.

"Olivia, open up. It's me."

Jen?

"Guess the dragon found out you left the tower," Wes joked, but his smile faltered when his phone lit up, his mother's name appearing on the caller ID.

"You can take it in the bedroom. I'll see what Jen wants."

————

Jen was the real deal. I'd seen her talk circles around producers twice her age until they were the ones trying to convince her of her good idea. As soon as I'd cracked the door, she rushed through. "Are you all right? Did they follow you home? I didn't see anyone downstairs."

Dressed in a deep purple sweater dress and matching knee-high boots, Jen was both beautiful and authoritative.

They said to dress for the job you wanted, and Jen dressed like she wanted to be on the cover of Vogue. Like me, she'd transitioned from modeling to movies, and it was one of the first things we'd connected on.

We were often mistaken for sisters. Same deep, wide-set eyes, same straw-yellow hair. Jen's was always cut perfectly straight. Never a hair out of place. Mine currently resembled the before version of a makeover.

"No, I'm fine. It was only one guy, and he backed off when we drove away."

"This is why I told you to stay inside. Why didn't you call me? If you needed food, I could have gotten someone to deliver. And if you absolutely had to go out in public, you really shouldn't have done it with Wesley. It's only throwing fuel onto a fire that refuses to burn out."

I was sick of this.

When I'd originally arranged for the photos of Bryson and me to be taken, I hadn't been naïve enough to think that it would pass without comment. The point had been to get attention. I'd hoped to push our relationship out of hiding. But I never expected it to result in a Jen-imposed house arrest.

"This is ridiculous. It's been weeks, and Wes and I have been friends for years. Everyone knows that. We've even milked it during promos for the show. I shouldn't have to hide away. How long do you expect me to keep doing this?"

The time between filming seasons used to be a relief. Two months to rest and decompress. When the only role I had to play was me. Last year, I'd hoped to spend it in Tahiti. I'd picked out the resort, a villa with a private pool. Nothing but sun, swims, and space. Then Jen had lined up a cross promotion shoot with Forever 21, and the trip had been rain checked.

I was sick of rain checks. Tomorrows. Somedays. I wanted to stop pressing pause on my life.

"Olivia, you've been through a lot. I know that better than anyone. And I stuck by you when you needed time to process what happened with your mom, but you need to let me do my job. This mess with Bryson, and now Wes, it's falling back onto you. It shouldn't, but that's the reality of it, and I'm doing everything I can to help you. I just need to know that I'm not doing it for nothing."

I deflated. "Of course. I'm sorry about today. You know how much I appreciate everything you're doing for me."

Jen stood at attention, hands on her hips and eyes darting around the room. She'd been here a million times, but I couldn't help but worry. Jen noticed *everything*.

I counted myself lucky that she sat without making a comment. I took the seat across from her, watching as her perfectly polished nails smoothed the wrinkles from her dress.

"I received a call today from the executive producers. There will be an official announcement tomorrow about the new show Bryson is heading up. The network will use it as a platform to thank him for all his hard work and congratulate Yvonne on taking the reins for the final season."

"Are they expecting us to make any kind of statement?"

"I've crafted something for you that will go out across your socials tomorrow. A little 'congratulations and excited to work with you' sort of thing."

"Thank you."

Her nod was quick and all business. "Now, we can expect to see an uptick in speculation that Bryson's move is related to your relationship, but there's nothing we can do about that."

From behind me, Wes scoffed but said nothing. I hadn't noticed him come back into the room. He stood, resting a hand on the back of my chair, keeping close. I shifted until I could feel the press of his fingers rustling my hair, reminding myself he was there.

"My suggestion," Jen continued, "is that you continue to lie low. And when I say that, I mean, don't be sighted having a romantic rendezvous with a man."

Show business. Proud proponent of misogyny since 1907.

"I'm not working. How much more of a break can I take?"

"Whatever you need to do to avoid the press." Her gaze flickered between Wes and me. "Events like today are not helping."

"That guy was an asshole," came from behind me.

I had to agree with Wes.

"What worries me is how it looks. You two spend a lot of time together."

"So she's not allowed to see anyone now?" Wes' face was stern. "I thought you were 'handling this'?" I could hear the air quotes.

Jen stood, face firm. "I am handling this, Wesley. But it would be a lot easier if you weren't fanning the flames."

I had to tip my head back to meet her gaze. It felt like a scolding when she was standing over me like this.

"As much as I hate saying it, if you can stay out of the

public eye, it'll let the media cycle move on and give the network time to decide what to do."

"What's there to decide?"

"Wes, stop." I stood up, needing to move. I shouldn't be the third wheel in a conversation about my life.

Every muscle in Wes' body looked taut. He only ever looked like that when he was preparing for a fight. It didn't matter whether stunts were involved. I touched his arm, relieved to find that it cut through the storm, his face softening as he turned to me.

Jen looked calm, but the glare she leveled against Wes was intense. "There are rumors floating around after your date this afternoon."

My heart did a small backflip. The open fire grill, the delicious food, how good it felt to be the sole focus of Wes' attention. It wasn't a date, but it could have been. I liked the idea.

Scared that this realization was playing out in real time on my face, I pulled a piece of hair out of my ponytail, looping it over and over my finger as I stared at my feet.

What would dating Wes look like? Probably gifts and spontaneous dates. Sweet nothings whispered in my ear. Warm hugs and extra marshmallows.

I remembered how gently he'd touched me when removing the necklace, and the memory alone brought a flush to my neck.

"In the past, I would have told you to ignore them. Rumors spring up on their own and will frequently pass by unnoticed. But—"

The full force of Jen's message was being directed at me. Over the years, I'd been photographed or filmed in everything from a cloak to a bikini. Never had I felt so naked as I did right then. I wondered if Jen really had tracked down the source of the Bryson photos. The real one.

"After what happened with Bryson, I would urge you to take this seriously. Neither of you have signed a contract, and no details have been announced. Mike and Alicia can do whatever they want, and if they decide that all of this press is damaging the brand of the show, they won't hesitate to cut one or both of you out of it."

I couldn't—wouldn't—allow that to happen.

"I know you two are friends, but right now there are people out there with a lot of time on their hands, and they're combing through years of photos and interviews, trying to sleuth their way into making you two an item."

I chanced a look at Wes. It hadn't escaped my notice that he had gone quiet beside me.

"It would be best if you aren't seen together for a while."

Oh.

Beside me, Wes said nothing. It would have been so simple to reach for his hand, thread our fingers together. He probably would have let me. Like every time we'd curled up next to each other during a movie. It would have been easy to throw a leg over his, press the last of our bodies together. With every hug, I'd eyed the hollow of his throat, tempted to breathe him in. Leave a kiss.

He would probably let me do those things, too.

But nothing could happen. Not here, with Jen's constant presence and the possibility of a fan around every corner. But what if we weren't here? What if it was only us? The mere spark of the idea excited me. The two of us, hidden away, no show, no expectations, no rules.

"What if I left the state?" I asked. I'd have to be careful. Jen would say no if she knew what I was thinking. I looked at Wes. He'd said he wanted to be partners. Clyde better be ready, because Bonnie was about to blow this joint.

Jen was apprehensive. "Where would you go?"

"Home to LA. I could stay with my dad." It wasn't a lie. I *could* stay with him. But I didn't intend to.

Jen hummed, unconvinced. Wes did exactly what I knew he'd do, which was back me up. "Great idea. No one will know where you are, and he can help you lie low."

I flashed him a grateful smile.

"I can't say I like this," Jen said.

Wes didn't look like he cared what she liked, but when he spoke, it was without anger. "It won't be any different from if she was holed up here. A week away from all this might help."

Jen looked skeptical, a single nail tapping in quick succession on her thigh, but ultimately, she agreed. "All right. I can't force you to stay if you're determined to do this." She stood gracefully. "In the meantime, I'll use the speculation to push Mike's hand on the spin-off. He won't be happy about today, but I'll remind him that it keeps people talking about the show. Hopefully we can sign the contract before anything else happens."

Wes' expression tightened in a way I couldn't read, but I was simply happy she'd agreed to let me go.

———

As the door shut behind her, the nerves crept in. Would Wes want me in LA with him? If he said no, I really could stay with my dad, but it would hurt. Sure, we'd spent almost every day together these past few weeks, but that didn't mean he wanted me there. He was probably looking forward to the break. And now I'd gone and invited myself. Talk about clingy.

The seconds ticked by as I struggled to talk. As soon as I opened my mouth, we were going to talk about it, and he might say no.

"So," he said.

Shit. Was it hot in here, or was it me?

He turned to me. "I guess you're coming to LA." His expression was frustratingly devoid of clues.

"Is that okay? I know I said I'd stay with my dad, and I can, but I hoped I could stay with you, if you don't mind. But I get it if you do. I didn't exactly give you a chance to say no. And I won't be offended if you want to. But this way we can keep each other company." I twisted a long strand of hair around my finger.

Finally, he smiled, crossing the distance between us. He rested his hands on my shoulders, rubbing calm into my skin. "Liv, stop."

He waited while I took a deep breath. Rosemary, thyme, and Wes. *Better.*

"I can't believe I'm going to say this, but I might agree with Jen. Maybe it's best if you stay here. I'm not saying you can't go, but if we're seen flying together, the press will have a field day, and Jen might finally explode."

"That's easy enough to get around. We just don't fly on the same day." I didn't see the issue. "Come on, I have to lie low, and you have to go to your parents' party. You always said your parents' place was big enough to house a small circus. They probably won't even notice I'm there."

He paled. "We're not staying with my parents. I, uh, have my own house in the hills. I'll take you."

"Wherever is good. As long as I'm with you."

I didn't say that the idea of him going away had made

me feel like I was wading into ice water. I didn't tell him that these last few weeks had been the most comforting I'd had since my mom had passed away. How I'd realized that my feelings for him were becoming increasingly non-friendly, and I didn't know what that meant for us or how to deal with it.

But I knew I wanted this.

I reached for him, crossing the small distance to hook my pinkie finger around his. Maybe if he didn't want to be my Clyde, I could appeal to his knightly duty. "Come on, Wes! Save me from the tower. Be my hero."

"Okay," he answered, and only then did Jen's warning about the show come roaring back into my mind. But it'd be fine. It was a week away with a friend. What was the worst that could happen?

8

WES

SO MUCH FOR a quick trip to LA. Now I'd be spending a week with Liv, just the two of us, with specific instructions to *lie low*.

Not that I had a problem with lying with Olivia. Shit. Nope. Thinking about that wasn't going to help.

I couldn't stop picturing the hope in her eyes when she asked if she could join me. She'd expected me to turn her down. Maybe I should have, for both our sakes. Liv always was smarter than me.

As if there was a universe in which I'd say no to her. I could only hope extreme exposure would somehow break what the last six years of friendship hadn't been able to. We'd get sick of each other after being in one another's pockets for a week, right?

Maybe then I would get it through my thick skull that this was never going to happen, and I'd stop wanting to kiss her every time I saw her. Or it would be a disaster, and I'd spend all week jerking off and hating myself.

A sleek black BMW picked me up at LAX, courtesy of

Penny. The driver took my suitcase without giving me his name and then refused to take me anywhere other than my parents' house. Great. It had already started.

I'd have to find my own way to my place. Because if there was one thing I wasn't doing this week, it was spending more time with my parents than was absolutely necessary. I could only handle avoiding one giant problem at a time, and I'd choose my ill-advised feelings for Liv over my brother.

Even the thought of the party on Saturday was stressing me out. I'd rather be frozen in the ninth circle of Hell than have to put on a happy face and pretend to enjoy myself with my parents' pompous friends. Maybe Dante had been wrong. Maybe there were actually ten circles, and the last one involved political small talk with out-of-touch millionaires.

Silence greeted me when I entered the house, but that wasn't unusual. I could count on my third nipple how many times they'd greeted me at the door. Oh wait, I didn't have a third nipple.

If I had to guess, Dad was at the country club. Bar or green, take your pick. If he had ever worked at the real estate firm he owned, it must have been when I was too young to remember it. These days, he had his minions do all the work and only showed his face at the parties where he could shake hands and get his commission.

Mom was where I expected her to be—pacing the length of their oversized kitchen, phone to her ear, metaphorical soapbox beneath her feet, with Penny, her assistant, shadowing her movements and looking overwhelmed.

Home sweet home.

"Oh! Wesley just showed up. I'll call you back." Mom thrust her phone into Penny's waiting hands.

"You made it," she said, walking over to hug me. "I was starting to worry."

I nodded, holding my tongue. *Not like I had any other choice.* "Where else would I be?" Was what made it out instead.

"Have you seen your brother yet?"

"Mom, I only just got here."

"Don't use that tone. I'm just asking. He's got a lot on his plate at the moment, so it'd be nice if you could help him out." She resumed her position at the kitchen island, plucking the phone from Penny's hands and effectively dismissing me.

Okay, I guess that's it then. Time to go find my ride.

My father, like most discerning rich people, liked to look rich but hated to spend money. What a problem, huh? Most of them picked one thing: the house, the toys, the "private donation to a college my kid couldn't get into otherwise." Whatever. They all had ways of putting their wealth on show.

For Dad, it was cars.

He had his everyday driving around town cars, black and silver sedans that cost six figures but were apparently pedestrian enough to be his work vehicle.

Then there were the ones too special to drive.

Those cars were kept safe in a second garage a short walk from the main house. The cavernous space was white and bright. And I mean, *bright*. All the better to see the dollar signs, I guess. That and the hand-buffed hoods.

A dozen cars, with little in common except price tags. Kept in pristine condition. Oil changed, tanks full, hoods waxed. But never, under any circumstances, driven. See, dear ol' Dad wasn't actually a car enthusiast. No, what he liked was anything that made him look more successful, whether it was the latest sports car or the picture-perfect family.

It's not like he would notice.

It was a crying shame to keep these treasures hidden away. I'd be doing the world a service. And I'd only be borrowing it.

My first instinct was to take the Mercedes. It was more practical than the Lambo, though not as fast as the Porsche. But if I was going to borrow a car, then common sense would dictate I take the one I really, *really* wanted to drive.

The DB11.

What a beauty. Hand-stitched leather interiors. Clamshell hood. Sleek curves. The midnight black sports car looked primed to strike, like a panther waiting for its prey.

I spent my childhood loving its predecessor, and I'd been crushed when Dad traded it in for the upgrade last year. I'd never get the chance to drive the 9, but now the 11 called to me.

It had to be a sign.

Getting my hands on the keys was laughably simple. The combination to the key safe hadn't been changed since I was a wayward teenager, and honestly, if he was going to make it this easy, it was his own damn fault.

Mom was still in the kitchen when I returned for my bags. "Off somewhere?"

Nice of you to notice. "Yeah. I'm gonna grab my bags and head over to my place."

"Oh." Her disappointment surprised me. Had she really thought I'd stay here? "We prepared a room for you."

Yeah, not happening. "That's okay. I've got a friend

arriving tomorrow. We'll stay out of your hair until the party."

"A friend? I didn't know you were bringing someone," she said with interest.

"We work together, that's all."

She didn't believe me, but what did she know of my life? She could speculate all she wanted. It wouldn't make it true.

"Well, have fun with your *friend*," she said, already typing something into her phone and turning away from me. "And call your brother."

Sighing, I took the fastest path out the front door, packing my luggage into the Aston. When I slipped into the cool leather seat, I straight up moaned. Every inch was soft to the touch, and the curve of the seat cupped me in an embrace that should only be reserved for a lover. Seated this low to the ground, I could practically feel the scratch of the asphalt against my ass.

Shit. I totally understood now how people became obsessed with cars. This was an out-of-body experience.

The engine roared to life with the touch of a button, the thrum of power rumbling into my bones. It was a double shot of adrenaline and sex. I was officially ruined for all other cars.

A small blur raced out in front of the car, making my heart jump into my throat as I slammed on the brakes. I parked and was out of my seat as soon as possible, spotting the culprit immediately. "Jesus, Baxter, you gave me a heart attack."

No sooner had I finished talking than I had a face full of tawny brown Staffy, jumping and licking what he could get to. He was huge. When I'd left for Chicago, he'd only been a puppy. It had killed me to leave him behind, even though he wasn't mine.

"Weren't you supposed to be getting pampered right now?" I laughed as he continued to lick my face.

Mom had gotten him on a whim, adopting him as part of a dog shelter charity luncheon she'd hosted one year before realizing she had no idea how to take care of a dog. I'd been the one to raise him when I'd still lived here, housing him at my place while mom complained that he'd dug up the garden again.

You know, like puppies do.

Without a second thought, I waved Baxter into the car, only sparing a small wince at what his nails might do to the leather seats. *Oops.*

It was strange being back. Back in LA. Back in this house.

When I moved to Chicago for the show four and a half years ago, I hadn't expected to return. I could have sold it or rented it out, but I'd either have to tell my father or go through one of his competitors. So I'd left it. Treated it like a hotel.

It was fine. Comfortable, private. Somewhere to store all the crap I'd taken with me when I moved out of my parents' house. The gym was fully equipped, even if all I had in the kitchen was beer and dog food—thanks to a quick detour on our way here.

I tossed Baxter another treat. If I had to be home—and I did—this was where I'd rather be.

The buzzer on my front gate went off.

I didn't travel with any sort of security, but that didn't mean I didn't appreciate a bit of distance in my own home.

When I reviewed the security panel and saw who was here, I groaned. Lucas.

I couldn't have one day to myself?

I opened the gate for my brother and tossed back the rest of my beer, walking to meet him outside. The faster this was over with, the better.

He looked equally unimpressed as he exited his car, tossing a sharp look at the Aston. He recognized it as well as I had. I smirked back at him.

"Lucas."

"Wes."

Standing there in a light-gray suit and tie, he looked like a carbon copy of our father. The only exception was his crop of our mother's signature black curls.

When I didn't move to invite him inside, he sighed, shoving a hand into his pocket. "Mom told me you arrived. I would have picked you up from the airport, but I had to finalize a sale this morning."

Of course he did. All I ever heard about was how swamped he was. Too important to be around. God, he really was becoming our father.

"You're a busy guy. What's new?"

He shifted, looking uncomfortable. Good. That made two of us. "Yeah, well, between work and Mom and Dad's anniversary, I have a lot going on, and I'm doing it all on my own."

There was a sharp edge to his voice, matched by the challenge in his eyes.

Once upon a time, we'd been inseparable. We could be fighting one minute and best friends the next. Now it was like talking to a stranger. I never knew what to say to him, not without it devolving into a fight.

I missed talking to him. I missed having a brother.

But I had no idea how to even start getting back to that, or whether we ever could.

"You could have asked me."

His only answer was a disbelieving huff and a shake of his head.

"You could have. If you weren't so busy being Dad's pet."

"Are you kidding me?" he started, then stopped when his smart watch beeped. "No. I'm not doing this."

He held out a thumb drive.

"What's this?" I asked.

"It's for the party. We're going to show a video reel before the speeches, and I don't have time to do it. This is a copy of some home videos. All you need to do is cut together about three minutes of footage before Saturday. If you can squeeze that in."

I stared at the thumb drive, making no move to take it. Every video on there would be a lie. I'd already lived it once. The last thing I wanted to do was sit through it again. "Do you know how many wannabe videographers there are in this city? Why am I the one stuck doing this?"

"Jesus, Wes. Stop being so selfish. Do it because I asked you to. You've done nothing else for them. You know they wanted you at the house, but you just had to be alone. Like always."

"Wow."

We'd reached a new low. From hello to fighting in less than five minutes. I gave him an exaggerated once over.

"It's uncanny. Dad gives you a job, and now you're the spitting image of him."

"Not all of us get to play pretend, Wes. Some of us have responsibilities."

Unbelievable.

"You're not the only one with responsibilities, Lucas."

"Oh really? Tell me one thing you've done for our family lately. You never visit. Mom practically had to beg you to come here for this. I know you don't care about us anymore, but the least you could do is suck it up for one party."

My gut churned. "Fine. Give me the damn drive." I held out my hand, and he passed it to me, then turned to his car. When he reached the door, he paused and looked back at me.

"You're lucky, you know that? You get to do whatever the hell you want, and you're still their favorite."

His words stunned me, keeping me frozen in place as he drove away.

I'd never been the favorite. Ever since Lucas was a baby, he'd had their attention. He still had it. Lucas was the golden child who could do no wrong, whereas I never lived up to their expectations. When I chose acting, I'd become the example they used for what not to do.

How could he not remember who had taken care of us while they were busy socializing? I'd been there to help with homework, to talk to him about his first girlfriend, to celebrate when he graduated. It was always just the two of us, thick and thin, no matter what.

Now look at us.

9

WES

LIV EXITED LAX in a backward cap, oversized sunglasses, and a pink patterned romper. Her hair was tucked behind her ears, sticking out the back of the white cap, and she wore a wide smile that had broken out as soon as she'd noticed me.

I took a deep breath, willing my frantic heart to stop skipping in my chest. Just the sight of her made me happier, loosened the knots that had formed overnight. Barely a day apart, and I'd missed her. I needed to get a handle on this soon or I'd be truly screwed.

Would I ever stop having this reaction to her?

"Nice car."

Liv slipped into the passenger seat quickly, casting a worried glance around. I'd picked her up from an exclusive exit so there was no chance of anyone seeing us, but her attempt to be stealthy was cute.

She narrowed her eyes as I chuckled, then she jumped in her seat when a cold nose bumped her elbow.

"Holy shit!"

I laughed harder, scratching Baxter's forehead. His tongue lolled to the side in a smile. "Liv, meet Baxter. Baxter, Olivia."

"Hi Baxter." Liv held out her hand for him, and immediately, he stretched forward to nuzzle it. Lucky bastard.

Liv's smile grew as she patted him. "When did you get a dog?"

"He's actually my parents' dog, but they're busy with all the party stuff and planned to ship him off to a dog spa, so …"

"You have a problem with dog spas?"

"Of course not," I laughed, "But I haven't seen him in a while, and I thought it would be nice."

"It is nice." She reached over and squeezed my hand, and a familiar thrill ran through my body. "You're a real sweetheart under all that bravado."

"You getting sweet on me, doll?"

I'd meant to deflect, all too aware of how the glow of her smile and fire of her touch had sent my pulse skyrocketing. But as I watched her cheeks flush, I realized that it only made things much, much worse. Instead of distracting me, all I wanted to do was pull her to me and feel the warmth of her skin beneath my lips.

Baxter, at least, was not deterred, barking loudly enough to break me out of the spell. Hell. Even the dog could tell I was too far gone. Clearing my throat, I pulled out of the spot, navigating my way out of the maze that was the airport parking lot. It was a hell of a lot easier to keep my focus firmly on the road and not on the beautiful woman next to me.

The one I was about to spend a week with. Alone. In my house. Where I'd be tortured by her presence every day.

A jerk in a BMW cut me off on the 405, and I gleefully retaliated by changing lanes and accelerating past him. This car was a dream. In my periphery, Liv gripped the door.

"I forgot that you drive like a maniac."

"Says the Sunday school driver. Some of us actually like to use both pedals." It had been a few years, but I still remembered what she was like behind the wheel. Slow. Anxious. At least when I drove, we got to where we were going in record time. "Complain all you want. You'll remember that I've never been in an accident."

"You've gotten lucky." She quickly held a hand up in warning. "Don't make the joke."

I laughed. "You set it up." Tapping my hand on the wheel, I asked, "Would you rather drive?"

"In LA? I don't have a death wish."

It was a good thing I had to keep my eyes on the road because that backward cap had raised her kissable factor by 80 percent. It didn't stop me from glancing over when I could. She was leaning against the window, observing the traffic with a soft smile on her face. It was a relief to see some of the tension drain out of her. No matter how hard this week might be for me, I wouldn't regret having her here if it meant giving her the chance to relax.

I'd just spotted our exit when she asked, "You'd really trust me with your car?"

The answer came easily. "Of course."

She already had my heart. At least if she broke the car, it could be fixed.

———

Baxter bounded out of the car as soon as he could, tripping over Liv, who hadn't expected forty pounds of excited dog

to get in her way when she opened her door. The closing
security gate rumbled in the background while he relieved
himself on the bushes by the front door. Dad would have
thrown a fit.

Good dog.

I turned back to help Liv with her bags, surprised to
find her holding a single carry-on. "Huh. I kind of
expected more than that."

She shrugged. "I packed light. I don't plan on wearing
much this week."

Two or three breaths later, my mind skittered back into
existence. This was going to be a long week. Lots of cold
showers.

Liv continued into the house, unaware.

She dropped her bag inside the entryway, making a
beeline through the living room to the outdoor pool. "Wow,
this place is amazing."

"It's not much. My parents' house is five times this size.
But it's secluded, and the view isn't bad." I didn't know why
I was downplaying it. Liv knew my background. But this
wasn't about impressing her. Not the way I would have
when I was a cocky twenty-two-year-old. I didn't want Liv
to like me because of what I had, but because of who
I was.

That said, the view was second to none. The hills
stretched out before us, the city a beacon in the distance. At
night, it would feel like standing above the stars, the lights
glittering below us. Liv's jaw dropped as she took it in.
"Whoa."

"Right?" Fine. I wasn't above admitting her wonder
made me happy.

"It's stunning." A breeze swept her hair into her face,
and I ached to brush it out of her eyes. Being this close and

wanting to touch her wasn't new, but it felt different, more intimate, out here with no one else around.

Liv tucked the hair behind her ears, staring in wonder at the view. I couldn't tear my eyes away from her.

"I might never leave," she said.

I might never let you go.

Liv turned back to the house, head tilted in thought. "You could get some really cool shots from this angle."

"Why don't you?"

She leveled a look at me that I recognized as "be serious, Wes."

"I'm serious," I said.

"No one is just going to hand me a camera."

I took great pleasure in proving her wrong by pulling my phone out of my pocket and holding it out to her. "Go on. Tell me what you want me to do."

She stared at it, biting her lip. Fuck. Backward hat *plus* a lip bite? It was official. This week was going to kill me.

Eventually, she took the phone—like I knew she would. "What do you want to do?"

"You tell me. This is your shoot, Liv. You're in charge."

She stood a little straighter. Determination looked damn good on her. "Go back inside. Come through the sliding doors and walk toward the pool. Slowly. Keep the glasses on."

And shit. Getting bossed around by her was hot.

I did as directed, keeping a cool, detached expression while she filmed. Baxter got bored halfway through the second take and trotted off on his own. Liv was in her element, eyes focused, making small adjustments as we went. She was always attractive, but Liv in boss mode was sexy as hell.

"Done," she said, taking another minute to edit the video before handing the phone back to me.

I watched it back, and … damn. All I'd done was walk a few feet, and Liv had transformed it into a moody one-shot akin to a designer ad. She'd even ended it by capturing the reflection of the pool from my aviators.

"This is really cool, Liv." I was so fucking impressed with her talents. Why the hell wasn't she directing already?

I didn't hesitate, posting it to my Instagram. Even if I couldn't tag her—thanks, Jen—people needed to see this.

"It's all right," she said, shy.

It was my turn to wear the "be serious" look. "You made me look fucking cool."

Liv turned away from the compliment, looking back to the house. But I had definitely caught sight of a grin. Good.

"It's easy to make you look good," she said. "And this house. I still can't believe this is yours."

I shrugged, dismissive. It wasn't my favorite topic of conversation, even if I felt like a dick for being so nonchalant about my privilege. There were a hell of a lot of people who were worse off, and I knew that. But everything to do with my family stirred up complicated feelings in me.

Which was why I hated coming back here.

"Dad always went on about making sure Lucas and I were," I used air quotes, "taken care of."

Liv raised a brow in question.

"And," I continued, "his answer to that was to gift us each a house. Welcome to my twenty-first birthday present." I waved my hand in a sweeping gesture over the building.

"You don't seem impressed."

"He wasn't ever around. And when he was, he just

shoved gifts at us and acted like he was a great dad for doing it. Taking care of us? Yeah right."

I was still raw from my argument with Lucas yesterday. This was the most I'd ever opened up about growing up here, and I really wished I hadn't said anything. That nice, fun moment we were having? Gone.

Now that the words were out, I couldn't take them back, and I settled for staring out across the hills, feeling Liv's gaze on me but unable to meet it.

She seemed to understand that I didn't want to elaborate, though I didn't expect the conversation to be over by a long shot.

But she took pity on me, shifting closer and dropping her head to my shoulder, her arms snaking around my waist. The hug tugged at my heart, and an area farther south, both of which I told to *get bent* because my control was already stretched pretty thin.

But I was a glutton for punishment, so I pulled her closer, holding her tight as she relaxed in my arms. She let out a contented sigh and sagged deeper against me. It was difficult to remember this wasn't real.

"I should put my stuff away," she finally said, pulling away when our hug had gone past the point of friendly.

"Right." She followed me inside, and I led her down the long hallway that ran through the center of the house. "I'll be in the master bedroom at the end, so you'll be in here." I gestured to the first bedroom on the right. There was a second bedroom beside it that was full of junk. Technically, I had no use for either room. It wasn't like I ever had guests stay here, but the guy I'd paid to furnish the place had set one up as a guest room anyway. And thank fuck, because I could not handle a whole "one bed" situation on top of everything else.

Light streamed in from the window, which overlooked the view she'd admired earlier. "There's a bathroom on the other side of the hall. I've got an en suite, so we won't have to share."

"What's downstairs?"

"Home theater and a gym." She looked impressed.

"No maids' quarters?"

I laughed, shook my head. "Not yet."

She unzipped her suitcase and started unpacking, and I realized I was hovering. We'd spent a lot of time together recently, but never like this. She'd be sleeping down the hall from me. Showering mere feet from where I did.

Shit. *Don't start thinking of her in the shower.*

I backed out of the room. "I'll order dinner."

———

"Wow. I'm so glad I traveled across the country to watch you on your phone," Liv grumbled from the other side of the couch.

"So put a movie on. There's a TV right there."

She reached for the remote. "I'm sure your girlfriends won't mind if you're MIA for more than an hour." She sounded pissed, and when I looked up, her mouth was a flat line. Definitely pissed.

Wait.

Was she ... jealous?

"That wasn't who I was—" I stopped. "The women I talk to ... None of them are ... It's not serious."

She looked at me like I'd just said the sky was blue. "Yeah, I know. Everyone knows you don't do serious."

Well, that hurt.

"If you ever fell in love, I'd fall over from shock," she added.

I bet she would.

"Yeah, that would be crazy," I joked, but there was nothing light in my voice, and a smile wouldn't materialize.

"Hey, I'm just kidding, Wes."

Shit. *Get it together, man.*

But my mouth had other ideas. "Is it really so unbelievable that I want to fall in love?"

There was a flash of surprise, but she covered it quickly. "Of course not. I guess we've never really talked about it, and you've always ... been you. You flirt and joke about sleeping around. I never knew you wanted all the romantic stuff."

Because it was easier than the truth.

"Well, I do."

"Wow." She nodded slowly. "So why haven't you been in love yet?"

This was skirting too close to dangerous territory. But being this close to the fire only made me more reckless, not less. "Who says I haven't?"

"Have you?"

Desire rattled the chains around my heart. *Open up. Let her in. Get closer.* Maybe I could stand to loosen them a little. If there was anyone I wanted to know me, it was Liv.

Trust was a sword encased in stone, and Liv wielded it easily. I envied that. She was fearless in a way I could only fake. I was better at pretending.

"No," I lied.

Silence descended again. Liv gazed out at the now glittering lights that spanned out across the horizon.

"I don't think I've ever been in love."

This surprised me. I'd always assumed that she and

Bryson were serious enough. "Not even with …?" I didn't want to say his name.

Liv shook her head. "No. I thought maybe we could be. But now I know better." She tipped her head back, eyes on the ceiling. "I remember what my parents had, and I want that. It's what I imagine true love is."

I thought about my parents. Love wasn't the word I'd use to describe their relationship. Everything I thought I knew about love had come from a book or movie. And Liv.

"What do you think true love is?" she asked.

In my experience? Heartache. "I think it's loving someone with your whole self. It's unconditional. Endless. You're happier than you ever imagined when you're with them, and being without them makes you feel like you're missing a part of yourself. And when it's the right person, you'd rather let your heart break than see them unhappy."

"Wow. I really hope you find it someday. You deserve it."

Our eyes met, and I couldn't look away. Her big rich brown eyes that had the ability to completely captivate me.

From where she sat tucked into my side, it wouldn't take much to lean in and show her how I felt. Barely anything at all. And, god, the way she was looking at me, soft and inviting. I felt the pull in my chest, heat curling below my skin.

I could barely breathe.

I could risk it.

It would be so easy to give in. But it was also scary and complicated, and it was so much easier to leave things as they were.

10

LIV

Dumped! Bryson Green is replaced as showrunner on popular show The Guild. *But it's not just the show that's moved on. Our sources say—*

WES PULLED the phone out of my hand, cutting off the caption.

"Okay, that's enough." He kept the phone out of my reach as he backed away. "You were complaining about me being on my phone, but all you've done for weeks is check your mentions and stalk the gossip sites. No more."

I stalked after him, plucking my phone out of his fingers and stepping close enough to feel his breath against my cheek. Suddenly, my body was sparking to life, lighting up like pyrotechnics in a Michael Bay film.

"Is that right? And how do you plan to stop me?"

His eyes dropped to my lips so quickly I almost missed it. Any longer and I might have dared him to do it.

It was odd, sometimes, to look at a person and know you've kissed them, even if it had been in front of your boyfriend and dozens of crew members. And then broadcast for millions of people.

The kisses on *The Guild* weren't real kisses. I knew that. They were too staged. Always at the right angle. Not too much pressure. Keep it tight and dry. I knew what it felt like to kiss Wes, yet I still wondered. What would it be like to *really* kiss him? No script, just passion.

Wes was a good person to kiss for the cameras. He was gentle, respectful, he never ate beforehand, and he always worked to get the details sorted out so there were no surprises—no tongue, hands kept to safe zones—hair, face, upper back, arms. Wes had a knack for improvising on set, but I liked how seriously he took the intimate scenes. I'd known a handful of actors—of all genders—who liked to "see where the moment led" and used it as an excuse to cop a feel they knew they wouldn't otherwise get.

Wes never did. Sometimes I wanted to shatter through that care, pull our hips together, and lick the seam of his mouth, see what it felt like, but I didn't. And I'd tried very hard not to think about why the urge existed in the first place.

"I thought asking you nicely might work, but I can restrain you if I need to." There was fire in his eyes. A dare.

I couldn't speak. Couldn't move.

I'd been a shy child. It was why I got into modeling so young. Mom had wanted to help me build up my confidence, and for once, my bird-like features and giant goggly eyes had been a plus. I had a *haunted quality*, they'd said. It helped that I didn't talk much.

The confidence modeling gave me was immeasurable. By the time I turned eighteen, I was a different person.

That confidence was MIA at the moment. Otherwise, I might have kissed him. Touched him. I wanted to. I wanted to close the distance. Forget everything Jen had said and follow this urge to its natural conclusion. I wanted Wes to want it, too.

But I couldn't.

I was already risking enough by being here. If a single person had caught me getting into his car yesterday, Jen would be on the next flight over to fire me herself. Wes might not believe that the network would get rid of us, but I wasn't so sure. I hadn't believed Bryson, either, and look how well that went.

I loved my job, and I knew how much the show meant to Wes. I would rather quit than mess this up for him.

I stepped back, cradling my phone to my chest. I needed to cool down. "Your pool is real, right? It's not just for show?"

"Sure. Why?" His voice was low, rough. Sexy.

I'd started to overheat. Was the ice bucket challenge still a thing? "I'm going for a swim."

————

The real world felt like a distant memory as I floated out here. I could be anywhere, anyone.

Do anything.

Mom had been the rebel in our family. When she was eighteen, she'd hopped on a plane and traveled around Australia for a year. Studied marine biology and spent the summer on a Catamaran off the east coast. Learned to surf.

Mom believed that if you wanted something, you went for it.

Sometimes I wondered if that trait had skipped a generation.

I was often asked what I would do if I wasn't acting. The easy answer was modeling, even though it wasn't true. I'd liked it for a while, but now I hated the feeling of being hired out as a blank canvas, a prop for someone else's pleasure. At least with acting, I could speak. Act, move, be.

Now I wanted more.

While we dated, Bryson had helped me. And from the moment he'd handed me a camera and walked me through framing, something clicked.

I'd gotten the same thrill yesterday when Wes had given me his phone. And I'd liked it. Liked taking charge. Finding the angles, playing with the light. It helped that Wes was easy to look at.

My eyes drifted closed, nothing but the sound of birds and the occasional breeze filling my senses. "This is heaven."

Wes hummed his agreement.

This was why I was here. No Jen telling me where to be. No stylist telling me what to wear. No makeup or hair to prep me before I walked out the door. No handlers, no assistants, no direction, no management.

Just Wes and me.

It should have felt selfish, hiding from Jen and everything back home. Instead, all I felt was relief. I took another long inhale, focusing on the lap of the water against my skin, between my fingers, through my hair.

Feeling fearless, I asked, "Do you think Jen was right?"

"No," he said, fiercely. It was easy to think Wes was frivolous, but he packed a lot of passion underneath his playful side.

I swam over to where he was sprawled out on a sun

chair, hanging on to the side of the pool and resting my chin on my hands. "You don't even know what I was going to say."

The sun bathed him beautifully. It was truly unfair how gorgeous he was. I knew women who would pay a lot of money for those cheekbones. A lot of people had written him off because of his looks. His strong jaw contrasted the smooth lines of his youthful face. The curls that called out to be touched. But it was his eyes that took my breath away. Deep pools of dark chocolate.

For someone who could revert to an oversized kid, he had a regality. Tall, so tall, and loose-limbed. Like the sapling of a redwood. Or a teenage Groot.

But he was also strong. He didn't have the bulk of Jackson, but he was lean and agile. It reminded me of the movie heroes of old. Errol Flynn or Gene Kelly. Gentle giants who could just as easily sweep you off your feet with words as they could with their arms.

He lifted his sunglasses. "I don't need to know. You're worried she was right about the show. She's not."

He looked tired. Even more tired than usual. I'd caught him staring at an innocuous USB multiple times today. It'd been wedged between a succulent and a cookbook dedicated to Christmas cookies.

I had no idea what the device held, but I noticed the tension on the edges of his smiles and the taut way he was carrying himself, so unlike the Wes I knew.

"Everything okay?" I knew his family played a part, and I hoped he would open up to me about them.

"I'm with the sexiest woman on earth. What could I possibly complain about?"

I preened under the compliment, even though I knew it was a diversion.

I wished he'd let me in. I wanted to help. He'd done so much for me lately. I was determined to return the favor.

That's all it was. Not the growing and undeniable need to be near him. Hear his voice. Make him smile.

Because we were friends, and that's what friends did.

Sure. Totally normal to want to bury your fingers in your friend's hair and wake up breathing him in.

Even in my wildest imagination, I couldn't sell that lie.

I couldn't put a word to what we were. The word "friend" didn't begin to encapsulate everything he meant to me.

He had become my sanctuary these past few weeks. The first I'd felt since mom passed. She used to be my go-to, at least until she got sick. Even after the diagnosis came —stage four, originating in the lungs—she rallied hard to keep everything the same for as long as possible.

But nothing was the same.

I spent as much time as I could with her. Watching a new show she'd discovered or laughing at a comedy special she liked—anything funny she could get her hands on. She loved to laugh.

Just like Wes. No matter how bad I felt, he could always make me laugh.

"It's nice having you around," I said.

He laughed. I loved his laugh. I never wanted to be without it. "You're just realizing that after six years?"

"You were a bit of a dick when we first met. It's taken this long to like you."

"And yet you're always talking about my dick," he said, then his smile dropped. "Is that really what you thought of me?"

"Well, yeah," I joked, then realized he'd stopped

smiling, and I immediately felt terrible. "I know you're not, though."

He didn't look convinced.

"Come on, you didn't like me at first, either."

"Of course I did. I've always liked you, Liv."

He looked so serious and still a little hurt. Shit. How could he not know how much he meant to me?

"I like you, too." It wasn't enough, but it was the truth. I liked Wes. A lot. Maybe a little *too much*.

11

LIV

I'D FORGOTTEN how overblown houses in the hills could be. Every room in Wes' place was cavernous. I could have held a small dinner party in the guest room alone, and the rest of the house only got bigger.

It wasn't just that every room was larger, lighter, and more comfortable. There were extras you'd never even think of. The floors were heated. There was a sound system connected in every room. The guest bathroom had a free-standing tub fitted with an automatic bubble bath dispenser, and the shower had a steam setting. It was completely unnecessary and utterly fantastic.

Despite Wes' frustrations with how he'd gotten the place, there was no denying how impressive it was.

It didn't feel right, though. I missed the Muppet chair and the lumpy couch. All the touches that made Wes' place his own. This must be how he felt when he visited my apartment.

Baxter trotted after me as I explored, my own personal

guard. Or perhaps he was making sure I didn't venture out of bounds. Then I got an idea.

The stakes might be small, but if I wanted this, I needed to step up. *Take charge.*

It took the gift of one treat and the promise of another before Baxter let me follow him. I hunched over to get the shot I wanted, filming on my phone as he ventured from kitchen to living room to kitchen again.

The clip of his nails on the floor reminded me of when I'd last seen Jen. I stifled a laugh, then let it free. Fuck it, I'd add music before I posted the video anyway. It felt good to let loose.

I played it back. Nothing groundbreaking, but the angle and the shakiness added a unique twist. I liked it.

I posted it before I could second-guess myself.

Wes was busy working out downstairs, so I called the other main man in my life. Dad picked up on the third ring. "How are you, honey?"

It was a relief to know that he wasn't asking because of everything that had happened recently. He, thankfully, didn't follow my career online. Dad only occasionally used Facebook, and that was only because he pen-palled—because he refused to call it anything else—his second cousin in Miami about wood lacquers.

The exciting life of a retired architect.

"I'm good." Understatement of the century. In the span of twenty-four hours, I'd gone from keyed-up in Chicago to feeling more relaxed than I had in years. If anyone asked, I'd say it was the calm. But I knew better. It was the Wes effect. "How are you?"

"Fine."

Not this again. Was there a vocabulary shortage? What was it with every man in my life always being "fine"?

"You're not overworking yourself, are you?" I asked.

"No." *Yes.*

"So you're not still walking Mrs. Williams' dogs?"

"Of course I am. Who else is going to do it?"

I rolled my eyes, moving down the hallway toward the bedroom that was currently unoccupied. I expected to find a mirror of the room I was in and was surprised to find it resembled every spare room in a *Hoarders* episode.

That was a slight overstatement. I could still see the carpet. But the packed bookshelves and stacks of filled plastic packing tubs spoke volumes.

"I don't know, maybe someone who didn't have hip surgery last year?"

"It's healed, and I need the exercise."

"You're supposed to be taking it easy. I thought that was the point of retirement."

"And do what? Sit around all day?"

"I don't know, Dad, just be careful, all right?"

"I always am."

Though my curiosity was nagging at me, I walked past the bookshelf to the half-opened wardrobe, finding a dozen suit bags filled with various designers. Before yesterday, I would have assumed these were new, bought after the show had become a success. Now I wondered how many were gifts from his father. Payment in exchange for affection.

"Your aunt Lucy tells me you're dating your boss."

I turned to rest my head on the cupboard door. "Dad."

Baxter's cold nose nudged my leg, his concern fading when I scratched behind his ear.

"I know you're old enough to do what you want, but—"

"Dad, stop. We're not even together anymore."

Stacked high in the wardrobe were more games than I'd

ever seen in one place. I didn't even know Wes liked to play board games. I'd have to ask him what his favorite was.

"I'm sorry to hear that. Was it serious?"

"No, it wasn't."

Gosh, this was hard. If it were mom, I would have dived in, told her all about the photos, the breakup, asked her what she would do if she were me. But I wasn't talking to Mom. Dad and I … we rarely had heart-to-hearts. And no matter how much I wished I could talk to him, the words always got stuck in my throat.

"It's been a little rough, but I've got work to keep me busy. And Wes."

"Ah, okay. Is he …?"

"We're just friends, Dad." A truth that felt more like a lie with each passing day.

I left the bedroom with a mental note to talk to Wes about the games. How often had we watched a movie because it was what I wanted to do? It would be nice to do something he enjoyed for a change.

"How is Aunt Lucy, by the way?" I asked, quick to distract us both from the topic of Wes.

"She's good. The shop is doing well." And from there, he gave a quick roundup of status updates. From Mrs. Williams ("her grandson turned eighteen last week. They must have been up until three a.m.!"), to my cousin Eddy who was getting his pilot's license ("It's the third career change in as many years, so hopefully he sees it through this time."). It was funny how much easier it was to talk about everyone else's lives and not our own.

And we never ever talked about Mom.

I'd always felt like my mother's daughter. A pale imitation, maybe, but I was working on being a better reflection of the best parts of her. We'd had so much in common—movies, music, our universal love of the scene in *In & Out*, where Kevin Kline dances to "I Will Survive."

But *Dad*, a man who had somehow managed to keep the same job for thirty years, who now spent his time tending to lawns in his retirement or volunteering at the local library ... I didn't know the first thing about how to connect with him. What did we have in common, except for the loss of the woman most important to us?

It had been four years since she passed, and we still hadn't worked out a way to bring her up to each other.

———

Wes returned, flushed and sweaty from his workout. "How is your dad?" He pulled his shirt up, patting his face dry and revealing the prominent V of his hips, the smooth expanse of his stomach, and the hint of hair trailing down. It led my eyes and my brain to filthy places.

"Doll?"

A pleasant tingle ran up my spine like I'd just held Lizzie Bennet's hand as she stepped into her carriage. *Doll.* Any time Wes said it, my whole body lit up.

I cleared my throat, even though it did nothing to clear the images from my brain. "The same."

I'd woken up this morning to find Wes shuffling around the kitchen in cactus boxers and cartoon taco socks. I'd had to physically restrain myself from marching over and plastering my body to his like I was a human koala bear.

"Still walking the neighbor's dog?"

"Of course he is. He won't listen to me. If mom were still around ..." I trailed off.

"She'd probably have changed the locks so he couldn't

get out of the house," Wes finished for me, making me smile.

"Exactly." His comments about his own father gave me pause. It was the most I'd ever gotten out of him. I wondered if was hard for him to hear about my dad when he was so distant from his own. "It's frustrating, but I still love him."

He looked pained when he sat, and I knew it wasn't from his workout. I shuffled closer, laying my hand on his, offering solace.

"Did I tell you my father refused to pay for film school?" he said.

I shook my head.

"Said if I wanted to waste my future, I'd have to spend my own money. It was an empty threat. I'd already gotten my inheritance when I turned eighteen. He just wanted me to know that he disapproved."

"That's horrible."

"That's him. We had a big fight, and I told him that I hoped I didn't turn out anything like him."

"What did he say?"

"That makes two of us."

I squeezed his hand. "Wes …"

"Hey, it's okay."

My heart clenched. He deserved so much better than that.

"We weren't ever going to be close. Not like you and your parents."

I had the sudden urge to call my dad back and tell him I loved him. Even when the conversation stalled or we tiptoed around our grief, I never doubted his love for me.

"Dad used to cook us pancakes every Sunday," I said, sinking into the memory. He'd put on the radio and hum along, a dishtowel thrown over his shoulder, throwing an occasional wink at mom. Then she'd swipe the towel and chase him around the kitchen.

My throat grew tight. "Does it make you angry? That you didn't get that?"

"The traditional *Full House* home life?" he asked.

I nodded.

"Sometimes. But then I might not have wanted out so badly. I wouldn't have started acting, and I wouldn't have met you."

There was so much going on behind those long lashes. I was desperate to know what he was thinking.

"Do you remember our first exam? When we had to write and perform a ten-minute monologue?" he asked.

"About our childhood. I remember."

"I almost quit that night. I didn't want to remember my childhood, let alone dissect it in front of everybody. But you convinced me to stay. You didn't even know you were doing it, but when I asked you why you wanted to be an actor, you said—"

"I don't want to. I have to."

"And I realized I felt the same way."

"I had no idea."

"Without you, I wouldn't be here."

My heart skipped a beat. Did he have any idea how much that meant to me?

"You would still be here." I was sure of that. Wes had a star quality that drew everyone to him. If it hadn't been me, it would have been someone else. "I didn't do anything."

"Liv ..." Wes' eyes were dark, his conviction clear. When he got like this, he was immovable. What would it feel like to be the focus of all that passion? "You changed my life."

"I ..." I'd lost the ability to think. I had no words. I just kept staring into Wes' eyes, overwhelmed by the combustion of feelings. It was electric.

"I wouldn't be here without you, either," I finally choked out, and I'd meant here, in this house, on this trip. But I also meant here, my hand in his, prepared to face the future, as long as he was by my side.

12

LIV

BESIDE ME, my phone lit up with a message. From Wes. Who was sitting next to me.

When I whipped my head in his direction, he pretended to be fully engrossed in the movie, but I could see the tug of a smile pulling at the corner of his mouth, and my own lips curled up in response.

Wes: get off your phone

I rolled my eyes, smiling wider.

Me: stop texting me and I will

His phone beeped loudly, and he silenced it. I tried to ignore his typing, but it was difficult to deny the buzz of anticipation. Which was silly. We weren't doing anything different, and yet ... I had butterflies.

Wes: stop distracting me, I'm trying to watch a movie

Luckily, the dark room hid the blush that rose to my cheeks. I wasn't sure how much longer I could feel this way without exploding. I needed to decide what I was going to do about it, and quick.

If what Jen said was correct, then getting involved with

Wes was a bad idea, but one I couldn't stop myself from wanting. And Wes was so convinced that Jen was worried for no reason that it made me want to believe it, too. The last thing I wanted was to put his job at risk. His happiness meant a lot to me.

But what if, my heart wondered, what if I could have both?

Yes, I'd made mistakes in the past. Bryson being one of them. But I'd also decided to leave modeling to act. And I'd taken the role of Meira, which had meant moving away from my family for a show no one expected would succeed. Even this spontaneous getaway was my idea. Maybe some risks were worth taking, even if they failed.

I knew what my mom's answer would have been.

I turned to him. He looked like the same old Wes. Messy dark hair, brown eyes, impish grin. The NASA T-shirt he wore smelled like shaving cream and fresh cotton, same as his shirts always did, but right now, it made me want to rip it off him and follow that trail all the way down.

Every fantasy I'd locked away raced up to the surface. The soft caress of his thumb on my neck was not helping things.

I turned my attention back to the TV, my face hot.

———

I leaned against the glass balustrade by the pool, admiring the row of tall trees that hid Wes' house from its neighbor. I could see why houses like this were so popular among the rich and famous. Privacy was a commodity that sold well in this area. Even street view didn't reach this far.

I could relate.

After being stuck inside my apartment for the last few weeks, standing freely in the open air was a luxury.

It would be a few hours before the sun would dip below the horizon, and the cool breeze felt amazing against my flushed skin. This end of the house was shaded, and I'd spent an hour filming the shadows playing off the water earlier today. I was no Spielberg, but it was the most fun I'd had in ages.

Yeah, the clips I'd posted were getting lots of likes and comments, but it wasn't about anyone else. I was finally doing something for me.

And it felt amazing.

Wes came out of the house to join me. "Everything okay?"

I nodded. "I keep thinking I should feel worse about lying to Jen."

"You shouldn't." He mirrored me, his pose relaxed and effortless. His hand touched mine where it rested along the thick glass. He brushed his finger along mine, and sparks fired through my chest, like I'd inhaled a bag of Pop Rocks and they were going off in my lungs.

Damn. I loved it when he touched me.

"You know why you shouldn't feel bad?"

I pressed my lips together in an effort to dampen my smile, a difficult feat when he was looking at me with his eyes lit up. I shook my head.

"Because this is the most relaxed I've seen you in a long time." His fingers ghosted over mine, sending a pleasurable tingle through my body and my mind straight into the gutter.

Suddenly, the afternoon breeze was not enough to cool me down. "Hey, can you bring me some water?"

His cheekbones came into sharp focus when he smiled.

We both knew he'd go, but without this playfulness, he wouldn't be Wes. "What, am I your assistant now?"

"Shut up. You're closer to the kitchen."

As he started to leave, I grabbed his arm, spinning him to face me. "Oh shit."

Startled, Wes whipped his head around to check if I was okay. "What?"

"Your clothes are wet."

He looked down, puzzled. "What? No, they aren't—"

It only took one quick shove to push him into the pool. "Ah!"

All those hours he spent in the gym, and I could still get the better of him.

I was already laughing when he hit the water, but it doubled when his face breached the surface, covered in a curtain of dripping curls. "You look like a drowned poodle."

In retaliation, he shook his head, flicking the water in my direction.

"Do you have any idea how much these jeans cost? You better hope they aren't ruined."

"They're so tight I'll be shocked if you can get out of them." I laughed.

"Try'na get in my pants, doll?"

I was glad for the sun beating down on me so I could blame it for the blush creeping up my neck.

"Trust me, you'd know if I was coming on to you." Emboldened, I added, "And if I wanted to get you out of those pants, I wouldn't need to drown you to do it."

He looked surprised, then offended. "Are you calling me easy?"

"If the extremely tight pants fit …"

He cupped his hands and showered me with water,

drenching me from head to toe. After taking in my now dripping hair and soaked clothes, he laughed, the sound lighting me up.

Oh, it was on.

Shaking my head, I catapulted myself into the water, lunging for him when I resurfaced, ignoring the weight of my now soaked clothes as I pushed him under.

For the first time in weeks, maybe even years, I felt childish and carefree. My cheeks already ached from smiling.

Wes got the upper hand when I tried to swim away, catching my shirt in his fingers and keeping me close. A dangerous, exciting thought appeared, and I felt just wild enough to entertain it.

Hooking my fingers underneath his, I lifted the shirt over my head, relishing the cool water on my heated skin, grateful that I was wearing a sports bra.

"That's better."

There was a startled beat before his eyes met mine, dark with desire and mischief. My smile widened, knowing he wasn't immune to this electricity.

"I think I need to even the playing field."

His eyes never left mine as he removed his shirt, the soaked material peeling away from his skin in a caress I ached to reenact. Rivulets of water traced a path from his neck down his smooth chest.

Even looking like a drowned rat, he was gorgeous.

A shiver rolled through my body.

His smile was playful, but with an edge of something serious beneath. We were so close to a line we'd never crossed before. Was he only flirting like he normally did, or did he mean it?

I was all too aware of the heat of his palm on my waist,

making my mind hazy, want driving me to inch closer. His hand shifted, and my breath caught when his fingers slid along my skin. Everything was on fire within me. Wes stilled, desire evident and dark in his gaze. We watched each other, sharing breath, the outside world a faded memory.

I want him.

It kept repeating on a loop. I couldn't avoid it any longer. I thought I'd done a decent job of forgetting it, but how else could I explain my constant need to talk to him, to touch him?

Wes was my best friend, and nothing I wanted to do to him right now was friendly.

Could he tell what I was thinking?

Time ticked by as he searched my face, and my breath caught when his gaze lingered on my mouth.

There was a blur of movement to my right, and then Wes and I were covered in a fresh wave of water.

"Baxter!" Wes laughed, stepping back, purposefully putting distance between us.

I felt the moment slip away. But I hadn't imagined that. Wes wanted me just as much as I wanted him. And I wasn't going to run from it anymore.

My heart was telling me to take the risk. Now I needed to convince Wes to do the same.

13

WES

I'D KNOWN BEING HERE WOULD BE hard. Coming home, dealing with my parents. With Lucas.

But I'd thought it would at least distract me from that pesky heartache I had going on.

Then Liv had come along. I'd known it would be a glorious mix of heaven and hell to be around her.

But I hadn't expected this.

Shit, I'd almost kissed her yesterday. If Baxter hadn't interrupted, I would have. Christ. I'd have to work harder to keep myself together or I'd ruin everything.

Her hips swayed to a silent beat as she moved around the kitchen. She'd had coffee pods overnighted and was currently on a mission to understand the never-been-used machine. I tried not to stare at the way her tiny cotton shorts hugged her curves, but it was easier said than done when she was moving like that.

She was trying to kill me.

When she turned around, my eyes flew up, but I knew she'd caught me looking. *Shit.*

But if she thought anything of it, she didn't show it. Ridiculously, I felt disappointed. What had I hoped for? That she'd suddenly feel the same way?

I was losing it.

And then she leaned over the island, brushed her hand down my forearm and said, "Wait here. I have something for you."

And Jesus, the way my blood ran south. *Down, boy.*

She ran toward her room, and I took the opportunity to adjust myself. *Press junkets. Golf. Bryson.* But even those unsexy thoughts didn't work when she bounced back into the kitchen, as happy as a kid on Christmas morning, something hidden behind her back.

"What have you got there?"

"Okay. So, I know you don't like making a big deal out of your birthday, but …" she said.

I should have known. Every year, I tried to ignore it. And every year, Liv would find some small way of celebrating it.

My heart knocked against my ribcage when she revealed what she'd been hiding. The whiskey bottle clinked against the countertop. I reached for it, brushing her fingers.

"Tiff said this was a special batch."

It was. And almost impossible to get.

"Wow, this is amazing. You didn't need to do that."

Her hand was warm against my skin. "I wanted to."

The incessant thumping of my heartbeat continued to grow louder.

"Happy birthday, Wes."

And even though I was scared of what she'd see there, I held her gaze with my own. "Thank you."

"Have you heard from your family?"

The mention worked better than anything else to douse the lust coursing through me. "Let's see. I got what I can only assume was a message from my mother's assistant, saying that she hoped today brought many cherished memories. And I honestly don't think my dad remembers."

She slipped her hand into mine, squeezing tight. I felt my chest constrict in the same way. Pain had gathered between her eyes, and I desperately wanted to smooth it away.

I'd had years to acclimatize to my parents' neglect, but for Liv, who was so close to hers, I knew it was beyond understanding, and I hated that their actions were now hurting someone I cared about.

She'd walked in here smiling, and once again, I'd ruined the moment. Shit.

"Hey. Did you know that there's a chicken on TikTok with two million subscribers?"

I got the reaction I wanted, Liv's surprised laugh the only gift I'd ever need.

———

This was better. My arms strained with another rep. A guttural sound erupting as I pushed myself harder. Another curl of the dumbbells. And another. Until it pushed everything else out.

All that was left was the pull of my muscles, my heavy breath, and Baxter snoring loudly on the treadmill. Dropping the weights, I used my shirt to brush away the sweat from my eyes.

I envied Baxter. What a life. Eat, sleep, play.

No brother who had forgotten him, no fake parties with

fake parents, no unignorable urge to ravage his best friend until they were both fuck drunk and out of breath.

Okay, he probably could relate to that last one.

Damn, I'd missed him. I should get a dog. Could I even have a dog in my apartment? Maybe I could smuggle him back to Chicago. My parents probably wouldn't even notice.

"Wes?" Liv called from upstairs.

"Yeah?" I called back.

"Can you give me a hand?"

I followed the sound of Liv's voice until I reached the junk room. What was she doing?

When I got to the doorway, I froze. Liv stood on a chair, framed by the open doors of the cupboard, reaching for something above her.

Clad only in her bikini.

With miles and miles of bare skin on display.

Fuck.

All the breath left my lungs.

"Hey," she said, smiling over her shoulder.

"Hey," I choked out, ready to spontaneously combust.

Think of Bryson. Mike. Hell, think of Jen. Anything but how soft and warm she'd feel ...

I was never going to survive this week.

Liv's smile widened before she turned back to her search.

I couldn't tear my eyes away from her. Christ, the way the muscles in her ass shifted as she lifted herself higher.

"What are you, uh, looking for?" I sounded like I'd swallowed glass.

"I saw Uno back here. I just can't quite reach it."

"I'll get it," I said quickly. She needed to get off the damn chair before I had a panic attack.

"I can do it. I just need you to keep me steady." She looked back over her shoulder. Shit. That was twice today she'd caught me staring at her ass. Her smile widened. "What are you waiting for? Come over here."

Was she … flirting?

Swallowing hard, I stepped up behind her and felt the heat pouring off her skin. My hands hovered uselessly while I tried to work out where I could touch her that wouldn't destroy my control. Who was I kidding? That place didn't exist. I settled them on her waist, jolting when she gasped.

"Your hands are cold," she whispered.

"Sorry," I said, and tried to remove them, but she placed her hands over mine, keeping them in place.

"It's okay. I'll warm them up."

It was a struggle to breathe. Thank fuck she couldn't see my face.

"Are you close?" I asked, then wanted to slap myself. "To the game."

"I'm close." Those words wreaked havoc on my body, short circuiting every wire, spreading liquid heat everywhere until I was sure there'd be two marks branding her skin where my hands were.

"I just need to reach a little farther." She stretched, and my grip tightened.

She felt so damn good. I never wanted to take my hands off her. I wanted to explore every inch of skin, first with my hands, then with my mouth.

The string tie of her top was directly in front of my face. Suddenly, I was filled with the urge to lean forward and kiss the dip of her spine. I would tease her, hold her here, finding every sensitive spot with my lips and my tongue before taking the tie in my teeth and slowly unknotting it. She smelled of salt and sun, and my dick was too far gone. Christ.

If she didn't get that damn game soon, I wouldn't have time to hide my reaction from her.

"Got it!" And before I could move, Liv had spun around, hooked her arms around my neck and jumped down into the scant space between where I stood and the chair. We were plastered together from chest to knee, and my dick reached full mast immediately.

A strangled sort of moan escaped me, and I stepped back, desperate to get out of this room.

"You okay?" Liv asked, looking amused. Was there any chance she hadn't noticed?

"Fine," I grunted. Shit, my voice was gravel. "Gonna shower."

"Enjoy," she said, clearly intent on killing me.

———

Our empty plates cluttered the coffee table, and Baxter sniffed at the remnants of our dinner. His tail wagged faster when I moved the plate to the floor, and he dug in without waiting.

I flopped back onto the couch, trying to ignore how close Liv was. My blood was still singing from earlier.

The couch could easily fit ten people, and yet we always ended up sitting side by side. "I can't believe Jackson is getting married. He's only a little older than me."

"Technically older, yes. Maturity wise?" Liv joked, her giggle reaching a high pitch when I threatened to tickle her. Except her shirt rose as I reached, and when my fingers brushed her bare skin, we both went quiet.

I pulled my hand back. "He'll make a good dad."

"He will," Liv agreed. She shifted beside me, her knee pressing gently into my thigh. "What about you? Do you want a family someday?"

I took a deep breath, and the resulting sigh threatened to deflate me. "Sometimes I think I do, but I don't want it to be like my childhood. I can't imagine putting anyone through that."

"You wouldn't."

"I hope not." But what were the chances? I couldn't even figure out my love life. How could I possibly take care of a kid? "But yeah, I think I'd like to have kids someday. What about you?"

She nodded. "Definitely. But I think maybe I want more than one. I loved having my mom to myself, but it was lonely. If I had a child, I'd want them to have a brother or sister." Her voice was wistful. "I think it would be nice."

"It was nice. My brother was my best friend growing up."

"Sorry," she said, resting her head on my shoulder. It helped. "I know you and Lucas don't talk anymore."

I stared out at the darkening sky, grateful Liv couldn't see my face or the emotions currently brewing inside me. "It used to be so different. Mom and Dad were never around, but we had each other. We'd waste whole days just playing games and messing around. As we got older, we'd stay up all night talking. I told him everything."

"I can't believe he cut you off after you moved."

I shrugged, hoping I looked unaffected by it all. All this time, and it still hurt that he'd chosen our parents over me.

"Do you think it'll ever change?"

"Maybe. Probably not. He can't even stand being around me."

She threaded her fingers with mine. "I'm sorry, Wes."

"It's not so bad." I pressed a kiss to her forehead and hoped it wasn't too obvious how much faster my heart beat when she hugged me tighter. I might not have had my brother anymore, but at least I had Liv.

I cleared my throat, forcing lightness into my voice. "Can we stop being sad now? It's really harshing my vibe."

She looked up. The "be serious" pout was back. Pink and perfect and so damn kissable. "Sometimes it scares me that you're older than me."

"What can I say?" I made a show of leaning over, batting my eyelashes like a cartoon, and dramatically sighing. "You make me feel young."

Pushing me away, she laughed. "You're ridiculous."

I winked. "Doll, I'll be whatever you want."

14

LIV

MY HEART WAS HAMMERING in my chest as I checked the time. Midnight.

Wow. I hadn't had a dream like that in a long, long time.

The imprint of Wes' lips had been so real, I could close my eyes and feel the ghost of them pressing against my throat. My legs squeezed together, remembering how incredible he'd felt against me, hard and warm and demanding.

I was shaking all over.

If a dream could have this effect on me, I don't think I'd survive the real thing.

I blinked into the darkness. What was I waiting for?

If I wanted this, I had to go for it. It was clear Wes wanted me back.

My hands traced where his had held me earlier today. The way they'd tightened and set my skin on fire. I'd felt how interested he was. Right before he'd run off.

Ten minutes later, my pulse had slowed, but sleep continued to elude me.

My bedroom door creaked as I opened it, and I quickly turned toward Wes' room, afraid I'd wake him. But his door was already open, pale light hitting an empty bed. *Huh. Guess I'm not the only one who can't sleep tonight.*

Even though he was likely awake, I snuck as quietly as I could down the hall, feeling my way through the dark.

As I entered the living room, I paused. Even in darkness, Wes' form was an unmistakable blob on the couch.

"Hey," I croaked.

"Hey. Can't sleep?" His voice was clear. He must have been up for a while.

I hummed.

"Bad dreams, or …?"

"Too many thoughts. I was hoping tea might help."

"It can't hurt."

"In that case, should I make two?"

"Sure." He followed me into the kitchen, taking a seat at the counter. He looked adorably disheveled, half asleep with frizzled hair. Like a cuddly Oscar the Grouch.

"Have you been up for a while?"

"Not really," he said. "Maybe an hour or so. I try not to check the time on nights like this."

There was a lot to unpack there. All those mornings where he looked like an extra from *Shawn of the Dead*. I'd always assumed he'd been partying, but the way he talked about it made it obvious that this was a regular occurrence.

My heart fell. He was going to burn out if he wasn't careful.

"Bad dreams?" I asked, repeating his question to me.

"Nah. It's not really anything," he lied. "I just don't

sleep well. I've gotten used to it. Most women like it when I'm up during the night."

This was a theme with Wes. Keep quiet and soldier on, then smile and make an inappropriate joke. I wondered how many things he'd been *getting used to.*

Was this why he'd run off earlier?

I abandoned the tea in favor of reaching over the counter to cover his hand with mine. "Well, whatever it is, I'm here if you want to talk about it. I mean, you're pretty much stuck with me for the week, so we might as well, right?"

"Thanks, but I'm fine."

"Liar."

A corner of his mouth curled up into a smile, but he said nothing else. I went back to my task, quietly happy that I knew my way around Wes' kitchen after only a few days.

Any time I looked over at him, I caught him watching me, setting off a familiar flutter in my belly.

Eventually, we returned, tea in hand, back to our favorite place—the couch.

I waited for Wes to sit first. It made it easier to snuggle into the space next to him. The scent of mint and … what was that? Lavender? Wafted up from the mug in my hands, and while it smelled amazing, the taste was …

Well, let's just say there was I reason I didn't drink tea.

But the warm cup and calming scent were soothing, so I kept a hold of it as I sat down.

"What are you watching?" Wes' laptop was open on the coffee table with what looked like a home video paused on the screen.

His expression was cold as he reached over and closed the laptop. Darkness enveloped us, leaving only the imprint of Wes' shape in my vision, the warmth of him beside me.

It was too quiet. Dropping a hand from my mug, I felt for Wes', exhaling when our fingers finally met and he didn't pull away.

"They're home videos. Lucas dropped them off before you got here." The words were clipped.

"Why didn't you tell me? I'm guessing it didn't go well?"

He didn't answer at first, but I waited him out while my eyes adjusted to the darkness. I watched as he took a sip of the tea and bit back a smile when it became obvious he found it as unappealing as I did.

I tugged on his hand, reminding him to answer.

"He called me selfish for staying here. Said I was taking advantage of Mom and Dad's hospitality when I never do anything for them."

Wes was uncharacteristically quiet. He never talked much about his relationship with his brother. Not even to me.

He continued to stare at the closed laptop while I inched closer. The night was silent around us, and I found myself matching the quiet with a soft voice, treading carefully around the fragile moment, sure that one wrong move would close the door on whatever Wes was feeling.

"For what it's worth, he's wrong. You're the most caring person I know."

Shadows obscured my view of his face, but I recognized the incredulous snort of breath he let out, felt the movement of him shaking his head. It didn't surprise me that he didn't believe it.

It frustrated me, but it didn't surprise me.

Suddenly, I was determined to prove it to him. I put my tea to the side, then his, so I could take both his hands in mine. "Don't do that. I don't care if you don't believe me; it's the truth. You've been nothing but selfless in the last few weeks, looking out for me in interviews, giving up your free time to keep me company. I don't know what I would have done without you."

I couldn't make out enough of his face to get a read on what he was feeling.

"Wes," I said when the quiet had gone on too long. I pressed closer until I was almost in his lap. "You didn't have to do any of that, but you did. And I'll repay the favor, no matter how long it takes me. For a long time after mom died," I paused as my lungs squeezed beneath my ribs, "I didn't feel close to anyone, not even Bryson. But you, you've become ..." and I stopped. Because the truth was he'd become *everything* to me, but that felt like too much, too big to say. "My best friend," I finished, knowing it didn't come close to defining what I felt for him.

He pulled me into a hug, his hand gently stroking along my spine. God, it felt good.

"There's nothing to repay. You know that, right? I'm here for you whenever you need me." Then, right on cue, the deflective joke. "Unless it involves any more of that tea. Then you're on your own."

I curled a hand around his knee, knowing it was the only spot he was ticklish. "Jerk. You'll drink that tea and you'll like it."

He jolted away from my fingers, then grabbed a hold of my wrist to pull my hand away.

"Come on." I looked up, my heart beating faster when I realized how close our faces were. If I just stretched up, our lips would be touching. Tingles burst across my skin at the thought, and my voice became breathless. "Talk to me."

Time stopped as his gaze flickered to my mouth, just for a millisecond, but long enough to catch my breath until he looked away.

"I need to edit together a happy memories video for Saturday. But what happy memories were there? Everything on those videos is a lie." He scoffed. "Probably the best acting I've ever done."

Huh. Apparently, the way to get Wes to open up about one topic was to present him with another topic he wanted to talk about even less.

And apparently that other topic was his attraction to me.

I didn't know whether to be flattered or insulted.

But his family took precedence.

I sat back, my hand falling from his grip. "Thirty years, though. There must be something there if they're still together after all this time."

"You don't know my parents." That was true.

"This isn't about love. It's just another performance. A way for them to showcase how perfect their lives are and make all their friends jealous." His voice was thick with emotion, and the ache in my gut intensified.

"I'm sorry, Wes."

I reached for my phone, which I'd pocketed out of habit. I unlocked the screen, my mom's bright smile shining back at me.

I couldn't imagine how I'd feel in Wes' position. I'd been so close with mom, and even though Dad and I didn't have the same relationship, I'd grown up knowing I was cherished and loved, and it killed me to know that Wes hadn't had the same thing.

There weren't many secrets I didn't tell Wes, but this was one of them.

"Can I play you something?"

I pulled up my voicemails, selecting the first one and putting it on speaker.

"Hey sweetie. I'm just standing here, looking at the stars. Wanted to hear your voice, which I've now done! Um, I would have loved to talk to you, but oh well. Not to worry. Love you lots, bye."

Tears pricked my eyes. The ache to be touched—held —overwhelmed me. Wes didn't say anything, rubbing soothing circles on my shoulder.

"I found them after she died, and I haven't been able to delete them. It's just so nice to hear her voice again."

Wes wrapped me tightly in a hug. "It's good that you have these to remember her by." He pressed his cheek against my temple, his lips brushing my skin, making me tremble. "I know that if I missed someone the way you miss your mom, I would give anything to hear them again."

Turning my face against his chest, I breathed in the scent that was so undeniably *Wes*. To my shaky heart, it smelled like comfort and laughter and *home*. At that, the dam burst, tears falling steadily, dampening the material beneath my cheek. Wes continued to whisper words of encouragement as he held me.

The thick ache in the pit of my stomach didn't ease, but it shook free, rising until it was gripping my heart, clenching around my pulse until my lungs pushed against it.

"Tell me a good memory," he said.

I hummed in thought, stretching out the moment a little longer. I wasn't ready to pull away from him just yet.

"Did I tell you about the time she caught me stealing from a craft store? It was the only time she ever raised her voice to me."

Wes' surprised "What?" jolted a laugh out of me.

"Didn't know I was a rebel, did you?"

He humored me. "You're a regular Bonnie. What happened?"

"She yelled, made me take it back and apologize. They

weren't happy, but they let it slide. Afterward, she said we were going to talk, and I spent the entire drive shitting myself. I'd never seen her so quiet. But we got to this dinky little diner and ordered milkshakes, and she asked me why I did it." I could still remember the smell of grease in the air, the stickiness of the floor beneath my shoes. "We ended up talking for hours. About everything. It was the first time I felt like an adult, and after that, it became a regular thing. Mom would pick me up from an audition or a class, and we'd find somewhere to sit and talk."

Hours upon hours of conversation, and we never ran out of things to talk about.

"The cancer hit so suddenly ... she'd been hiding how she felt for a while. After she was diagnosed, she was tired all the time. So instead of going out, we stayed in. Watching the movies we loved and quoting them back to each other."

I dared to voice another secret I'd been holding back, grateful for the dim light in the room and the way Wes' arms around me made me feel bolder.

"I haven't visited her grave since the funeral. I just ..." I swallowed around the lump in my throat. "It's so final. Being there. Knowing I won't see her again. When I listen to her voicemails, I can almost pretend. Like I could call her back, and we'd pick up where we left off."

Wes brushed a kiss to my temple, and I closed my eyes, savoring how safe I felt.

"I don't have the first clue about how to deal with what you're going through, but I'm pretty sure there's no right or wrong way to grieve. I think it's pretty great that you have those messages and can hear her voice whenever you want. You shouldn't feel bad, Liv. You miss her."

I sank into his arms, moving with Wes as he rearranged

us on the couch until we were lying down, wrapped up together.

"When did you get so good at this?" I asked, sleep pulling me under.

"I'm not," he whispered, sounding as tired as I felt. "It's only for you."

15

WES

WHEN I WAS A KID, I slept like the dead. Anywhere. Anytime.

There was a particular anecdote that my mother loved to throw out at parties about how, at the age of four, I'd disrupted one of their dinner parties by falling asleep under the table. They'd continued the party around me, and I'd slept through until morning.

Then I'd grown up.

In the last few years of school, Dad had become increasingly judgmental, always on about my grades and insisting that I get a business degree. He set up meetings with advisors for colleges without telling me and ambushed me with applications. I had nightmares of working in an office and being called "Conrad Jr."

He hated that I wanted to act. I'd thought taking the role on *The Guild* and moving to the other side of the country would fix my sleeping problem, but no dice.

So to wake up with the sun after a full night of rest? I couldn't believe it. And yet, here I was, my neck aching from being propped on the arm of the couch, and my arms full of the warm body currently curled into me.

Liv.

Her even breaths fanned over my throat. Her head was resting on my shoulder, and she had one arm thrown over my stomach. Over the course of the night, we'd tangled and wrapped ourselves around each other.

It felt right. I didn't want to move.

I dipped my head, breathing her in. We couldn't stay like this. Eventually, she'd wake up, and I wasn't ready to face the uncomfortable questions that would come after.

It was hard enough keeping my true feelings from seeping out when we worked side by side. At least on set, I could channel my frustrations into the show.

But last night, when she'd fallen apart in my arms and opened up to me about her mom, all I'd wanted to do was throw open the vault that was my battered heart and lay myself at her feet.

Lying here, in the warmth of the early morning sun, her fingers curled into my shirt and the soft sounds of her breathing swirling in the air, I knew I never wanted to wake up with anyone else.

There was no one for me after Liv.

Baxter's nails clipped against the hardwood as he walked into the room, his excited breathing breaking the silence. Soon, there was a cold nose persistently nudging at my arm, and I knew the fantasy had come to an end.

Closing my eyes, I memorized the exact feel of her in my arms, then pulled away, careful not to wake her.

"Come on, buddy. Let's get you some breakfast."

———

"Shouldn't you be working on that video?"

I glanced up from the game we were playing. The one I'd suggested specifically to avoid the very video Liv was asking me about.

"I will. I'm just busy right now."

"Yes, this game of Hungry Hungry Hippos is very important. I'm glad we managed to find time for it despite our busy schedules."

I laughed. The more she relaxed, the more sarcastic she became. I liked it a lot. "You're the one who ransacked the spare bedroom for games—hey! Only one hippo in play at a time."

Liv laughed as I smacked her hand away.

"You're avoiding the question."

I was avoiding a lot of things right now. She'd have to be more specific.

"I forgot what it was."

"Liar," she said, low and flirtatious, and I looked away because I was getting very close to pushing this board out of the way and tasting that smile.

I bet I could give these hippos a run for their money.

After waking up with her this morning, I couldn't stop thinking about the last few days. Maybe I had finally lost it, but Liv had been getting closer than usual, always finding a reason to touch me. If I didn't know any better, I'd say she was flirting, but … that wasn't something we did.

We were friends.

I had to be imagining things. That was it. I'd spent so long wanting her that I was now hallucinating signs of her feeling the same way.

Liv stood to get a drink from the kitchen, and I eyed her long legs. Her denim shorts perfectly cupped the curve of her hips and ass, and her bikini pulled against the swell of her breasts. I tried not to stare at her, but it was hard. All of me was hard.

I groaned into the empty room. In the last few hours, I'd discovered that there were freckles on the soft of her stomach, near her belly button.

I'd never noticed them before. Never been close enough to see.

Dammit. I needed help.

Liv bounded back into the room carrying a glass of water for each of us. She handed mine over with a wink.

I was going to die of horniness.

My poor dick was having a hard time, literally, figuring out what the hell was going on. As was I. Every time I convinced myself it was only my overactive imagination, she'd wink or flirt or run her hands along my arm.

And I would swear to Hades that she had purposefully brushed her ass against my crotch this morning while she was making breakfast.

Across from me, Liv pulled her hair into a ponytail, leaving her long neck on display. We'd been swimming earlier, the ends of her hair still damp.

I imagined she'd still taste like chlorine and sweat.

Shit. How the hell was I going to make it through the rest of this week?

————

I'd never loved Baxter more than right now. Best impulse I'd ever had, especially because it meant walking him. Which meant leaving the house. Which meant getting time on my own away from Liv and whatever the hell was going on.

Having her so close and not close enough was slowly driving me insane.

It was wrong, but I pulled the "we shouldn't be seen in public together" card when Liv asked if she could join us. The disappointment on her face made me hate myself a little more.

Fuck. I was the worst type of asshole.

Baxter pulled me along, and I was happy to let him lead. My head was too full of Liv to be of much use.

My control was slipping. Years of working with her, and it had barely taken four days for me to crack. Ridiculous. How many times had I kissed her in front of a camera? I'd lost count. But I hadn't slipped.

How many nights had she curled up next to me on the couch with that damn sit-wriggle-sigh and fallen asleep on my shoulder? The number had to be in the triple digits. But I hadn't slipped.

It hadn't been easy, but I'd managed it. Somehow in the last few days, I'd forgotten how. Everything Liv said felt like a come-on. Every look, each soft smile, only seemed to drive me crazier.

After two blocks, we turned a corner, Baxter pulling on the leash like he knew his way around. He sniffed around an electric pole that was obviously a dog favorite, and I took the opportunity to spy on my neighbors. The sun was beating down in the late afternoon, but the street was lush with greenery, a series of manicured lawns perfectly aligned (and likely never touched by anyone except the gardener).

I watched as a pristine white SUV pulled up to a house not far from where we were standing, followed by a red Model S.

Curious, I walked closer, then stopped in my tracks when the door of the SUV opened and Lucas hopped out.

This must be his work car. I watched as he walked with the Tesla owner to the front door, talking the whole way (no doubt some spiel Dad had taught him), and after the other guy walked into the house, Lucas turned and caught me watching.

I could have walked away. Said nothing. But he was my brother. He might hate me, but I didn't want to hurt him. So I steeled my shoulders and made my way over to the house. Lucas met me halfway, and I wondered if he was about to tell me to get lost. I'd never actually seen him work before, and even in what I could tell was a three-thousand-dollar suit, he looked uncomfortable.

Good, I thought, unkindly. His comments from the other day still stung, and every time I forced myself to watch a few of the videos he'd given me, my insides twisted.

"Hey," I said, annoyed at myself for feeling awkward. He was my own brother, for Christ's sake. I nodded toward the house. "One of yours?"

He stuffed his hands in his pockets. "Yeah. Just showing a client around."

Baxter nosed around the gravel as Lucas and I struggled to fill the awkward silence.

"Think he'll buy it?" I was grasping at straws. *This was awful.*

To my surprise, his expression turned disdainful, a sliver of the old Lucas shining through the primped veneer. "I fucking hope so. This is the third time this week he's asked to see it, and if I have to listen to him talk about his juice empire one more time, I'm going to run him over."

I barked out a laugh, shocked and practically joyful to see the real him again. Maybe there was hope. "Make sure you do it while he's not driving. I'm pretty sure those Tesla's have a no-vehicular-manslaughter mode."

"Shame," he quipped, smiling back. I relaxed a little further. So far so good. "So, did your girlfriend arrive okay?"

"Not my girlfriend," I corrected. "But uh, yeah. She even managed to find all our old board games. Do you remember that marble one?"

"With the sticks? Wow, you still have that?"

I shrugged. "Yeah, I kept everything. There are a lot of memories there, you know?"

"Yeah."

I was struck by how young he looked. There were only two years between us, and I knew he hated being treated like the baby of the family, but these days, it was easy to forget he was only twenty-five.

Not that it mattered. Once a big brother, always a big brother.

We could be in our fifties, and I'd always want to protect him. Even when we barely knew how to talk to each other.

Man, I missed him so much it ached.

"Is she coming to the party? Your not-girlfriend?"

I nodded. "Liv, and yeah, she'll be there."

"Cool. It'll be good to meet her."

Lucas shifted awkwardly. It was good to know I wasn't the only one who felt that way. "Happy birthday, by the way. I would have come by, but I wasn't sure you wanted visitors."

"It's fine."

I didn't know what to say. We were in uncharted territory here. Five minutes, and we hadn't fought yet.

"If you've finished that video, I can come by and collect it when I'm done here."

Spoke too soon.

Avoiding eye contact, I shuffled, guilt climbing uncomfortably up my throat. "I haven't done it yet. Been busy." It was a stupid lie. One I knew he would see through.

His expression shut down. "Yeah, you look really busy. Jesus, Wes. I should have fucking known." He shook his head, looking down. "Is there anything you didn't take from the house when you got here?" He gestured to Baxter, who was now pulling on the lead, ready to leave. *Me too, buddy.*

"The Aston, the dog ... do you want me to bring over Dad's Rolex while you're at it?"

"Fuck you." I turned quickly, not looking back at him as Baxter led me back the way we'd come.

How dare he? Didn't he realize how hard it was? To watch those clips and remember those years and all the shit we'd been through?

Did he seriously not remember?

16

LIV

WE WERE two-thirds of the way through Skyfall when Wes paused the movie. Again.

"Did you know the DB10 was the first Aston designed solely for Bond? And it was actually never released to the public?"

Okay, fine. I didn't need to be into cars to find Wes' enthusiasm cute. Really, really cute.

"I think I prefer the older films. My favorite will always be Connery."

"You have to admit, Craig has done a good job."

Knowing the reaction it would bring, I said, "Eh, Brosnan was better."

He narrowed his eyes. "You know, everyone thinks you're so sweet, but they really have no idea how evil you are." Wes stole the bowl of popcorn from my lap, holding it high so I couldn't reach it.

"Hey!" Two could play at that game. Only, I wasn't planning to play fair.

As I straddled his lap, Wes let out a surprised grunt. *Let's see you run away this time.*

My hands fell to his chest, my body heating at our position. His eyes were dark and hungry. Was the movie still playing? I had a vague sense of something happening in the distance, but I was too caught up in the heat under my hands and the way the air seemed to crackle and pop between us.

He was still holding the popcorn above his head. I wondered how long he'd let it hover there. What he would do if I sank into him a little more. Would he push me off? Lose control?

I needed to know.

Reaching up, I looped a curl around my finger. Silky soft. What the hell did he condition with? I kept looping, around and around. Heavenly. I wanted to thrust my hand in his hair, like a kid in a candy store. My imagination shot off like a rocket. It was long enough to softly graze my skin if he leaned down to kiss me. How would it feel against my neck? Between my breasts? My legs?

Shit.

My ringtone shocked me, and I scrambled off Wes' lap to catch the call. The number had a local area code. Odd. I didn't normally answer unknown numbers, but what if something had happened to Dad?

"Hello?"

"Hi, my name is Sym Padilla. Am I speaking to Olivia Davis?"

I stilled. I hadn't known the number, but I recognized the name. Sym was one of Hollywood's most influential talent managers. Why was Sym calling me? "Yes, this is Olivia."

"Wonderful. I hope you don't mind the intrusion. I

heard you were in town for a few days, and I couldn't miss the opportunity to invite you to lunch."

I looked at Wes, who wouldn't meet my eye. "That's a very kind offer, but—"

"Please. Let me take you to lunch. I know you have representation, and I'm aware of how passionately Jen fights for her clients. The last thing I want to do is make you uncomfortable. One conversation, that's all. No pressure."

For some reason, my mother's voice appeared. *Take the risk.* "Okay, sure."

"Fantastic! Where would you like to go?"

The question stunned me. "Me? I don't really know." Even if my mind hadn't blanked out the name of every restaurant I'd ever visited in LA, I couldn't imagine a single one of them was good enough for a lunch with Sym Padilla.

"Not a problem. I'll take you to my favorite spot. Do you like pancakes?"

I voiced my approval.

"Fantastic! I knew I'd like you. Okay, give me ten minutes, and I'll send you the details."

I was still in shock after we hung up.

"Who was that?"

Wes' question had my senses rushing back to themselves.

"Like you don't know. Were you going to tell me that you'd given my number to them, or was it more fun for you to watch me get blindsided?" I didn't let him answer. "I don't know how many times I have to tell you this. I'm happy with Jen. She's done so much for me. I can't just turn my back on her now."

"Why not? She runs your entire life, Liv. Have you ever

asked yourself why? What's in it for her if she chooses your furniture or drives you to the set every day? She's trying to control you."

"That's ridiculous! She's doing her job."

"Then why doesn't my manager do those things? Or Jackson's? I don't trust her."

"That's rich after what you just did. You went behind my back. I can make my own decisions, Wes. You should have asked me."

Bond was still paused as I stormed out of the room.

———

I stared down at Sym's message. It had been a few hours since fighting with Wes, but I couldn't shake my frustration. Did he really think I wouldn't be mad? And now I had to turn down one of the best talent managers in LA. I'd be lucky if Sym ever considered working with me in the future.

I'd never wanted to talk to Mom more. I needed her advice.

Wes had disappeared into the gym over an hour ago. He could be down there for the rest of the night. If anyone knew how to avoid a difficult conversation, it was him. I stopped and started three different movies before realizing I was too restless to watch anything and stepped outside.

I'd hoped the fresh air would calm me down.

It didn't. When I finally grew tired of pacing, I sat in the sunken seating area to the far right of the pool and called my dad.

"Hey, honey, how are you enjoying the hills?" I could tell he missed being closer to the city. Dad had moved up to Fresno after mom died to be closer to his sister. Being near family kept him busy.

"There's not much to tell," I lied. There was a lot to tell. All of it different shades of exciting, confusing, and arousing.

I watched with interest as Baxter scampered over to the steps of the pool and hopped down, dipping his head in the cool water before jumping out and shaking it off. He looked like a small, happy sprinkler.

"Sounds like you're having fun," Dad said.

Baxter spotted me and walked over, nudging my leg until I scratched his ear.

"Yeah." I closed my eyes and sighed. "I am." Despite my argument with Wes, I couldn't deny that I'd felt more like myself in the past few days than I had in years. It had been so nice to wake up and make every decision by myself. Actually finding time to be alone ... I hadn't even realized how much I'd missed it.

"I'm glad," he said. "You deserve it."

I looked out at the view. Mom would have loved it here.

The sunset was breathtaking, the horizon awash with burnt reds and oranges fading into soft yellow. The valley was already growing dark, not yet glittering, but taking a moment to revel in the beauty of nature. Soon, the stars would be out, barely visible over the lights that crowded the land below.

This in-between, where the sky was a shifting, evolving canvas, had always been my favorite part of the day.

Beautiful.

I wanted to enjoy it with Wes. But I was still too annoyed with him.

Even if a tiny part of me wondered if he was right.

"Do you think I was wrong to take this job?" I asked, caving to the nagging voice in my head. It sounded suspiciously like Wes.

"No. Why? Do you think it was the wrong decision?"

"No?" Not most of the time. "Sometimes I just …" How could I put it into words? "I don't really feel like I'm in charge of myself anymore."

"Have you spoken with Jennifer about it? If you don't like how things are, you should find a way to change them."

I hummed. If only Mom were here.

Dad seemed to understand what I was thinking. "Sorry. I know your mother was better at this."

"No," I reassured him. "Well, yes, she was. But I'm glad I can talk to you."

"I might not be much help, though."

A blanket had been draped over the bench beside me, reminding me of what I'd told Wes about decorating. "That's okay."

"What do you want to do but can't?"

The outside air still held a warm edge, but I knew it could drop at any moment. I wrapped a blanket around my shoulders.

"I really want to direct someday."

"Then you should do that." Quick. Decisive. Like it was that simple. Bless him.

He interpreted my silent disbelief correctly. "You know what your mother would say."

I did know. "There's no regret in trying."

My heart clenched in my chest at the memory. Everything about her was so vivid, even after four years.

I thought about it. Was I really in a position to make anything happen? I didn't doubt my capabilities, but I was barely a name, and now I was a name with a scandal.

With the spin-off role up in the air, I needed to think about what I wanted to do next. And what better time to take a chance on myself? On my future?

And hadn't I already been testing it out? Weren't the videos I'd been posting my way of dipping my toe in while still playing it safe? And even if I wouldn't have contacted them myself, I now had a lunch meeting with one of my idols.

Maybe it was time to try. No risk, no reward, right?

The last of my anger fell away. "Thanks, Dad."

———

Wes appeared soon afterward, fresh clothes and damp hair, sheepishly approaching with his head hanging low.

"Liv, I'm sorry. I shouldn't have gone behind your back."

I patted the seat next to me. He smelled of cotton and soap and a bit of lingering sweat. It sent my mind into a tailspin, even as I felt the comfort of his presence. I knocked his shoulder with mine. "Don't do it again, okay?"

"Scout's honor."

For the first time in hours, I laughed. "You weren't in the scouts."

17

WES

EVERY INCH of the view was covered in shades of pink and purple. It touched everything, even us. Liv stared out, the hurt from earlier replaced with a thoughtfulness.

It had been a stab in the gut to fight with her. No matter how much I questioned Jen's motives, Liv was right. I had been just as bad as Jen, not giving Liv the choice.

A breeze blew cool air from the north, and Liv wrapped the blanket tighter around herself. With her hands occupied, she couldn't do anything when her hair fanned over her cheek. I reached out, brushing it back behind her ear.

Our eyes met. Color rose to her cheeks.

She was beautiful.

The pale light painted the soft curves of her face. I'd always found Liv attractive, but in the last few days, she'd been intoxicating.

Relaxed. Playful. Flirtatious.

It wasn't my imagination. Something had changed, and Liv had been trying to show me for days. What I didn't know was what to do about it. How I felt about her was too strong. I couldn't cross that line for something fleeting.

If all she wanted was a rebound, it would break me.

Liv, like always, noticed my concern. "Are we okay?"

Were we?

"Let's get out of here for a bit." I needed to think.

"Where? We can't exactly grab dinner somewhere."

"We'll go for a drive. The Aston's tinted, and it'll be dark soon."

Her eyes sparkled, glittering in the sunset. "All right. Let me get a sweatshirt first." She stood, and it was hard to hold back my smile. She walked inside, Baxter following her, and it suddenly felt like a different reality. One where this was our home and tonight was a regular night out.

It was a nice dream.

———

Liv played with the radio, unable to find a song she liked for more than sixty seconds. Between us, Baxter had stuck his head between the seats, content to stay there, breathing wetly on my elbow.

Every once in a while, I would catch Liv's eye. We'd both smile, and then I'd focus on the road again.

It was while someone was singing "this is how you fall in love" that I felt Liv's hand on mine, and I shifted my grip on the stick to stroke her fingers with my thumb.

This felt right. And I decided I wouldn't worry about what this was or what would happen later. I'd just enjoy it.

One perk of having a father who was more invested in his work than his family was that he owned multiple properties, one of which was a piece of land east of Malibu, directly overlooking the coast. I hoped he hadn't done anything with it since the last time I was there. I'd always found it the perfect spot to think.

We stepped out of the car and leaned against the hood. Maybe it was sacrilegious to do that on such a beautifully crafted car, but it meant getting close to Liv, and that trumped pretty much everything for me.

Liv sat beside me, quietly pulling at the strings on her hoodie. The one I'd given her. It felt like a statement. A confession. Or, more likely, another sign that I was lost in my own sentimentality. I was being ridiculous again. It hadn't really been mine to begin with.

Out here, under the starlight, she was a goddess. Ethereal and magical. Time had no meaning. It was a mere inconvenience that could be ignored while we shared this moment together.

I wondered if she was still mad at me. I hated the thought.

"I gotta apologize again. I shouldn't have done it. But I just," I stared up at the stars, "I know you want more, and I want that for you."

She gave me a soft look. "I know what I want, but what about you? What do you want?"

Where do I start? "I'm pretty happy right now." It was true for this moment as well as for my career. "If the spin-off goes well, I'll focus on that."

"You don't worry about the future?"

"I worry about a lot of things. I try not to count on anything being around long term."

She chewed on her bottom lip, drawing my attention there.

"What do you want, Liv? And don't tell me something Jen thinks. Tell me what you think."

"I really want to direct. And produce."

We fell into a comfortable silence, the muted noise of cars barely reaching us. Liv nestled her head on my shoulder, a perfect fit at my side. It felt natural to rest my cheek there, breathing her in. My heart gripped with the enormity of the love I had for her.

There was nothing in this universe that mattered to me as much as her happiness.

"What would you do if you weren't acting?"

"Real estate, probably."

"Be serious." A small elbow nudged my belly while I chuckled. "If the spin-off doesn't go ahead—"

I cut her off. "It'll go ahead. No matter what Jen says."

She stiffened a little at Jen's name, and I mentally kicked myself for going there so soon.

"Do you have a backup if it doesn't?" she asked.

"No." I didn't need one. There wasn't a single bone in my body that believed that Mike and Alicia, hell, that the network, was stupid enough to cut free their biggest earners right now. Rumors be damned. "I'm just lucky I didn't get killed off in season one like they'd planned."

"That's because fans loved you too much. And now you're about to get your own show."

"We are," I corrected her. "The network doesn't care about a couple of rumors. And even if we were dating," I paused, feeling her still in my arms, "Meira is the heart of the show. Ares is nothing without her. They'd be crazy to not see that."

"I guess." She twirled a strand of her hair around her finger, and I was reminded of how incredible it had felt when she'd done the same thing to my hair earlier.

Liv sighed. "I love playing Meira, but I think I love it because of the people it's brought into my life. The fans I've been able to reach. But I always viewed it as a stepping stone to something else." Her fingers intertwined with mine, a tether I held tight to.

"The fans love you. You know that. We're up for best kiss, remember?"

She didn't look convinced. "I guess you're right."

"Of course I'm right."

She turned to me. "I'm really grateful they cast you as Ares. Not only because I get to work with you, but because you really are amazing at it. You care about him, and it shows. Plus, you're one of the most dedicated actors I know. Even Jackson agrees."

"That guy won't remember a single one of us after he's left."

"What are you talking about? You're friends. He won't forget you."

I shrugged. "We'll see."

Jackson had the quintessential all-American good looks and easy charm. From day one, I'd known he'd go on to bigger and better things. It made sense that he'd be done with the show after this season.

Which left Liv and me. Good. That's all I needed anyway. For as long as she'd let me hang around, I'd take it.

Silence descended again, occasionally broken by the sound of Baxter's collar jangling nearby.

"Are you happy?" she asked, surprising me.

"Mostly."

"What would make you happier?" Liv asked.

"The only thing I really want is the one thing I'm not sure I'll ever have."

"Which is?"

"Love. A family."

"They're good things to want."

"What's your one thing?"

"I don't want to be afraid. I want to go for what I want. Take risks. Be bold. I want to get to the end of my life, no matter when that is, and be proud of myself. Know that I did something. Know that mom would be proud of me, too."

I was constantly in awe of her. After Rebekah passed, Liv had grown a thick skin, but there was so much more beneath that. I'd never met anyone so capable. I fully believed that she could do anything she wanted.

I knew I couldn't cross that line. But it was getting more and more difficult to remember why. To not read into the way she leaned in to me, her touch sparking a fire that had been burning for so long, I wasn't sure it would ever go out.

"You know she is."

"I think I'm letting her down," she admitted softly.

"You aren't," I assured her, the words whispered but full of conviction. "You couldn't."

"Sometimes I'm afraid to be happy without her."

"You know she wouldn't want that."

"I know. She said it a lot near the end. 'Don't hold back. Be happy. Look after your father.'"

"Good advice."

"I don't know that I've been doing any of them very well. But I want to."

I held her tighter. There wasn't any doubt in my mind that Liv was destined for great things. And if that left me on my own, well. I'd have the memory of this week and the feel of her in my arms to keep me going.

18

LIV

WHEN WE GOT HOME, Wes had ordered dinner, and we'd watched a movie, but I couldn't tell you which one. I was too restless.

It was late. Much later than I'd normally stay up, but I wasn't tired. I couldn't let another day, another second, go by without kissing him.

Wes brushed my ankle with his feet, gentle and tender. And, wow, when had my ankles ever been an erogenous zone? But here I was, tingling all over and clenching in places I shouldn't be equating with my best friend.

He did it again, and my eyes snapped up to meet his, all breath leaving me in a rush at the sight of affection on his face.

Overwhelmed, I pulled my foot away. "Stop that," I said, breathless.

He stretched his foot closer, amused. "Why? Are you ticklish?" Bending forward, he wrapped a hand around my other ankle, brushing his fingers along the skin, and my heart jumped into my throat.

"I ..." I couldn't think about anything other than his fingers on my skin, the way his curls hung loose around his eyes, the rich red of his lips.

No more waiting. What I needed was action. And from the look of Wes, who was currently scowling at his laptop again, I wasn't the only one.

"All right, mopey, that's it. We're gonna have some fun."

I took the laptop from his lap and pulled on his arm until he stood, making him follow me into the kitchen.

"Is that right?"

Instead of answering, I picked up the bottle of Glengarry and poured two glasses. Two generous glasses.

"Hey." Wes chuckled. "Damn. You trying to get me wasted or what?"

"No, but I thought you might need a little liquid courage." I knew I did.

"What for?"

I pulled out my next trick. A question-and-answer game simply titled "Confessions." Technically, the game was made for a group, but tonight wasn't about following the rules.

"I want to play this. But I've made up a few of my own rules."

"I see how it is. Are you trying to learn my deepest, darkest secrets?"

"Who says I'm not the one with a confession to make?"

"Has Bonnie been bad again?"

Okay, wasn't expecting to add that to my list of kinks, but here we are. Goddammit. *No. I can't think of Wes holding me down and whispering that or I'll never get through this.*

I took a gulp, wincing as it burned the back of my throat. My eyes watered as I recovered, smiling at the amusement on Wes' face.

"Are you okay?"

I could only squeak an affirmative as I blinked back the tears, then all thoughts left me as Wes reached out, his thumb catching a stray tear as it fell down my cheek.

"Maybe we should slow down," he whispered, his hand searing a brand into my skin. I fought the urge to turn and press a kiss into his palm.

Suddenly, my heart was beating out of my chest, my whole body thumping like a reverberating drum.

Between the whiskey and Wes, it felt like my pulse was pounding in my throat, and I wondered if he could tell. Reluctantly, I pulled away, looking down at my empty glass.

Why was this so hard?

Everything was about to change, and I was terrified.

Wes stepped back, and I waited for my mind to clear. Suddenly, catching a single thought was impossible. All my attention had narrowed to the space between us and the need to have him touch me again. To touch him.

I eyed his still full glass. "Are you going to drink that?"

"I guess I am." He followed suit, throwing it back, easy as anything. As he swallowed, I couldn't help but watch the line of his throat, tracking the movement and feeling my temperature rise.

All right. *Let's do this.*

I moved to refill our glasses, but Wes stopped me, taking them out of my hands and rustling through the kitchen cupboards.

"If we're going to do this, we need different glasses. I should have some tumblers in here somewhere." Another door opened, then closed as he searched.

I raised a brow in question. "Are you becoming a connoisseur?"

"Tiff may have mentioned some things that I

remembered. And Jackson invited me over for a few tastings."

"And then you became a little obsessed."

"Enthusiastic," Wes countered, smiling as he placed two new glasses on the counter.

"Uh-huh," I joked. "It's cute when you're passionate about something."

He poured far less than I had. Spoilsport. "You mean it's sexy and mature."

"Adorable." Wes had never cared about labels, so I knew he was only playing with me.

"Manly. Like James Bond."

I laughed, taking the drink he offered. "Bond drank martinis. You're more like every lawyer in a film or TV show who's about to lose their case and is cramming their closing remarks in a dark office."

"Are you saying I look tired and depressed?"

I smiled. "If the shoe fits."

He shook his head, hiding his smile in his glass. I watched eagerly at his lips, openly staring at him. No more hiding.

"Okay, then. Show me." Forget the game. I had a feeling things were about to get far more interesting.

Wes' eyes snapped to meet mine. "What?"

"Teach me. I'm your eager subject."

Wes choked a little on his next sip and took a moment to clear his throat, his face flushing red. When he finally spoke, his voice was hoarse, a thick rumble that did terrible things to my self-control.

"You sure you're ready for that?"

"I can take whatever you give me."

His expression stilled, some kind of battle happening in his mind, until I worried I'd stepped over a line. These days, it was like I had trampled all over the damn thing. I could barely see it anymore. But I wasn't the only one.

I was five seconds away from throwing myself at him.

Wes disappeared for a moment before returning with the bottle I'd gifted him.

"So," I watched as he unwrapped the cork, "am I right in saying that bourbon is whiskey, and scotch is whisky, and whiskey is whiskey?"

He froze and raised his head, brow wrinkled like he didn't know if I was joking or not.

"Okay, to make it simple, yes, but," he said, popping the cork on the bottle, "don't ever say that to someone who likes whiskey. They'll probably lose it."

"You know that's ridiculous, right?"

"Hey! I didn't make the rules. I'm just enjoying the results."

Wes poured mine first, and I reached forward to take the glass, brushing my fingers against his. My head felt light, giddy from the precipice I was inching closer to rather than the booze.

I tasted the whiskey. It was dark amber, smooth, smoky. Potent.

I looked up. Had Wes moved closer or had I? I took another sip, my gaze locked with his.

He watched. Didn't move.

The warmth of the whiskey eased my nerves. The rush of Wes' attention was overwhelming.

It made me bold.

Slowly, I licked my lips, heat unfurling in my gut as Wes tracked the movement with his eyes. I stepped closer, my fingers brushing his chest, the glass the last thing between us.

"Good?"

I hummed, satisfied. "You should try it." I took another sip, leaving my lip wet.

All his attention was focused on my mouth as he moved closer. "I want to. You don't know how much I want to."

"Wes," I sighed, breathless. *Do it. Kiss me.*

Suddenly serious, he held my gaze, pools of dark chocolate staring down at me. He was beautiful up close, beautiful from any angle, but it wasn't the perfect cheekbones or impish smile or tousled curls that made me want him. It was the way he looked at me now, with care and desire; mirroring the longing I felt.

He took the glass from my hand, moved it to the counter. Now there was nothing between us.

"Tell me to stop," he whispered, his breath ghosting my lips. We were barely touching, and yet I could feel him everywhere. The anticipation of it spread goosebumps along my skin, a wildfire of longing taking over my body.

He needed to kiss me. *Right. Now.*

My heart knocked against my chest, but there was no fear. Only a thrill. Because it was Wes. The same Wes who reached for my hand when I was scared. Who let me drool on his shoulder when I fell asleep during a movie. Who walked two blocks out of his way to bring me hot chocolate. With extra marshmallows.

"Don't stop."

As I felt him inch closer, I thought I knew what to expect. I'd kissed Wes on the show. Dozens—maybe hundreds—of times.

I knew how it felt. And it was nice. More than nice.

But *oh*, I was wrong.

A split second before his mouth hit mine, his tongue was there, gently caressing my lips, tasting the whiskey, before he engulfed them with his own. Heat coursed through me and left me lightheaded. *Holy hell.* He'd never kissed me like this before. I let out a soft sigh and pulled him toward me, wanting more.

With no cameras in sight, this kiss blew away any memory I had of stage-kissing Wes. Hell, it blew away every other kiss I'd ever experienced.

He nipped gently, pulling my bottom lip between his. Changed angles and deepened the kiss, devouring me slowly. Purposefully. Taking his time.

I was happy to let him.

When I thought he might stop, he continued, capturing my lips and curling his tongue around mine, hungrily licking into my mouth. It was easily the most erotic thing I'd ever experienced, and I couldn't get enough.

"You've never kissed me like that before," I said when we pulled apart, trying to catch my breath.

"The way I want to kiss you isn't rated for general audiences," he softly joked. His thumb skimmed my cheek as he pressed a kiss to the corner of my mouth.

"Lucky me." I dived back in, lured by his mouth like a moth to a flame.

I needed his hands on me. No amount of acting with him had prepared me for Wes' kisses, so I was going to throw out all my assumptions and rewrite them with the truth. And I needed to start as soon as humanly possible.

I pulled him closer, even though there was no space left between us, no place we weren't touching. He devoured the little sounds I made. Of course he never kissed like this on the show. It was way too hot for TV. But then another thought occurred to me. *Is this how he'd been kissing everyone else?*

Possessively, I licked into his mouth, wanting to make this good for him, wanting to erase the taste of anyone who had come before me. He moaned, low and rough, then pulled back slowly, peppering me with more kisses, his thumb stroking my cheek.

Wes kissed me slow, tender. Determined. His mouth sought mine with a care that was agonizing and addictive. I melted on the spot, bones liquified under the force of his lips, his tongue.

"I've wanted to do that for a long time," he said.

"You have?"

"Always." He pulled me into another slow kiss, one I felt down to my bones.

19

WES

HAVING her lips on mine was more than I'd hoped for. I was half expecting to wake up from a dream, except that for as many times as I'd imagined this moment, the reality was so much better.

There were no cameras, no crew, just Liv's plush lips beneath my own, little puffs of breath against my cheek as I held her close to me, not willing to break the kiss. She tasted amazing, whiskey sharp and sugar sweet, tentative and tender beneath my tongue.

Once I started, I couldn't stop. Learning the shape and movement of her mouth with my own. I could feel the heat of her in my arms, and I drank in every sound she made.

God, I couldn't get enough of her.

It was everything I'd wanted. Lips, teeth, tongue. Desire flared, white hot, down my spine when her fingers skimmed the bare skin under my shirt, lust racing through my veins.

Liv's ringtone pierced the silence, and I pulled back, my heart pounding. It felt like I hadn't taken a full breath since we'd started, and Liv looked dazed. She huffed out a nervous laugh, and I opened my mouth, then found myself at a loss for words. I was still too blown away by how incredible that kiss was.

The phone rang again.

"I should get that." Liv sounded as breathless as I felt.

She looked at the caller ID, and I could tell from the look on her face it was Jen.

Of course it was.

Although, honestly, I was thankful. I could use a minute to pull myself together after that firework of a kiss.

Liv took the phone call outside. Clearly, whatever Jen wanted would take more than a five-minute conversation. But that was good, too. Because even though my breathing was back to normal, my pulse was still racing, and it kind of felt like my body wanted to vibrate out of my skin.

I moved into the kitchen, found my own phone, and dialed.

"You what?" Jackson asked, understandably surprised when I explained why I'd called.

"We kissed, man, I don't know. I'm kind of freaking out."

We'd been drinking. Maybe not a lot, but enough to make it possible this was a misfire of alcoholic logic and, I don't know, Stockholm Syndrome? I was afraid of hearing Liv tell me this was a mistake.

"What did Liv say about it?"

"Nothing. Jen called." I pushed a curl out of my face. "Tell me you have some great advice for handling this."

"I'd probably start with not freaking out."

I let my head fall back against a cupboard with a thump. *No shit, J.*

"Just talk to her. It won't be as bad as you're expecting, I'm sure of that."

"I know we need to talk, but we've been drinking. What if she tells me it was a huge mistake?" Suddenly, the weight of what we'd just done hit me. If Liv said it was a mistake, I'd accept that, but my heart would be broken.

"Somehow I don't think she will."

"J. I've spent years never thinking this could happen, and now that it's a possibility, I don't want to screw it up." I closed my eyes. Jesus. "This is everything I've wanted since I met her."

"Then you should start by telling her that."

———

It was appropriately awkward when Liv stepped back inside. "Hey."

"Hey. Everything okay with Jen?"

"Yep. Yeah. Absolutely fine." She hadn't moved and didn't seem to know what to do with her hands. I wasn't the only one left a little off-kilter from our kiss. "It was just. You know, work stuff."

"Right."

Man, this was awkward. Like we'd forgotten how to act normal in front of each other.

"How are you?"

"Fine. You?" We'd been reduced to small talk. Great.

She nodded so slowly it was like watching her in slow motion.

What were we doing? We'd known each other for years. We worked together. This shouldn't be so hard.

The ridiculousness of the situation caught up with me, and I burst out a laugh. "Sorry. Why is this so awkward?"

A relieved smile broke out on Liv's face. "Right? Thank god it's not just me."

She walked toward me, and I met her in the middle, cupping her cheek. "That's better. Let's start over. Hi."

Her smile widened, her arms wrapping around me. "Hi." She was glowing, and pleasure swelled in me. I did that.

"That was some whiskey. I should tell Tiff to be careful who she serves that to."

She laughed softly, just a brush of air across my skin.

Then her smile faltered. Just a little. She bit her lip.

She needed to tell me something, and I wasn't going to like it.

Shit.

Did she regret it? Want to pretend it never happened? Was I just supposed to forget how incredible her lips felt?

I hoped to god I hadn't just ruined everything.

"Wes." Liv's eyes searched mine, hopeful. "I'm glad I kissed you. I wanted to. And I want to do it again. But if you don't want—"

"I do," I said quickly. She needed to know that. "I don't regret kissing you. I couldn't even if I wanted to." I could still taste the sharpness of the whiskey on her tongue. Could hear the little gasp of surprise when my lips had first touched hers. "I wanted to. Still want to. But I won't if it means losing you."

"Me, too. It's," she ducked her head, and I caught the pink tinge to her cheeks, "kind of all I've been able to think about lately."

I framed her face with my hands. "That makes two of us." It was easy to lean down, take her mouth again. Standing close, cradling her head, angling her right where I wanted her. Pushing in deeper. Being rewarded with her barely there sighs, her fingers gripping tighter around my arms.

To think, we could have been this doing all week.

"Wait." I didn't want to stop kissing her, but something was nagging at me. A replay of the last few days flashed through my mind. "So all of that was on purpose? 'Wes, give me a hand; keep me steady,' that bikini. All of it?"

"Um …" she trailed off, not looking sorry at all.

Christ.

"You have been bad." And fuck, the way her eyes darkened. I barely had a chance to process it before she gripped my hair and pulled me down into a hot, messy kiss.

I grabbed her waist, hauling her tighter against me, destroying any distance that might be left between us. Days, weeks, years of desire licked up my spine. I was hard, and I was fucking ready. Her body felt amazing. Her mouth was divine. If the ground opened up beneath my feet, I'd happily submit myself to purgatory before I gave up this kiss.

Liv's hands fell to my shorts, teasing me through the zipper. I growled into her mouth. Fuck. I wanted to have her. Right now.

Which was exactly why we needed to stop.

Abruptly, I pulled back, my breathing coming hard and fast. "Wait. Wait."

I let out a breath. Control. I could do this. I took another step back when she inched closer.

"Hold up a second, we should …" Be kissing, that's what. On every surface in this house. And never stop. No. Shit. Kissing her was incredible, but what happened after? Tomorrow? Was I just some escape she was taking? "We need to talk about this."

She stalked toward me again, and her smile almost did me in. "Or we could keep going and talk later?"

I thought I knew all of Liv's expressions, but I'd never seen this naked want before, and Christ. It was too much.

I pressed my palms into my thighs, fighting my instinct to pull her into me. I wanted to bite down on the lip she had caught between her teeth. Lick the sweat and sun from her neck. Taste the curves of her shoulder, her breasts, her hips.

Fuck. Stop.

Talking. That's what we needed to do.

"I'm serious." I laughed, and that seemed to get through to her. She stopped, standing close but not close enough to touch. Good. I might actually get through this.

"You need to know that you mean a lot to me. I don't want to lose this friendship."

"Neither do I."

"Liv, you have to know I like you. A lot. But," I looked deep into her eyes, "this isn't a casual thing for me. I need you to know that. If all you want is a—a …"

A flash of hurt crossed her face, pinching her brow. "What? A quick lay? You're not some itch I need to scratch, Wes." She looked away. "I can't tell you what this is, but it's something I can't ignore anymore, and I don't …" She searched for the words while my fragile heart cycled through every irrational fear it could.

I don't want you. I don't think we should do this again. It doesn't mean anything.

Her eyes were fierce when she returned my gaze. This Liv wasn't joking around. "It's not casual for me, either."

Sweet relief cascaded over me. I hadn't realized how much I'd needed to hear those words.

Without any more hesitation, I closed the distance, feeling the warmth of her neck under my palm. I traced the curve of her jaw with my thumb. Teased her plush lower lip.

"I know this might sound strange, but can we take it slow? I don't want to rush into anything."

Her fingers danced over my spine, a slow, delicious stroke that went straight to my cock. She looked up at me, eyes wide with surprise. "Wesley Owens wants to take it slow? Who are you and what have you done with my friend?"

"Are you calling me easy?"

She laughed. "Are you kidding? It took days of all my best moves to get you to kiss me. I practically had to tattoo it on my forehead. You are anything but easy."

"Excuse me for being a gentleman, doll." And, oh. That got a reaction. I'd have to remember that for later. "It's not every day my best friend tries to seduce me. I thought I was losing it."

"Gee, thanks. You really know how to make a girl feel special."

Smiling, I dipped down to brush my nose along her cheek, feeling her sigh. I was going to find every single way to elicit that sound, and I'd love every minute. "You are special."

This kiss was slower, softer than before. The gentle slide of mouths and sharing of breaths. I was happy to know that she wanted this, wanted me.

We broke apart when Liv struggled to stifle a yawn. She looked embarrassed, and I couldn't stop myself from kissing the pink of her cheek. "Boring you already?"

She narrowed her eyes, but the effort was ruined by another yawn. "Jerk."

I pressed a kiss to her hair. "It's getting late. We should get to bed."

She nodded sleepily. "Hey, Wes?"

"Yeah?"

"Promise me this isn't a dream?"

Affection blossomed in my chest, warm and comforting. Rich like the whiskey we had drunk.

I savored one last sugar sweet kiss. "I promise."

My eyes didn't leave her until she had disappeared into her bedroom.

Whoa.

So. That happened.

Years of control. Shattered. Everything was going to be different. Liv wanted me.

So why was I still worried? This was everything I'd ever wanted. But what was this for Liv?

She wasn't heartless, but what happened in a week, or a month, when she realized we worked better as friends?

Maybe it would be better to stop now, before we took things too far. Before we passed a point we couldn't come back from. Or maybe we'd already passed it. Who knew?

One thing was for sure. Whatever Liv wanted, I'd give her. And if that meant walking myself to my own destruction, I'd do it.

20

LIV

HOLY SHIT. That was some kiss.

Even a full night's sleep hadn't damped the memory of it. Wes' steady hands, his relentless mouth.

I buried a smile in my pillow. I couldn't believe it. Wes and I had ... and we could ...

Excitement had taken over every cell in my body. I hid a squeal in the soft down, then played the whole night over again.

I couldn't stop. And I wanted so much more.

Even before I rounded the corridor into the room, I heard the scuffle of paws and a mixture of playful growls and Wes' breathy laughter. When they came into view, I had to hide my smile behind my hand. Wes lay on his side on the floor, Baxter jumping on and over him.

For the last year, every morning had been the same. Wake up alone, preapproved breakfast, shuttled to the gym, preassigned workout, shuttled to work, have someone else do my hair and makeup.

Same routine, over and over. I hated it.

But this I could do. Waking up to Wes every day sounded pretty damn good to me.

"Morning," I said, and wow, I could not keep the smile out of my voice. The Wes effect had only grown more potent since that kiss.

We locked eyes. His hair was a beautiful mess, fluffy and erratic. I was officially obsessed with his curls.

"Hey." His smile sent my insides into a fresh tailspin. "Come here. I want to show you something."

I propped myself against the back of the couch, needing the barrier between us and knowing if I came any closer, it would be impossible to stop myself from kissing him. "What am I looking at?"

Wes sat up. "Sit," he directed Baxter, who followed the command. "Drop." Baxter laid down. "Roll." Baxter rolled to the left, completing a full turn until he was back on his stomach. "Squirrel." Baxter shot up to his feet, one paw in the air.

I tried to hold back my giggle, but it escaped as soon as Wes met my gaze, his pride apparent. I gripped the back of the couch, longing to climb over and touch him.

It was easy to see the bond between them, and it surprised me that Wes had never mentioned wanting a dog before. It was clear how much he adored Baxter. And how mutual that adoration was.

"Play dead," was the last command, and I watched as Baxter rolled onto his back, sticking all four legs into the air. He would have sold it better if his tail wasn't wagging like crazy. It was so adorable I wanted to cry.

Wes went through the game again, treating Baxter to a raspberry on his stomach every time he "played dead," a curtain of curls falling down as Baxter waggled his entire body in joy. My heart squeezed and jump-started. This was a facet of Wes he didn't show many people. Soft and caring, unrestrained. I treasured that side of him, and even though I wished more people saw it, I was selfishly pleased to be the only one who got this. So many aspects of our lives were shared with other people. Was it so bad to want some part of him to myself?

Except I was finding it increasingly difficult to stop wanting more than a part of him. I wanted it all. I wanted sleepy mornings and smiles over breakfast. Baxter snoring over a movie while we cuddled on the couch, Wes' heartbeat keeping time while I recited my favorite lines. I wanted him nearby when I was happy and when I was sad.

"Wait, do that again. I'll film it."

He did, and I made sure to keep him out of frame as I filmed, spinning the phone when Baxter rolled over, and adding a slow-motion effect to the last trick.

It only took a few minutes to edit and post the finished clip, and when I looked up, I found myself lost in the adoring smile on Wes' face. It very quickly slid into something dirty, and the reaction inside me was instantaneous.

Pleasure pulsated between my thighs, and as Wes crawled toward me, my mind filled with filthy fantasies of him on his knees, drinking down every drop.

My skin flushed as pink as my shirt.

From the floor, he slid his hand into mine, wicked thoughts reflected in his brown eyes. "I don't know what you're thinking about, but I'm going to guess it's good."

A quick tug was all it took for me to fall into his lap, tumbling into another kiss.

Oh, yes. I could definitely spend every morning like this.

———

Jen called. Again.

Considering she'd told me to "rest and recuperate," she wasn't giving me much space to do it. But telling her to back off felt selfish. She was working so hard; I shouldn't be ungrateful.

"How's your father?"

"He's good. Refuses to rest no matter what I tell him." I felt awful for lying to her.

"It's difficult when the people you care about won't listen to you."

Was I paranoid, or was she talking about me directly?

From where I was sitting, I could see Wes outside. He was standing and stretching beside the pool. Just another part of my life that was in flux right now.

He pulled his shirt off, and my eyes were suddenly not large enough to take in the miles of skin on display. There was no safe place to land. Only the dips and ridges of finely tuned muscles that my eyes followed and my fingers ached to touch. My mouth ran dry. After our kiss yesterday, my fantasies had reached a fever pitch.

There was nothing I hadn't imagined him doing to me. Nothing I wasn't desperate to do to him. I squeezed my thighs against the growing need in my core.

It was a relief when he dove into the pool, out of my sight. Then I realized that I'd soon have to face the same view, but this time, dripping wet.

Good god.

"Olivia?"

Right. Jen. Work.

"Sorry."

She hummed, sounding displeased. There was so much

to infer from that sound, but honestly, my brain was still running a montage of Wes and chest and water.

Wes popped up on the other end of the pool, curls agonizingly alluring. I'd become obsessed with getting my hands in them. Gripping. Pulling.

"Mm."

"Olivia, if you have something more important to do right now, I can hang up. It's only your career. I'm sure it can wait."

Shit. "Sorry. I—uh, have to help my dad with something."

"Fine. I have a million things to finalize anyway. Including chasing the network for your contract. I'll be in touch."

My guilt lingered after we hung up. I was being inconsiderate. Here I was, relaxing in a multi-million-dollar house in the Hills, thirsting, while Jen was working her ass off trying to fix a mess of my own creation.

As if summoned by my dirty thoughts, Wes stepped out of the pool, as sexy as I'd imagined he'd be, shimmering and completely lickable.

And when our eyes met and he winked, my whole body fired up. I might need to play it safe when it came to my work, but this was one risk that had definitely been worth taking.

Wes walked inside, no towel in sight. "Let me guess. That was your handler?"

I shot him a look, and he laughed. "Fine. How is Jen?"

"Stressed. She wanted to talk to me about starting a brand."

"Why? She knows you aren't interested in anything like that."

Which was exactly what I'd thought. "Without the

contracts in place for the spin-off, she wants to make sure I have another revenue stream."

"I keep telling you—"

"The spin-off is happening, I know. But it's not exactly a terrible idea to have a backup."

"Then she should be booking you auditions, not brand deals."

I hummed. I agreed, but I didn't want to talk about Jen. Wes was still shirtless and dripping, and I could think of far too many other things I wanted to do with my mouth.

"Liv?"

Water dripped from his hair down his chest, and I followed the path with my eyes. "Mm?"

"If you keep looking at me like that, I can't be held responsible for my actions."

"Then I guess you better stop me."

21

WES

I WAS DECIDING on lunch options when Liv placed the USB on the counter in front of me. Shit. Probably should have hidden it better.

"I thought I threw that out."

I didn't need to look up to know she was pulling the "Be Serious" face.

"You're avoiding again." Her fingers curled around my wrist. "I could help you. I haven't met your parents, but I could watch some of the videos, pick out some good bits?"

I shook my head. I didn't want Liv seeing them. It was too close. Too real. "You don't have to do that."

"I know I don't have to. Why are you trying so hard to not do this?"

"I'm not."

"You clearly are."

"Can we not do this? I know you think you're helping, but you're not. You were close with your mom, I get that, but it's not the same for me, and it won't magically change just because of some fucking video."

She flinched, and I wanted to sink through the floor, or maybe punch myself in the gut.

"I'm just trying to help. You don't have to bite my head off."

"I know. Shit, Liv, I'm sorry. All this stuff with my folks … I don't mean to take it out on you."

She studied me, and for once, I sat back and let her look. The scrutiny made me uncomfortable, but I deserved it for lashing out. She could look as long as she wanted.

Eventually, she found what she was looking for.

"You should scream."

All my thoughts screeched to a halt. "What?"

"Let it out. You're wound tighter than I've ever seen you. It was a trick my mom used. She said it worked better than a shot of tequila to get the blood flowing. Maybe it'll help."

"I know a few ways you could help get my blood flowing." I winked.

"Wes." *Be serious.* I laughed. It was too easy to tease her.

"Screaming, huh?" I wasn't convinced.

"It's worth a shot. Do it for me?" Now that was unfair. I should have known letting her know my weakness for her would backfire.

"Okay." I took a breath, then released it in a laugh. "This feels so dumb."

"Come on. I'll do it with you."

I really wanted to make the obvious joke, but Liv's expression stopped me. Fine.

Knowing I'd given in, she smiled, and my next breath came easier. I didn't know what I'd done to deserve it, but I was so glad she was here. "On three?"

"Sure."

"What if the neighbors think I'm murdering you?"

"Wes. Stop stalling. Your neighbors aren't close enough to hear, and even if they could, they'll just think you're eccentric. Or an asshole." She leaned up, my eyes fluttering closed as she pressed a sweet kiss to my cheek, whispering against the skin. "You'll feel better, I promise."

"Fine."

I took a deep breath, balling up the anger, drawing it deep, and imagined it forming in a solid block (guess Mr. Andrews had been onto something in that visualization class).

I shouldn't have felt nervous. How often had we practiced shit like this in school? But that was *acting*, despite how often they'd said to "draw on what you know," and *I had*. No point wasting good material, right? But that was fuel for a scene, not … this. Not *release*.

Closing my eyes helped, and I forced myself to stop thinking about how it would sound and focused on pushing out the pain and the self-doubt and every other toxic thought that had been dragging me down. My voice was rough as I screamed, and I could hear Liv chiming in.

When Baxter joined in, howling as much as a small Staffordshire could, we both burst into laughter. Suddenly, the space where I'd been harboring so much anxiety and fear felt light. Clear. And she was right. I did feel better.

I wrapped my arms around her. "Thank you. I guess I needed that. And I could use your help with the videos. If you don't mind."

She lifted her head from my chest and was suddenly so close all I could concentrate on were her pouty red lips. She smiled, soft and oh so sweet. "I offered, didn't I?"

I felt breathless. "Yeah."

The press of her mouth against mine felt natural, and I

was quickly becoming addicted to the sweep of her tongue, the hitch in her breath when I searched deeper.

This time, it was Liv who pulled away. "You're trying to distract me, and it's working, but you really need to finish this."

Quickly, I stole another kiss, then relented. "Fine."

I pressed play and tried to be objective as I watched. *Treat it like work.* Having Liv next to me helped. She offered comments and paused the video here and there to point out good places to edit.

It was far easier to watch her instead of the video. "She'd be proud of you, you know."

Liv smiled and kept watching, not letting me bait her into a distraction. Fine. The only way to finish this damn video was to suck it up and do it.

There was a large ballroom on-screen drenched in white linens and baby's breath and lace. People were everywhere, talking and dancing, barely a single person without a drink in their hand. Some turned to the camera, shouting their thoughts about the happy couple as the cameraman roamed through the ballroom. It was obvious from the late eighties clothes and terrible hairstyles that this was before Lucas and I were born.

"When was this?" Liv asked.

"'Bout thirty years ago. It's their reception."

"Wow, okay. That explains the sleeves." She laughed. "And the perms."

"I think you'd look good with a perm." I ran a hand through her hair, smiling when she let out the same soft sigh that always drove me crazy.

"Not as good as you do."

The footage cut to Dad, standing in front of the crowd,

giving a speech about how lucky he was and how much he adored my mom.

"They look happy," Liv said.

I scoffed. "They fake it well."

Liv looked like she was going to say something but instead stopped the video and saved it in a file marked "anniversary clips." After that, we settled into a routine, Liv starting the videos and asking questions, then moving the files we chose to the folder. I reluctantly pushed through, trying to be objective as my childhood literally played out before my eyes. Without Liv, I would have quit multiple times.

I lost count of how many we watched: birthdays, holidays, celebrations. All of them filmed from a professional, polite distance. These weren't private moments caught on camera. They were snapshots of my parents' achievements—trophies that marked different stages of their life. Here's Dad accepting an award, here's Mom opening a charity gala. Now watch as they show off their multi-million-dollar house.

Lucas and I were props, if we were included at all. Stand here, wear this, smile.

I had to hand it to them. The footage was impressive. If I didn't know better, I'd believe they had the perfect life.

The thought of compiling these lies into a curated celebration of their marriage made me angry. I was so tired of lying for them. Of pretending.

Fresh stubble scratched at my palm as I ran a hand down my face. I'd have to shave before Saturday. Couldn't look anything but perfect for their big day.

"Fuck. Why am I even doing this?"

Liv reached for my hand, squeezed. I was so lucky she was here. I couldn't have done this without her. "Because you're a good person, and despite everything, you want to do the right thing."

"Is that right?"

"Okay, it's because your brother guilted you into it, and you don't want to be an asshole."

"That sounds more like me."

"You're wrong. You're a better man than you think you are." A smile slowly set in when she leaned in and kissed my cheek. She'd been doing that a lot. I treasured every one. "I'm really proud of you for doing this."

I couldn't feel anything resembling glad, but I still remembered how angry Lucas had been, and I wasn't so much of an asshole that I wanted to hurt him.

The last still of the video remained on the screen, my parents posed on the couch, smiling, while Lucas and I sat on the floor beneath the Christmas tree, surrounded by shredded wrapping paper and laughing with each other, not even noticing the camera.

My gut turned over.

"Look at that. Hard to believe we were ever that close. These days it's like talking to a stranger. The worst part is seeing Lucas forgive them. Like he can just sweep all that shit under the rug like it doesn't matter."

Between one shaky breath and the next, Liv stretched up, one hand wrapping around my neck as she pulled me in, taking my weight as I leaned into her hug. Tenderly, she pressed kisses into my skin. My eyes fell closed as she made her way from cheek to cheek, my nose, my eyes, the corner of my mouth.

I felt exposed. Raw.

"You should talk to him. Tell him that you miss him."

Sure. I could imagine how well that would go.

"He doesn't want to hear it, Liv. Every time I try, we

end up insulting each other. He doesn't want anything to do with me anymore."

"He might."

He might also tell me exactly where I could stick it. "Maybe."

"Hey." She brought a hand up to my face. "Talk to me."

Her warm brown eyes offered a respite, a safe place to lay bare everything I felt, even though I was terrified of sharing it. It was silly. Liv was an incredible person. A great friend. But it'd been so long since I'd let anyone in. Exposing so much of myself was difficult.

It was safer to keep everyone at a distance.

Describing it was harder than I thought it would be. Like the feeling was too big to fit into simple words. "It's just ... there's a door, with everything behind it, and if it opens even a crack," my voice faltered, "I won't know how to close it again."

I knew I shouldn't hold back this much, especially with Liv. She'd been nothing but open with me, and she'd listened patiently, asked questions, distracted me when I needed it. I wanted to let go. I really did. *Especially* with her.

But, fuck, if it didn't scare the life out of me.

Opening my heart to her felt ... huge. Final.

Life changing.

Suddenly, Liv jolted off the couch, possessed by some driving force. "All right, I think we need a break. We've been doing this for hours. My ass is going to start trade negotiations with the couch at this rate."

"That's a terrible reference, and you should be ashamed of yourself."

That beautiful mouth slid into a cheeky grin. "You understood it, though, so it couldn't have been that bad."

She tugged me off the couch and pulled me along the hallway toward the bedrooms.

My heart pounded a little faster in my chest.

"Relax," she said as we walked into the junk room. "How about a game?"

I was still on edge from my previous thoughts, so it took me a moment to catch up. "What kind of game?"

Liv bent over—that wasn't helping me keep it together—to pluck a box from the floor. Monopoly.

"Anything but that."

But she ignored me, already setting up the game. She settled herself on the floor, then cocked a brow at me. "Well?"

She was teasing me, but the fond look in her eyes made my chest squeeze. Begrudgingly, I sat down. And she thought I wasn't easy. She didn't know the half of it.

"You better be ready to lose," I said, rolling the dice. The full force of her smile was so sweet it practically hurt.

22

LIV

"WAIT, SERIOUSLY?" I placed another house on Pall Mall and looked at the row of properties I'd lined up along this side of the board. Wes was going down. "He paid the biggest pop star in the world a quarter mil to sing at your party?"

"Oh, yeah. Dad never made it to a single one of my birthdays, but he had no problem throwing money at them."

Oh, Wes. I had no idea what it must have been like to grow up like that.

From the corner of my eye, I watched as his hand inched closer to Free Parking. Playfully, I hit it away. "Stop cheating," I said.

"Then stop taking all my money."

I laughed, relieved that a little of his good humor had returned. My heart still ached from watching those videos. I hadn't ever seen Wes so broken up. How long had he been holding that back? Did his brother even know how much pain he felt?

I'd never met Lucas, but when I did, I had a long list of bones to pick with him.

Wes rolled the dice, groaning when he landed on one of my properties. There was a smile as he counted his bills, but it didn't fully reach his eyes, and I knew now what was hiding behind them.

When he handed over his money, I caught his hand in mine, squeezed.

Finally, a spark returned, the corners of his lips curling up into a pulse-skittering smile. Geez. I was so finely tuned to him. All he had to do was look at me and tingles erupted.

He ran his thumb over my knuckles. "I'm sorry about earlier. You can see why I put it off for so long. Watching those videos just reminds me of why I left in the first place."

I was quick to shake my head. I never wanted him to be sorry for being honest. "Don't apologize. You don't have to pretend with me. You can be as messy as you want. Hell knows you've seen me at my worst."

Wes reached out to caress my cheek. "You don't have a worst."

I leaned into his palm. "Quit changing the subject."

"Thanks, Liv."

"For what??"

"Being here. Listening. You're," he paused, espresso eyes stormy when they met mine, full of emotion, "amazing. No matter what happens, I promise I'll be there for you."

My heart swooned, releasing a lovesick sigh in a single, reverberating thump within my chest. I closed my eyes against the onslaught.

Wes. A Romantic. Who knew?

He was watching me with a soft smile when I finally

opened my eyes. "You're really making it hard to enjoy this victory," I said, gesturing to the board. "I was going to wipe the floor with you, but that was so sweet I actually feel bad." I scrutinized him. "Did you do that on purpose?"

He raised a shoulder in a nonchalant shrug, but the sly gleam in his eyes gave him away. Clever. But he'd also made a mistake. Now that I'd discovered how much my flirting affected him, I knew exactly how to play this game.

"I guess it doesn't matter," I said, forcing a bored tone into my voice. "I'm ready for something different anyway." Holding his gaze, I brushed my hair over my shoulders, trailing a finger along my neck. My pulse jumped under my skin when his eyes dropped, first to my lips, then my hand, breasts, and back again.

I licked my lips. "You look like you need a swim."

"Is that right?" He was onto my game, but it didn't matter. I was making the rules up as I went, and everything was pointing to a win.

"Definitely."

"You think I need to cool off?"

He needed to stop eye fucking me and come over here and do it for real.

"I think you need something wet."

Pushing the game aside, he reached for me, pulling me in. I went along willingly, needing to feel his lips. Craving them. Craving him.

He didn't hesitate, his grip biting into my hips as he rearranged us until he had me pinned beneath him. Exactly where I wanted to be.

I melted against the hardwood, caged in by his arms. His thigh slipped between mine. Strong, deliberate. Just like during every fight I'd seen him train for. I ground against him, pulling at his shirt, needing to feel his skin. I couldn't decide where to touch first, my hands roaming his neck, arms, hair.

All the while, he devoured each moan straight from the source.

Wes broke the kiss, pulling back just enough to rasp a single word into my ear. "Bedroom," he said, but it was too far, and I wanted him too much.

"Too far," I shot back, stripping his shirt off, then reaching for the button of his shorts. The long, hard line of his dick was a tease between my thighs, and there were too many layers of clothes between us. I needed to get my hands on him.

Now.

He surged forward, trapping my hands between us, capturing my bottom lip between his teeth. I moaned so loud I heard it echo against the ceiling.

"Shit, Liv. The things you do to me," Wes growled, pushing my hands away as he licked a hot stripe up my neck.

I arched beneath him, needing more. When he undid my shorts, I buried my face in his neck, a habit so familiar and so new. "You smell so good. I've always loved how fucking good you smell."

Like hot showers and sheets fresh from the dryer. Fuck. I'd never again do laundry without thinking of him.

His eyes snapped up to mine. "Liv …"

"I know you wanted to take it slow," I started, but he shook his head.

"It's not that." His hand cupped my cheek, thumb stroking. There was so much depth in his eyes. "This isn't a game to me. I want you, I have for a while, and I—" he leaned into me, his fingers gliding over my neck as he gently brushed my hair back, "—I want to make it good for you."

My body was covered in goosebumps, tingling from where he'd touched me. Spinning from the force of the desire in his gaze.

Damn. I'd seen flashes of it this week, but I was starting to wonder how long he'd been looking at me like this while I hadn't noticed.

Well, I was noticing now.

My toes curled into the carpet when his hand trailed farther south, brushing deliberately over my nipple.

"I want you so damn much. You have to tell me what you want. Anything. I'll give it to you."

"Just touch me, please." It was all I'd wanted him to do for days now. Which was ridiculous because when wasn't Wes touching me? But I wanted more of it. Everything he had to give.

As long as he started right fucking now.

Propped up on his elbow, Wes dipped his fingers under my waistband, gently brushing along my pussy and dipping inside. I watched his eyes darken with lust.

He was feeling what I already knew. I was dripping. "Christ," he grunted.

My hand was already twisted in his hair, and I pushed up to kiss him, moaning into his mouth as two slender fingers entered me.

Yes. Finally. Every dirty thought I'd had about him flooded my mind. My skin flushed, running hot. Wes' hand down my shorts made movement impossible, and my hips squirmed. I wished we'd taken the time to get naked, but I didn't care enough to stop what we were doing.

All I needed was Wes.

His fingers were magic, building the intensity before teasing, and the change was driving my desire through the roof. The sound of it was erotic, wet and rhythmic as he fucked me with them, his hand curled so that his thumb was rubbing on my clit.

My panties were soaked, arousal dripping from me. Along his fingers, down my thighs. The scent of sex filled my senses.

Reaching for him, I fumbled with his pants until I had my hand on him. I wanted to do more, but then Wes was doubling his efforts, and pleasure took over.

I threw my head back as my orgasm hit, my eyes squeezing shut as I cried out. Wes' lips were soft against my throat. "That's it. You're so goddamn beautiful when you come."

Our lips met in unhurried, messy kisses between breaths.

And before I could do anything, Wes was reaching between us to grab his dick. I watched, mesmerized, as he worked himself over, his fist moving quickly, his fingers glistening with what I realized were my juices.

I wanted to taste him. "Jesus, that's hot," I said. Wes' eyes darted up to mine, and I saw the exact moment he fell apart. It was glorious.

We lay next to each other, blissed out. I was pretty sure there was a plastic hotel under my ass, but I didn't care. I could barely move.

"That was ..." I panted. *Incredible.*

Wes fell to the side of me, trying to catch his breath, his chest rising and falling. He nodded silently, out of words. That was a first. I could get used to making him speechless.

"Next time," he said, "I'll get you into a bed and take my time. I want to savor every part of you." He hooked a finger under my chin to pull me close, grazing my lips in a soft kiss.

Next time couldn't come fast enough.

23

LIV

I WAS PUTTING the finishing touches on my French braid when I heard Baxter coming down the hallway. His paws thumped excitedly against the hardwood as he bounced into my room, his excited breathing breaking the silence as he sat at my feet, tongue lolling out of his mouth and his tail sweeping the floor.

My bracelet jingled when I scratched behind his ears, and I knew I'd miss seeing him when we flew back to Chicago. I'd already gotten attached to him, the way he'd dig his nose under my hand when he wanted a belly rub or the sound of his little snores echoing down the hall.

He wasn't the only one I'd become increasingly attached to, either.

Wes was perched on a stool along the breakfast bar, staring down at the USB his brother had given him, when I entered the kitchen. He'd showered and changed from his swim shorts into gym shorts and a shirt that hung loose on him. He looked relaxed and comfortable, and it made me want to bury my nose in the soft fabric and breathe him in.

He looked up at the sound of my heels clicking against the tile.

"Wow," he breathed, and I preened. I knew the blush-pink sundress looked good on me, but seeing it reflected in his eyes made my stomach swoop.

He needed to stop that or I'd have to walk over there and tell him what I wanted.

Which was pretty much to jump his bones anytime we were in the same room together.

"You look amazing."

"Thanks, I'm nervous. What if I embarrass myself? Sym Padilla is a legend."

"You'll be great. How could they not love you?"

My skin heated at the wanton look he gave me. Damn, he was gorgeous when he did that. Okay, he was gorgeous twenty-four seven, but wow, it was like weaponized beauty at this range. If we didn't leave soon, we'd be replaying the events from yesterday, right here on the kitchen counter. Or the couch. I wasn't picky.

"Are you ready to go?"

Wes had arranged a suit fitting near the restaurant I was meeting Sym at. He'd said it was merely a coincidence, but we both knew that was a lie. He wanted to be nearby. I understood the impulse.

Still the same old Wes. A big ball of sweetheart under all that swagger.

"If we don't, I'm going to mess up that dress," he said, eyes traveling slowly over my body.

If we didn't leave now, I'd make him.

———

Local & Aesthetic was quintessential LA—picture perfect, from the walls to the servers to the food. Jen would have loved it. Even the name seemed like something a screenwriter would come up with.

The restaurant was tucked away, with a private terrace out back for days when the weather was fantastic and the photos would be as well. Days exactly like today.

I'd done my research on Sym. Fifty-six years old. They/Them. Industry heavyweight. Their mom had designed theater costumes, their dad had produced several big hits in the sixties. Sym had grown up around show business and now owned a bicoastal boutique agency which managed a third of the leads in this year's summer blockbusters and boasted a roster that was wonderfully gender fluid.

I spotted them immediately. Walking over, I knew I wasn't imagining the passing looks I received from other diners. No surprise. In LA, everyone was curious. You never knew who you were going to bump into.

"Olivia, thank you for joining me. It's so wonderful to finally meet you." Sym held a hand out, then preempted my response. "Please call me Sym."

I shook their hand. "Then I guess you can call me Liv." The informality was unexpected but pleasant. Seeing them up close felt surreal.

Sym Padilla knew my name, was sitting across from me, and we were about to have lunch. Crazy.

A light breeze carried through the courtyard, and Sym hurriedly reached into their pocket for a tissue, sneezing so loudly that a passing waiter jolted. Sym's eyes, already so kind and welcoming, shone with laughter. "Sorry about that. Allergies."

It was easy to feel comfortable in their presence. "We should move inside then."

Sym waved me off. "Oh, sweetie, you're so thoughtful to suggest it. But on a beautiful day like today? We must sit and enjoy it. My medication will kick in soon, so it won't be an issue."

The navy jumpsuit they wore had tiny flowers embroidered in red and yellow along the seams. Nestled in Sym's long dark hair was a pair of chunky enamel earrings, two bright yellow daisies. If I hadn't seen them in a recent Harper's Bazaar spread, I would never have known they cost four figures.

Sym was both exactly what I expected and nothing like it.

We ordered quickly; brandy and salted caramel pancakes for both of us. With a side of hot chocolate for me. It was exactly the kind of meal Jen would never have approved of.

When the waitress left, Sym straightened, their eyes not leaving mine. Looked like we were getting straight to business. Nerves fluttered in my chest.

"Do you enjoy acting, Liv? Does it make you happy?"

Oh, wow. That wasn't what I'd been expecting. Taking a deep breath, I gave the question some thought. I did enjoy acting, absolutely. But was it making me happy?

"Yes," I answered honestly. "But," came out before I could stop it, and I hadn't meant to elaborate, except Sym's curious gaze encouraged me to go on, "I've been thinking that I would like to direct."

They smiled warmly. "An admirable goal. One that I suspect you'll be quite good at. Have you been given many opportunities while working on *The Guild*?"

I wondered how much I should share. Did this

technically breach some sort of manager-actor confidentiality with Jen?

Sym surprised me by apologizing. "You know what? Let's not talk about work. I don't want to make you uncomfortable. How about we get to know each other a little? Enjoy this beautiful day."

Gosh, they had an ease about them. I envied it. It's what had drawn me to Wes when we'd first met. His was a different type of ease, one I sometimes thought was a cover for something else. A way to deflect. Sym's felt solid and steady. Hard earned and fiercely defended. Like they'd been through enough to get it and wouldn't let anyone take it away.

I liked Sym. A lot.

When our meals arrived, I salivated. A short stack of fluffy buttermilk pancakes drenched in syrup, topped with honeycomb shards, gingersnap crumbs and a generous scoop of mascarpone. Sym hadn't been kidding around.

Eventually, I could no longer bite my tongue, needing to mention *Mo & Jo*, the television show Sym had spearheaded ten years ago that featured a young woman traveling back in time to get her big break on Broadway. It was what had inspired me to try acting. "My mom loved it. We would always watch it together."

"Oh, thank you. It is still so dear to my heart. Everyone I knew told me that it would never work, but I knew I'd always regret not trying. I was convinced that it wouldn't get picked up past the first nine episodes, but we surprised everyone." Sym reached over and laid a gentle hand on mine. "It must have been very difficult to lose her. My own passed when I was still in school, and it is a bond that you can never replace."

I nodded, not trusting my voice.

They pulled back, digging into their food. "Do you like musicals?"

"I love them." I dropped the marshmallows into my hot chocolate, watching as they bobbed. I'd inhaled my pancakes already, and I was determined to enjoy this drink. "We actually recorded a musical episode on the show in season three. It was my favorite that year."

My lips curled into a smile. Wes and Jackson had hated it, neither of them being able to hold much of a tune, but it had reminded me of my mornings watching mermaids lose their voices or genies parade toward palaces.

Sym brightened. "I'm working on a special project that I think you would be perfect for. It's about a ragtag troupe of performers trying to set up their own theater, but everything is constantly going wrong. Think Howard Ashman and company revitalizing the WPA Theatre with the oddball satire of a Christopher Guest mockumentary."

"Wow," I said, genuinely excited about the sound of it. "So, kind of like *Starkid* meets *Faulty Towers*?"

"Exactly!" Sym's head tilted, their astute gaze assessing me. "See? I knew you would be perfect for it. And since it will be a small production, I think you would have a good chance of negotiating a directorial option."

What they were presenting sounded like my dream job.

So I knew it had to come with a "but."

"I assume that would only be an option if I fired Jen as my manager and signed with you." I pushed my plate away.

"You have a bright future, Olivia, and a quick mind. I can tell there will be many opportunities for you ahead, and I don't want to push you, but I will give you a piece of advice. Once you know what you want, don't let anyone else put you on a path of their own making. This is your life and your career. Don't regret the choices you didn't make."

I sipped my hot chocolate and thought about what Sym had said. I didn't disagree with them. It was something I'd heard many times from Mom.

I wanted to live without regrets. To be fearless. Go after what I wanted.

And I knew what I wanted now—directing. And Wes.

Despite Wes' complaints about her, Jen supported my goals and was helping me toward them. It was simply taking some time. She'd warned me that it wouldn't happen overnight. And sure, I didn't love waiting, or the hundred other things Jen kept me busy with instead, but I trusted her.

I just needed to be patient.

I stood. "Thank you. I can't tell you how much this has meant to me. I'm so sorry to have wasted your time, but I'm just not ready to leave Jen yet."

"It wasn't a waste at all. I'm glad we met." Their expression was soft and sweet, reminding me so much more of my mother than I had been prepared for. "You have my number. Save it. Any time you want to talk, even if it's about old musicals, give me a call."

I had to admit, they'd sparked something in me. As I made my way to find Wes, I replayed the conversation in my mind and realized with surprise that Sym had asked for my opinion and had never once made me feel bad for it.

24

WES

MY MEASUREMENTS HADN'T CHANGED since I'd last been fitted, but the attendant, who had helpfully introduced himself as Ken, wanted to be thorough, so I was whisked into a private changing room and given the full treatment.

Ken was a little grayer than any of my usual fans, so I assumed he didn't watch the show. He certainly never mentioned it. Although he had the air of someone who felt good service should be seen and not heard. It was such a massive change from the usual fawning that I felt a little like a kid undergoing an etiquette lesson.

His current suggestion was a custom velvet jacket matched with a classic black pant. It was fantastic, but better suited to a walk down the red carpet than an anniversary dinner. I could already picture my father's reaction to it. A weighted stare that said, "I expected better from you."

Well, he could take those expectations and shove them. He was lucky I was coming to this damn charade at all. But I wouldn't wear his costume and dance around for him, too.

At least I'd finished the damn video.

In the end, it hadn't taken as long as I'd thought it would. With Liv's help, I'd gotten it down to two and a half minutes, a simple instrumental track playing over it. There was still a sick churn in my gut when I watched it, but even I could admit that it looked good.

No, good wasn't the word. It looked like it should—a perfectly constructed fantasy.

Dad would be so proud.

I straightened the sleeves again. Were they too short or was that just me? I felt like a lady in the old west, nervous about showing my ankles. Ken shot me a critical look when I snorted a laugh to myself. He probably thought I was going crazy.

"Maybe a longer sleeve," I said. He nodded, then disappeared out of the room.

I already knew which suit I'd leave with. It was a pale blue linen blend that didn't feel too stuffy but was still perfectly tailored. Definitely not to my father's tastes, but that only made it more appealing.

I saw the door open in the reflection of the mirror and turned, ready to tell Ken to go ahead with the pale blue, when Liv slipped in carrying a large dress bag. Her smile was triumphant, and I found myself beaming back at her.

And I thought I had it bad before.

She laid the bag over a nearby chair, then raked her eyes over me in appreciation. "Wow. You look good." She bit her lower lip. "Really good."

Slow. I'd wanted to take it slow. Why was that again?

I shrugged, going for nonchalant, but really, I was ready to lock the door and take her up against it. "I clean up all right."

She hummed, her eyes hungry, making my body react. I

knew if I reached between those silky thighs, I'd find her wet and waiting. But getting caught fooling around in public was the exact opposite of what we were meant to be doing, so as much as I wanted her, I needed to—quite literally—keep it in my pants.

Ken returned, swapping the black velvet jacket with a more standard gray wool. He didn't react to seeing Liv in here with me. Dude must have seen all kinds of things. He deserved a raise.

He made a few small adjustments and stood back. "This is an option if you'd rather a more classic look."

"I look like my brother in this suit." I turned to the Ken. "I'll go with the light blue."

He nodded and left me to change, but not before I caught him looking between Liv and me.

I heard the click of the lock after Ken left. I was gonna need to tip him well.

"Have you talked to Lucas yet?" Liv asked as I shrugged out of the jacket. Quietly, she reached up and eased it off my shoulders, taking it from me and hanging it as gently as Ken had.

"I texted him this morning to tell him the video was done." He'd responded with a curt "Thanks." Don't ask me how I knew it was curt, but I knew. If there was one person who could manage to convey sarcasm in six letters, it was my baby brother.

As Liv slid her palms down my chest, I breathed in her soft perfume. Subtle hints of flowers I'd couldn't recognize but would forever remind me of summer breezes, barely there sighs, the gentle curve of her nose tucked into my neck.

My fingers stilled on the buttons of my shirt. Not the time.

"How did it go with Sym?"

"Strange. I felt like I was cheating on Jen. And I felt bad that Sym made the effort only to be turned down."

Only Jen could make Liv feel bad about that. And without even being here. Just the thought of it made me angry, but I knew Liv didn't like it when I badgered her about Jen, so I said nothing.

Liv teased the buttons above my waist. "Aren't you going to change?" There was a devilish glint in her smile.

I was hard already, my natural reaction to having her this close, especially now that I knew what she tasted like. My body was three steps ahead of my brain, already undoing the rest of my shirt without thinking.

I was having a hard time remembering why we shouldn't do this.

"Let me help you," she said, reaching down to unbutton my pants. My dick throbbed as she ran her fingers down the zipper, teasing. Cupping me, stroking through the material.

Oh, fuck.

It was difficult not to moan as she dragged the zipper down, licking her lips in anticipation.

"I've been thinking about this all week."

And before I could say anything, Liv dropped to her knees, pulled me free, and swallowed me down. I fisted my hands at my sides and let my head fall back.

I let out a low groan. "Oh, yeah." Shit. The things she could do with that tongue.

My gaze jerked over to the door. "Are you sure?"

Ken could be back at any minute. It would be torture to stop now, but I could handle a little delayed gratification if it meant keeping Liv out of an embarrassing situation.

No way I'd do that to her. No matter how good she was

at sucking cock. And she was really fucking good. I reached for her, brushing her hair behind her ear before cupping her cheek in my palm.

She licked up the underside of my dick, smiling as it twitched against her lips. "I'll be quick." Another lick. Christ. "Let me make you feel good, Wes."

Then she took me back down, humming like it was the best thing she'd ever tasted. I groaned when I hit the back of her throat and she swallowed around me. I'd never worked harder to be quiet.

The reality beat out every fantasy I'd had of having her mouth wrapped around me. Thank fuck I'd never known how good this felt. I wasn't sure I'd ever think of anything else again.

Her mouth was so fucking warm and wet, and the sight of her lips stretched around my dick was too much. I clenched my thighs, straining against the urge thrust deep into her.

The sight of her coming on my fingers yesterday was branded on my brain. More than anything, I wanted to lay her down, take my time, and watch her fall apart over and over again.

Liv was anything but shy in the moment, angling so that the tip dragged along the inside of her cheek, so I could feel it against my palm. Then she took me down and held me in the back of her throat, her big brown eyes blinking and shimmering.

Seeing her in control, with fire and lust in her eyes, was divine. This was what I saw when I looked at her. Power and pleasure, hidden under a sweet exterior. I'd wanted to help her explore that side of herself, and good god, if getting on her knees helped her do that, I'd happily support her. It wasn't a surprise to me that I'd let her do just about anything she wanted to.

Aliens could have dropped out of the sky, and I'd never know. I was too wrapped up in Liv.

Fuck, she was incredible. She swirled her tongue just as the pressure hit an all-time high, everything tightening. I had enough time to choke out a warning before she was swallowing every drop of my release.

It was a damn good thing I needed to be silent because every thought in my head at that moment was a spin of "I love you," the words sitting so close to my tongue I had to bite down to keep them from slipping out.

Returning from oblivion, I stroked the curve of her lips where she was stretched around me and swallowed back a groan when she hummed around my over-sensitive shaft, her long lashes damp with tears. *Jesus Christ.*

My voice was raw. "I thought I told you that I wanted to take my time."

She pulled off, as breathless as I was. I watched as she stroked her swollen lips, and even though there was nothing left in me, my dick twitched. *Down, boy.*

"And I didn't want to wait another second to have your cock in my mouth."

She was going to be the death of me. "You're incredible. Did you know that?"

"It's you. You make me feel like I could do anything."

"That's got nothing to do with me, doll. That is all you."

25

LIV

THE FIRST TIME I'd ever tasted champagne, I ended up having hiccups for an hour. Mom had snuck me a glass on my eighteenth birthday, claiming it was a tradition. It wasn't, but I liked the idea of us starting one together.

It hurt to know we would never get the chance to start any others.

The slip dress I wore was a pastel yellow, pale like the light of a new moon. Silk as soft as a lover's touch draped and hugged my curves with the appreciation of a sculptor.

Barely there straps left my shoulders and collarbone exposed.

It made me feel like a damsel in an old film. The ones where a swashbuckling hero would storm the castle or climb the outer walls to bust into her boudoir. My mom would have loved it.

I picked up the final touch of my outfit for tonight's party from the dresser. Two yellow gold earrings, delicate threads ending with single a white pearl. Mom had always saved them for special occasions, but when she'd gotten sick, she'd handed them to me and told me to wear them as often as I could.

"Christ, you look sexy."

Pleasure bloomed in my chest at Wes' words, setting off a chain reaction to every sensitive part of me. "You haven't even seen it all yet."

I spied his reflection in the mirror, my breath catching at the sight. Wes was … my heart stuttered as I admired him. He was gorgeous. I mean, *of course*, he always was, but … Wow.

Occasionally Wes looked like a kid playing dress up. It never failed to pull at my heartstrings something fierce. But not now. Now he was all man. Devastating. I couldn't take my eyes off him.

Every part of my body was on fire, completely overwhelmed with need.

The powder-blue suit hugged his body and made his eyes pop (hadn't I always said navy was the best? Well, I'd been wrong). Even the soft white T-shirt he wore underneath couldn't detract from how smoking hot he was.

In fact, the whole "casual" look, with his tousled waves artfully falling around his face and his hands stuffed in his pockets, took him from hot to scorching.

Straight out of my fantasies.

Exactly like the kind of boy band member I had a massive crush on ten years ago. Or even better, like the exact kind of man I had a massive crush on now.

Except this time, I didn't have to dream about what it would be like to kiss him. Because I already knew. I had several extremely vivid memories of it.

I slipped the last earring into place as Wes slid his hands around my hips, his body flush against my back. The heat of him obvious through the thin material of my dress.

I turned to face him, threading my hands around his neck. His hair was much shorter here than the front, barely an inch but still soft—and addictive to touch. But it was the look in his eyes that left me speechless.

Those deep, dark brown eyes looked at me like I was the answer to his life's pursuit. I was Rose at the top of the staircase. Or Annie at the top of the Empire State Building.

"Do you know how much I want to ravage you right now?" he asked.

I laughed breathlessly, feeling lightheaded. Joy bubbled inside me. It was my first glass of champagne all over again.

Having Wes look at me like this—talk to me like this—was turning my world upside down. "What am I, a dame in some regency novel?"

A deep smile pulled at his lips, and he dipped his head, brushing his nose gently across my cheek, whispering in my ear. "If I could, I would lay you down, strip you slowly, and savor every inch of you."

Oh.

"I'd start here." He slid a finger down my neck, teasing out every goosebump with ease. They continued all the way down my arm. "Then I'd kiss you here." He followed the line across my collarbone with his lips, his hair brushing my bare skin.

Desire licked at my skin, making me wet.

Our breaths sounded loud to my ears, and my body felt like a live wire, sparking at his every touch. Fuck, if only we didn't have to leave. I wanted him so badly.

"Wes, I really need you to kiss me right now."

His eyes were clouded over, and I imagined mine were, too. His thumb stroked along my jaw. "Can't mess up that makeup, doll, so I'll have to make do with this."

With a hand gently guiding my head back, he skimmed

his lips across the breadth of my throat, kissing with just enough pressure that I was shaking with want. He continued until he reached my ear, taking the tender lobe and the gold earring between his teeth. My fingers gripped at his sleeves. If he let go of me, I wasn't sure I could stand.

"I won't be able to take my eyes off you tonight," he said.

It was beyond obvious we were more than friends. I couldn't even remember what that was like. I didn't want to. Not being able to touch him was not an option for me anymore. But we still hadn't had sex, and the anticipation of it was making me crazy with lust for him.

"Maybe we should stay," Wes said, his breath tickling my ear. "Forget the party."

I wanted that more than anything, but I also knew we couldn't miss this. No matter how much Wes wanted to.

"As much as I want that, we need to go. Come on, the faster we leave, the faster we can come home."

I didn't miss the spark in his eyes as the word slipped out. *Home.* But that's how I felt. And it wasn't just the house I was referring to. It was him.

———

There should be a whole section of the thesaurus dedicated to describing LA mansions. Huge. Impressive. Imposing.

Wes hadn't been kidding when he'd called it a monstrosity.

Maybe it was because I grew up in a two bedroom with a bathroom I'd shared with my parents, but this was exorbitant. Seven bedrooms? Thirteen bathrooms? What kind of math was that?

I'd known Wes had grown up rich, but wow. This was ... excessive, even for Bel Air.

Overshadowing the house was the clear marquee that had been erected for the event. Tall enough to be visible from the driveway, I had to give Wes' parents credit. If their intention had been to intimidate their guests, they'd certainly done it.

A valet took the car keys from Wes, and we were directed to the party via the main house. Apparently, it wasn't enough to have the guests be impressed from the outside alone; we had to walk through the house as well.

Understanding hit me when we stepped inside Wes' childhood home. The large, minimalistic rooms that were too designed to feel lived in. Looming canvases watching as we moved. Chandeliers that hung ominously overhead. The cold, unfeeling palette of tiles, concrete, and paint that closed in around us.

High archways under vaulted ceilings.

It felt like a cave. A sterile, expressionless cave.

It was very pretty. There wasn't a single angle that would result in a bad shot. They could set it up as an attraction and conduct tours, probably make their fortune twice over.

But it wasn't a home.

Beside me, Wes' expression had tightened, a practiced smile set in place. I'd seen it many times, in interviews or at events.

As we exited the house and made our way into the marquee, we were handed glasses of champagne, and while there was certainly more of a vibe out here—music, laughter, mingling—I couldn't shake the eerie sense of staging that lingered. Everything—everyone—felt placed, like a prop, exactly right.

Suddenly, all I wanted to do was wrap Wes in a hug and never let go.

He squeezed my hand as we walked, and I could feel the clammy evidence of his nerves, even though I saw none of it on his face. I already knew he was a fantastic actor, but seeing it in this setting made my heart ache. That hard, distant mask slid into place so quickly, it was almost impossible to recognize the Wes I knew underneath it.

And he'd almost come here alone.

Suddenly, any last guilt I felt for lying to Jen disappeared. Being here for Wes tonight was more important than any job. I couldn't kiss him right now, but I clung just a little tighter.

We found a quiet spot at the edge of the party, and I marveled at the setup. It was clear a lot of effort had been put into tonight. If what Wes had said was true, Lucas had done an incredible job.

Drapery was strung across the center of the marquee, soft and romantic. Pendant lights hung like fireflies, a sea of glittering stars against the white clouds above. There were flowers everywhere, soft neutrals and pastels that shone like luminescence in the growing twilight.

It was beautiful.

Around us, the party was bursting with people, and I recognized far more than I had expected to. Politicians, sports stars, actors, two late-night talk show hosts, and at least half of an aging rock band my mom had loved when she was younger.

What surprised me most was the lack of family in attendance. Just Wes' parents, his brother, and him.

When I asked him, Wes shrugged. "Dad's an only child, and Mom's sister moved to Seattle after she got married."

"She didn't want to fly down for this?"

A sliver of Wes' mask dropped. "Tonight isn't really about family."

I squeezed his hand harder and threw back the rest of my drink.

It was going to be a long night.

———

Wes made a trip to the party planner to hand off the thumb drive, returning quickly. I wanted to ask if he'd had a chance to talk to his brother yet, but before I could, two familiar figures were suddenly in front of us. Familiar because I'd spent the last few days watching footage of them.

But nothing prepared me for meeting Wes' parents. After hearing Wes' stories and watching the videos, I'd thought I'd know what to expect. *Ha. How naïve yesterday me had been.*

Elizabeth cut an imposing figure, tall and lithe, with a mane of black curls cascading around her shoulders. It was clear Wes resembled his mother. Without hesitation, she stepped forward and hugged him.

Conrad stood next to his wife, looking sharp in a tuxedo. His more-white-than-gray hair and artfully peppered wrinkles did nothing to disguise his good looks. Here was a man who owned the room (figuratively and literally in this case).

And when he turned his smile on me, I knew exactly where Wes had inherited his charm. Not that I'd tell him that.

"You must be the lovely Olivia I keep hearing about. I'm so happy you could join us." He leaned in to kiss my cheek, and I quickly hid my surprise. Wes cleared his throat beside me.

"Thank you for having me, Mr. Owens. It's a beautiful party."

"Call me Conrad. And I'm afraid I can't take the credit. Lucas has done a fantastic job, and I dare say it's almost as beautiful as my wife."

Wes' mom laid a hand on his sleeve. "Aren't you lovely?" She turned her smile to Wes. "I'm very glad to have my family together for the first time in a long time."

Conrad's attention snapped to Wes, his tone turning sharp, even though his smile never wavered. Another trick Wes must have learned from him. "Son. What a surprise. When your mother said you were in town, I barely believed her. Especially since you haven't seen fit to grace us with your presence."

"I'm surprised you even noticed. You're usually too busy with your empire."

Elizabeth's hand smoothed a wrinkle on Conrad's sleeve. "Actually, your father's been making a concerted effort to spend more time away from the office."

"Yes, now that at least one of my sons has had the fortitude to continue the family business, I've been able to step back a little."

"It must be like looking in a mirror." Wes sneered.

It was uncanny how much tension emanated from these three smiling faces. I felt like an extra in a horror movie. Or a spectator at a political debate.

Maybe one of the servers knew morse code, and I could blink an SOS to them?

Conrad's eyes narrowed slightly. "How do you like the Aston?"

"It's a good car."

"I know, I paid for it. You should keep it since you like it that much."

"Yeah, right."

"Think of it as an early Christmas present."

"You're joking."

"A simple thank you would suffice. Although if it can convince you to stop ignoring your family, I'm sure your mother would appreciate you calling more often."

Elizabeth patted Conrad playfully, like he'd made a wonderful joke. "Boys, please. Take the gloves off for tonight. Wes, how about you get the lovely Olivia a drink?"

Wes was one step ahead of her, already pulling me away from his parents. "That sounds like a great idea."

26

LIV

OUR ESCAPE WAS THWARTED by the event photographer, who cooed at us and refused to leave until she got a photo. "Your parents are such an inspiration. Thirty years of marriage is practically unheard of these days. Big smiles."

With my arm around his waist, I could feel how tense Wes was, but it was me who stiffened as she brought the camera up, taking a series of photos of the two of us.

I needed to relax. What were the chances of these photos getting out? It was a private event, not the Emmy's.

After that, hiding was impossible. Wes was continually pulled aside by people who recognized him as the son of the guests of honor.

It was with growing annoyance that I noted that Wes' job or success was rarely brought up, although Lucas' name came up a lot. Along with the phrase "chip off the old block." I didn't know anyone still said that.

Each mention made Wes stand a little straighter, and I

wished more than anything that I could make it better. Already, I was counting down until we could leave.

The last two days had been a test of my composure. The more I got of Wes' touch, the more I wanted. My mind was a constant reel of dirty images and even dirtier fantasies.

I didn't know what would change when we returned to Chicago tomorrow, but that could wait. Tonight, I wanted everything Wes had promised me.

We just had to make it through this party first.

More than two hours passed before the speeches started. I recognized the ex-governor as he stepped up to the mic, introducing Conrad and then waxing poetic about their shared love of integrity, honor, and a few other things I didn't hear over the force of keeping a straight face.

It sounded like a rehash of his campaign speeches, and at least 80 percent bullshit. From the way Wes started audibly exhaling next to me, the number was probably more like 90 percent.

It didn't escape my notice that Elizabeth barely got a mention in the intro. Thirty years of marriage, and the girl couldn't catch a break. At her own anniversary dinner, no less.

I hugged Wes a little tighter.

Eventually, the lights dimmed, and a screen rolled down from the roof.

The video played. Clips I'd already seen flashed on screen, and I didn't feel the need to watch them again, too concerned with how Wes was doing. He looked pained, his brows pinched together, and I wanted to smooth them out with my fingers.

Wes' dad stepped up to the mic. For the first time all night, I spotted Lucas, a familiar set of black curls, as he stood beside his mom. He looked as stiff and uncomfortable as Wes did. Curious.

"I'd like to start by thanking everyone for attending, especially those who traveled to be here with us tonight. To my beautiful and long-suffering wife," he paused as everyone laughed, and I bristled at how casually he could joke about something that was likely true, "you are the light of my life. How can I possibly sum up thirty glorious years?" He lifted his glass, and the rest of the room followed. "Pearls are seen as rare, admirable, and beautiful, and I cannot think of a better metaphor to encapsulate the love that binds us together. Here's to the last thirty years, and for the rest of my life. May it be as wonderful."

The speech was met with thunderous applause. I dropped my arm from Wes to join in, and even he managed a light clap. Music began again, encouraging everyone back to their drinks and conversations.

I slipped my hand into Wes' and leaned in. "Want to give me that tour now?"

His lips quirked up. Finally, I saw a hint of my Wes looking back at me.

Then Lucas appeared.

"Hey." His tuxedo matched Conrad's down to the pocket square, which I could only assume wasn't an accident.

"Hi."

By mutual agreement, they came together to half hug, half pat each other on the back. It was an obligatory display of brotherly affection that involved as little touching as humanly possible.

In person, I could see the resemblance. Lucas' hair was much shorter, but the curls were the same, as were the gentle eyes and boyish good looks. Considering how strained they were both acting, I could bet there were a few other similarities, too.

Lucas' gaze fell onto me as he pulled back, and he offered another short nod. "Hi."

"I'm Liv." I stuck my hand out. "Wes' friend."

"Lucas," he said as we shook. "You play Meira on the show, don't you?"

"Yes," I said, surprised. Wes had never mentioned that. "You watch the show?"

"Every week for four years."

From the corner of my eye, I saw Wes' surprise. I reached for his hand, intertwining our fingers in a silent show of affection.

Lucas shoved his hands in his pockets. "So, uh, good work on the video. I think Mom and Dad really liked it."

"Good job with all of this," Wes said, gesturing to the marquee and everything else that surrounded us. "Maybe if the real estate stuff doesn't work out, you can take up event planning."

"If I thought Dad would let me, maybe I would."

"You could if you wanted. You don't have to do everything he tells you."

Lucas bristled. "Sure. Maybe I could just pack up and run off. Like you did."

Shit. And it was going so well.

"I did it for my career."

"You did it for yourself because that's the only person you care about."

Wes pulled away from me, shaking his head at his brother. "I'm not doing this."

I watched Wes walk back in the direction of the house. This was ridiculous. I couldn't take it anymore. I whipped back to Lucas, who at least had the decency to look guilty. Good. I kept my voice low, not wanting to cause a scene, but made sure Lucas could hear how angry I was.

"Do you know how hard it was for him to put that video together? He's been in pieces all week. Watching those memories and knowing how little you all care about him was excruciating."

Lucas opened his mouth, but I didn't want to hear it. I may not be anyone to him, but Wes was everything to me. I wouldn't leave without saying this.

"He misses you. Did you know that? He told me you used to be his best friend. It killed him when you stopped talking to him."

"If he missed me that much, he shouldn't have left."

"For as smart as you are, you're being an idiot. There's still time to repair this. I think you miss him as much as he misses you. I think you're both being too stubborn to talk to each other and realize it. And I think if you wait too long, you'll lose the one person who's ever cared about you." Suddenly, I was blinking back tears. "And trust me, that is something you never get over."

———

It took a few wrong turns and an awkward encounter with Elizabeth's assistant, Penny, to find Wes' room. The house was a maze, and I could see the benefit of that. It meant lots of hiding spots. Unfortunately for me right now, it was a pain in the ass.

When I finally found Wes, he was leaning against the wall just inside the doorway of a bedroom. Eager to get a glimpse of his childhood, I crossed the threshold but was disappointed to find a nondescript guest bedroom, lavishly furnished in multiple shades of white but lacking any character.

No, not lacking. Stripped of.

"Looks like something out of a magazine, doesn't it?" Wes asked, eyes not straying from the bed as I slid my arm around his waist, borrowing his warmth and taking another deep breath of soap and cotton. "It could give your apartment a run for its money."

I nestled my cheek against his chest. "Are you okay?"

He pulled me tighter against him, then pressed a kiss to my hair. "No, but I will be."

He said it so sadly, my heart broke a little.

I hated how quiet he was. Reserved and still.

The Wes I knew was always full of excess energy, like there was an engine running underneath his skin.

Once upon a time, I'd pictured it like the inner workings of Wonka, a boundless maze of machinery and sweetly singing minions endlessly operating, keeping up an unnatural but palatable outcome.

Now it felt like pulling back the curtain on the great and powerful Oz, peeling back the grandeur to see a single man pulling levers and working to exhaustion to keep up the outside appearance.

"Wes." I looked up, fingers gripping his lapel.

He met my gaze, and I watched as the mask fell away, until the man I was falling for was staring back at me. "Hey," I said, too relieved to see him to think of anything witty.

But it had the effect I wanted. Wes' smile formed slowly, but lit up his whole face.

My heart rattled around my chest like a hummingbird in a cage. Wes meant so much to me. Beyond attraction, beyond friendship. I cared about him. Deeply.

He cared for me, protected me, fought for me, supported me. He'd seen me at my worst and called me beautiful. He'd let me cry on his shoulder. Opened up about his family.

It felt too soon to name it, but was it? We might have only crossed the line a few days ago, but what I felt for him hadn't appeared overnight. It was years of hugs and bad jokes, of late-night movies and early morning texts. It was us, standing in a room that had been stripped of all its history, haunted by the ghosts of his past.

"Wes," I whispered, gripping tighter. "I have to tell you. I think I'm falling for you."

He kissed me more passionately than he ever had before, hunger and devotion stealing my breath, making it impossible to be anything more than an ember of need. It roared beneath my skin, aching for his touch, pulling me closer until I had crowded him against the wall, my hands possessively tight.

He pulled back from the kiss. "Liv, I've fallen so hard for you, I can't remember a time before it. I don't ever want to remember. I just want to be with you."

I couldn't get enough of his mouth, his hands, arms, hair—everything. He held me without an ounce of hesitation, kissed me like I was air itself. Crucial. Life-giving.

"Wes?"

His lips caressed my cheek as he spoke. "What do you need? I'll give you anything."

"Take me home."

27

WES

I COULDN'T GET us home fast enough, even in the Aston. One thing had stopped me from flooring it the entire way back: I needed time to think about how I wanted to do this.

The last two times we'd fooled around had been great, fucking more than great, but I was done letting distractions keep me from my goal. I wanted to worship her body. Kiss her everywhere, taste her, drive her as wild as she'd been driving me.

I didn't know how long Liv and I would last. Hell, maybe this would disappear the moment we got back to Chicago, but if tonight was all I got, then I was damn well going to make the most of it.

Liv kicked off her heels as soon as the front door closed behind us. As soon as she could, she threw her arms around my shoulders, pulling me down into a deep kiss. The silk of her dress felt amazing under my hands, and I took my time to explore, touching as much of her as I could.

If I had it my way, tonight wouldn't be our only night together, because I didn't think I'd ever get enough of this.

This time, I was determined not to rush. I was on fucking fire, passion burning through my body and making me ache for her, but we had all night, and I wanted to revel in it.

We made slow progress to my room, stopping multiple times to make out against whatever surface we bumped into. After tonight's shit show, I wanted to forget everything else and focus on the one good thing in my life.

When something slammed into my ankles, I jumped, completely knocked off balance. Catching myself on the door to the master bedroom, I looked down at Baxter's curious face.

My stomach was in my throat. "Shit, buddy, you scared me."

He jumped again when I leaned down to pat him, looking like he wanted to join the game Liv and I were playing.

Liv's breathless giggle brought my attention back up to her. Lips pink and swollen from kisses, wet as she ran her tongue over them. I couldn't stop myself from touching, running my thumb across her lower lip, leaning in to taste.

Baxter jumped at my legs again. Someday I was going to teach him that being a good wingman meant knowing when to leave. "Okay, okay." I waved him down, then snuck one last kiss from Liv. "Let me put him to bed."

"What should I do?" she asked coyly.

Another kiss, longer, until she sighed into my mouth. "Get naked and wait for me."

Baxter looked so excited as we walked back through the house, probably thinking it was time for a *w-a-l-k*. I wanted to apologize for disappointing him, but what would I say? Sorry, bud, but I'm about to spend the next few hours pleasuring the best damn woman I've ever met, and you're not invited?

I was more than grateful that Liv had suggested feeding him earlier because it meant all I had to do was make sure there was enough water by his bed (there was) and then say my goodnights before closing the door at the end of the hallway.

I didn't want any more interruptions tonight.

Whatever I'd expected when I got back to my room paled when compared to the fucking vision before me. Liv was laid out, naked as the day she was born, punching the air out of my lungs. Golden hair and creamy skin. Full breasts and rounded hips. An altar of every delicious craving I'd ever had.

Fuck.

Steadying myself on the doorframe, I took a breath, needing to collect myself. Lust surged within me. I was hard and throbbing. My hand came down to stroke myself through my clothes, long and slow. Taking the edge off.

"Good fucking god, you're beautiful."

Liv flushed the perfect shade of pink. In a few long strides, I had crossed the room, desperate to touch.

"Really?" She nibbled nervously on her lip. "How do I compare to all the models you've been with?"

"Liv." I cupped her face in my hands, drawing her attention back to me. I needed her to know how serious I was. "I was always comparing them to you. They never lived up."

She surged up to kiss me, and we worked together to remove my jacket. When she reached for my pants, I stopped her, kissing each palm before laying them back on the bed.

Her skin smelled honey sweet, and I took my time

tasting every inch. There was no part of her I didn't want, no sight I hadn't craved for as long as I could remember. She deserved to be treasured. Adored. I wanted to throw myself at her feet and worship her from the ground up. I made do by kissing the breath from her lungs instead.

"Wes," she whined. "Please."

I deliberately slowed down. "Give me a minute. I want to savor this."

"You're killing me here," she groaned, but there was no weight behind it.

I pressed my smile into her skin, dropping kisses across her shoulder, down her arm, in awe of how soft her skin was beneath my lips. I dragged my nose over the sensitive spot inside her elbow, followed it down to her palm. Her fingers curled around my cheek and found their way into my hair. I went willingly as she pulled me back into a kiss, heaving a contented sigh against her lips.

"You're so beautiful," I breathed, still in awe that she was naked in front of me.

"You said that already," she whispered back.

"Gorgeous," I whispered against her collarbone.

"Stunning," was kissed against the soft pillow of her breast. I sucked kisses into the flesh until she gasped, then tasted the sweet bud of her nipple as it hardened against my tongue.

Fuck, she was a gift. Good-hearted and generous. Stronger than Kratos and more beautiful than Aphrodite.

With her nails, she ran light scratches against my scalp. The rumble of her pleased sighs under my lips working up my own arousal. I shifted in my pants, the friction not nearly enough. Moving to kiss the underside of her breast, I asked, "Who's killing who here?"

"Still you," she breathed.

"You are absolutely—" Feeding off her soft moans, I placed a series of reverent kisses down her stomach, over the freckles that had teased me for days, following a path to her hips and taking in the heady scent of her arousal as I gently stroked my tongue along the seam of her thigh. "—incredible."

Liv whined, high and needy, and I pushed down against the mattress to stave off my own desire, which was climbing higher with every taste of her.

"Wes, *please.*"

My senses were overloaded. I sucked a kiss on her hip, enjoying the way she bucked against my lips, then ghosted a series of kisses across the bare flesh, reaching her pussy. She was glistening.

Repositioning myself between her thighs, I coaxed her wider. Fucking gorgeous. I teased her, tracing the lips of her pussy with gentle fingers, kissing a smile into her inner thigh when she chased my touch for more.

Having so much control over her pleasure was intoxicating. I'd wanted her for six years, but now that I had the opportunity, my only goal was to make this as good for her as I could. I was going to cherish her. Give her everything she would ever want.

I leaned in, drawn by the desire to taste, nosing gently at her flushed clit and eliciting a broken gasp. Without waiting, I licked deep into her. Her surprised, "Fuck!" all the confirmation I needed.

"Please," she whined again, and I couldn't wait any longer.

As quickly as I could, I tore my shirt off, sick of the constriction, but left my pants as they were. My dick was hard and heavy, but I didn't care. This was about her.

About showing Liv everything I'd wanted to for the last few days, for the last few years.

I kept my pace slow, deliberately teasing. Circling her clit, then dragging my tongue slowly down her lips. She was hot and wet. No amount of muscle would ever make me feel more powerful than I did right now, with her body pulsing beneath me.

Liv breathed heavily, letting out these little whining sighs that gradually grew higher. They had officially become my new favorite sound. Sorry, Montero, this was all I would be playing on repeat in my head from now on.

I looked up, watching as her head dropped back against the pillows, bottom lip trapped between her teeth. "Let me hear you, doll."

I sucked on a spot just above her clit, and her hand tightened in my hair.

"*Oh!*"

She was so damn wet. I was on edge from the taste of her alone.

Not letting up, I continued the assault on her senses, using every response she gave to direct me in what to do next. Every sound she made, the chant of *oh, fuck, yes, right there, more—shit, Wes, your tongue*—had me leaking.

I couldn't have gotten harder if I'd tried.

No more teasing. I needed to make her come. Doubling my efforts, I continued to lick and suck as she started to fall apart.

My heart was beating so fast, I spared a passing concern that I might pass out. Taking a deep breath didn't help because it only brought more of her into me. Sweat and skin and sweetness. I was high on adrenaline and her.

Her thighs trembled under my palms, her breath hitching increasingly between her soft cries. My name was a plea, scrambling my brain. Fresh pleasure spiked on my tongue. Her skin was so fucking soft I wanted to cry.

I wanted her so badly I felt like I would break apart.

The powerful rumble of her beneath my lips matched the roar of my own desire, my dick straining and trapped against the mattress. I was fighting my control, determined to make this about Liv. But with every gasp, she was undoing me. And when her legs clamped around my ears and she bucked, throbbing as she came against my mouth, it took everything in my power not to come.

"Liv." It was a breath, lost in the darkness. An ode. A promise. "I need to be inside you."

"If you don't," she panted. "I'll never speak to you again."

Our lips met, teeth clashing as I laughed.

As I stripped out of the last of my clothes, Liv rummaged through the side table, pulling a few condoms out and throwing them on the bed. More than a few. I looked at them appraisingly. "Your confidence in me is flattering."

"Wes, if you think I'm letting you out of this bed before we've used all of these, you're crazy."

She curled a hand around my neck, pulling me down for a kiss that was all tongue. "I just hope you can keep up."

"Not gonna be a problem, doll."

I made quick work of putting a condom on before fitting back into the perfect space between her thighs. Slowly, I pushed inside her until we were nose to nose, our lips sliding softly against each other, my dick pulsing within her exquisite heat.

Fuck, she felt incredible.

With Liv's legs wrapped around me, her hand stroking gently down my back, my heart clenched, overwhelmed with feeling and too big for the confines of my chest. I ducked my head so that we were cheek to cheek, my eyes slipping closed.

"There's never been anyone else, Liv." There would never be anyone else.

I moved, capturing her soft sighs with my lips. When our kisses got rougher, I pushed up, digging my knees into the mattress and sliding deep into her. She was hot and wet, grinding against me. Meeting me thrust for thrust. The slap of our bodies was the most erotic fucking thing I'd heard, but it was the sight of her, flushed and free and primal, that drove me fucking wild.

I eased my fingers along her thighs to her hips. My thumbs fit perfectly. I tightened my grip to bring her closer with every thrust, finding just the right angle to make her gasp.

The room filled with the sound of our ragged breathing. The slide and slap of flesh a sharp drum beat.

This meant so much more to me than getting off. Holding her close, feeling her heat under and around me, our sweat mingling and lips colliding, was fucking amazing. I never wanted it to end.

"Wes, I'm, I'm gonna—" Liv said, and I worked harder, faster. There was a sharp gasp, then she cried out. Her back arched, and I couldn't hold back a deep moan as she pulsed around my dick.

It was the view of her, cheeks flushed, lips parted, skin glistening, that did me in. Blinding hot pressure built up, pooling at the base of my spine. Need took over, animalistic, pushing my body into her again and again. I cried out as I came.

Satisfied and spent, I rolled to the side, tying off the condom and discarding it. I didn't care where it landed.

Right now, all I cared about was Liv. She was on her side, curled toward me. A few sweat-slick hairs had caught on her cheek, and I brushed them back, moving in for a slow kiss.

What I felt for her scared me. It made me want to open up to her, trust her with every truth and hope it didn't scare her away. To lay myself bare.

It was terrifying.

But holding it back was beginning to break me.

I'd held back for so long that I had no real practice in moderation. It was all or nothing with Liv. And I wanted it all. To give her all of me. She already had my heart.

Had for years, even if she didn't know it.

I palmed one of her breasts, loving the feel of her nipple hardening under my palm. "I'm never letting you get dressed again."

"So we're not going to leave the house?" She didn't sound upset about that.

I traced a line to her waist, flexing my grip around the soft skin of her hip. "We're never leaving this bed."

She made me want to let her in. The words were hard enough, but the act of cracking myself open like that in front of her, of trusting someone again, made my chest ache. I'd fortified myself from rejection all these years by telling myself it was better that we were friends. That friendship was enough.

"Liv. I need to tell you something." I kissed her, just a press of our lips together, before pulling back. "I need you to know that you don't need to say it back, but I love you. I've loved you for a long time."

Once they were out there, once my heart was opened, there was no closing it again.

"Wow, Wes, I …" The silence hung as she pulled her lip

between her teeth, seemingly debating her next words. "How long have you felt this way?"

"About you?"

She nodded.

"Since I met you."

There was a sharp intake of breath before Liv was pressing closer, her lips ghosting mine. "I wish I'd known."

"You know now." I pulled her closer. "Liv, you are incredible, and you deserve the kind of love people dream of. The kind poets write about, that fairy-tales are made of."

"You make me want that."

"I want to give that to you. More than anything."

"Tell me again."

It might be too soon for her to say it back, but I didn't care. I'd been holding it inside for so long that lying to her now felt wrong. Impossible.

With her arms wrapped around me, her heart beating against mine, I whispered the words I'd been holding back for six years.

"I love you."

28

LIV

MY LAST MORNING in LA was bittersweet. I'd woken up to Wes peppering a line of soft kisses along my shoulder. Then my alarm had gone off.

I'd booked my flight a week ago, before anything had changed between us, and I'd stupidly thought a morning flight was a good idea.

When I'd complained to Wes that we didn't have enough time, he'd pinned me to the mattress and shown me he could make me come just as hard when there was a deadline.

My legs were still a little shaky when he dropped me off at LAX an hour later. I lingered in the car, not ready to leave. The last few days had been a wonderful blur, and I still couldn't get Wes' confession out of my head.

Was it too late to cancel my flight and stay? Maybe forever?

"Will you be okay?" I asked.

He'd only be a few hours behind me, but first he needed

to return the car, and unfortunately, Baxter, to his parents. But I didn't like the idea of him seeing them alone.

Wes leaned across the center console, twisting himself so he could cup my face in both hands. I loved it when he did that. "It feels like my heart is about to fly across the country while my body stays here, but apart from that, I'm fine."

I placed my hands over his, leaning in to kiss him. Once, twice. He sucked my lower lip between his. Dammit, I didn't want to leave yet. Leaving meant work. And Jen. And responsibilities.

And I just wanted to stay here in my perfect Wes bubble a little longer.

"You keep saying things like that, and I'll never leave."

Dropping a series of soft kisses across my cheek, he whispered, "So don't leave."

I made a sound, half sigh and half groan, gripping his shirt in my hands. How was he even real? Baxter whined from the back seat, and Wes chuckled. His lips were warm as he kissed me, just a light press against mine. It felt like goodbye.

"Don't worry, doll. I'll see you in a few hours."

———

Who needs a man when you have friends in high places? Olivia Davis surprised everyone when she was spotted at a trendy café in downtown LA this week, with none other than Hollywood bigwig Sym Padilla. Are they planning a takeover of show business? Where do we sign up?

I closed the app, guilt sitting uncomfortably in my stomach. Jen would have seen this, but she hadn't called yet. I didn't know if that made it better or worse.

The flight back to Chicago passed quickly. I assumed it was because my mind was completely preoccupied with replaying every moment of last night.

Jesus, I could still feel Wes' hands on me. How was I going to sit next to him in an interview now and pretend that we were just friends? Like he hadn't become so much more than that over the last seven days?

The last week had taught me so much more about Wes than I expected. Here was a man who would sacrifice himself for the happiness of others, who would put himself through hell because someone asked him to. He'd spent so long accepting nothing in return. It broke my heart to think about it. I wouldn't do that to him. I would do everything I could to make sure he knew that. To show him.

———

I'd stopped and started three different movies when the knock I'd been waiting for finally came. I bounded over the couch, eager to see Wes. It had been five hours, and I missed him something fierce.

But when I answered the door, it wasn't Wes on the other side. It was Jen.

"Jen! Hi." My voice rang loud. Too loud.

"May I come in?" And her calm demeanor only made me more worried.

"Of course. Can I get you anything?"

In a few short steps, Jen had crossed the apartment and taken a seat. "An explanation might be nice."

I swallowed down the lump of nerves that clogged my throat and sat in the armchair across from her.

It felt like déjà vu. Jen sitting primly in the white armchair, her French tipped nails tapping against her tailored black pants. They would have looked plain if she hadn't paired them with a neon pink crop, its asymmetrical neckline highlighting the puff of the single sleeve.

There was no way she owned a single pair of sweats. I bet she even did yoga in designer leggings.

She raised a single brow. "Were you going to fire me yourself or have Sym do it?"

Shit. I knew I should have called as soon as I'd seen the post.

"No, you've got it all wrong. I'm not firing you. Sym got my number somehow," I said, keeping the knowledge that Wes was involved to myself, "and we met for lunch. I told them I was extremely happy with my current representation, and we left it at that."

Jen's face was still tightly controlled. The thought that I'd disappointed her hurt.

"I promise."

"You should have told me."

"I know."

"Do you know how humiliating it was to find out via TMZ?"

I could imagine. My gut twisted.

"I swear, it was only lunch."

"Even you aren't that naïve, Liv." Her face had fallen, and I felt awful. She continued, "I know I don't have the same experience as someone like Sym, but I thought that we understood each other. I thought you recognized how much I was putting in to your career, and that even if we weren't friends, you at least respected me enough to be honest with me. I have always respected you."

Lead lined my stomach. I couldn't believe how callous I'd been. So wrapped up in Wes that I'd completely forgotten that I'd only needed to go away in the first place because Jen was cleaning up my mess. Looking out for me, while I went behind her back.

"Of course I respect you. I know you're doing a lot more than you expected to. I've been asking a lot from you lately, what with Bryson and the spin-off. I'm not ungrateful."

"But you want more."

"For me, not from you."

Jen brushed a hand over her knee, re-aligning the ironed crease into position with delicate fingers. She was so refined. I looked down at my mismatched skirt and print tee. The shirt was brand new, but the logo was faded, a *Top Gun* reference to the USS Enterprise.

Sometimes I really wondered why she kept me as a client.

Jen sighed. "I know you want to do more, and I'm supportive of that, but you have to remember that it's a process. You've achieved more than most have by this time in their careers. And I was the one who made that happen for you. You're allowed to want more, Olivia. In fact, I'm glad that you're ambitious. But you need to understand that for now, your sole responsibility is to do your job. Everything else you need to leave to me. That's what you pay me for."

Feeling chastised, I nodded.

For the second time today, there came a knock on my door, this time musical and jokey. I knew who it was immediately. So did Jen, who held her hand out when I moved to answer it. "No, let me. I think the three of us need to have a little chat."

Jen's heels clicked ominously as she stalked toward the door.

"Glad you could join us, Wesley."

29

LIV

AS JEN TURNED and walked back, I finally got my first look at him. He must have come straight from the airport. White tee, dark sweats, and a sight for sore eyes.

Our eyes met over Jen's shoulder and he mouthed, "Missed you," with a smile.

The tightness that had curled around my chest finally loosened. "You too," I mouthed back.

"Sit, Wesley," Jen said, and as he did, his expression shifted into something flatter. It reminded me of his parents' party, and I didn't like it.

Wes took a seat beside me on the couch, keeping close and reaching for my hand. The simple gesture did more to calm me than anything else could, and I held tight, giving him a gentle squeeze.

Jen stayed standing. "Now. I'm going to assume you lied to me, and you haven't been staying at your dad's. Do you know how I know?" She pulled out her phone, clicked on something, then turned it to face us. Shit. It was the photo from Wes' parents' anniversary.

"But how?"

Jen looked smug. It wasn't a good look on her. "The photographer recognized you. She emailed me asking if she could get permission to post the photo to her business account." She pocketed the phone. "You're lucky this was a private event and that I was able to ensure it can't be released."

And just like that, the last lingering thread of my good mood was gone. Not only had Jen caught me out in my lie, but this was not the way I'd hoped to let her know about Wes and me. His thumb stroked my knuckles, grounding me.

"I told you not to be seen together. I warned you." She shook her head. "How long has this been going on?" she asked, waving between us dismissively. My hand tightened around Wes'.

A lifetime? I thought hysterically and caught myself before I could laugh. I hadn't planned on giving Jen, or anyone, the details of our relationship, but I figured some honesty would help get her back on my side. "A week."

She sighed. "Okay. I think I can fix this."

Wes shot out of his chair, furious. "Fix what?"

"Thanks to your little charade," her eyes bore into me, "Mike and Alicia are preparing to fly here to talk to you."

Wes scoffed. "That doesn't mean anything. They're probably bringing the contracts for us to finally sign."

"Oh? And when was the last time they were in Chicago?"

She was right. They hadn't visited since before the first season started filming, over four years ago. It wasn't a definite sign of trouble, but it did mean something. Ice spread through my chest.

Jen stood her ground, unruffled, even as Wes towered

over her. "The speculation about you hasn't died down. That they are prepared to come all the way here should tell you how unhappy they are."

My fingertips went cold, goosebumps rising over my forearms. I didn't like this. "Are you sure? Apart from that one photo, we were really careful."

Jen smiled, but there was no humor in the gesture. "Were you?" A few taps on her phone, and then she was playing one of the videos I'd posted, Baxter trotting around as master of the house. She then brought up a photo Wes had posted, and while Baxter was half hidden by the couch, it wouldn't take a genius to see it was the same dog.

"Fans are already talking. It would be bad enough if they were grasping at straws, but it appears they aren't. When you're caught—"

"If we're caught," I interjected.

"When," Jen emphasized. "You can count yourself out of the spin-off. And you can find yourself a new manager."

Wes wasn't having it. "Bullshit. I don't buy that for a second. We're two-thirds of the show. I don't know what your game is here, but Mike and Alicia aren't about to fire us."

Jen smirked. "And I suppose you think going public is a great idea right now."

"People are already saying we're together and nothing has happened. We should play into it."

"Would you still feel that way if it meant giving up your career?"

Wes didn't hesitate. "Yes."

All the air left my lungs in one go. It was easily the most romantic thing anyone had ever suggested and completely terrifying to imagine.

She scoffed. "Then you're more reckless than I thought, and I'm glad I don't work for you."

Wes made a low, unhappy noise beside me. "That makes two of us."

I jumped in, finally standing. "We'll be more careful, I promise."

"That won't be enough. Not anymore. Now, I know Jackson is getting married in a week, but with the producers flying over and the fresh rumors going around, you'll need a plus-one for the night." She was looking directly at Wes.

I felt sick.

"No. I'm not doing that." Wes was adamant.

Jen ignored him, stepping closer to me. "Liv, please. I know you've been going through a lot recently, so I've shielded you from the worst of it. Maybe I shouldn't have. Since the photos with Bryson came out, I've had multiple brands back out of deals and producers stop talking to me about future projects."

Oh. I hadn't known that. Of course I hadn't. I'd left Jen to deal with it all while I was hanging by the pool and getting on my knees at Tom Ford.

"If you absolutely refuse to listen to me on anything else, at least wait until after we've spoken to Mike and Alicia. If I'm wrong," her gaze cut to Wes before returning to me, "then I'll apologize. But if you don't at least try to dampen these rumors, you'll be putting both of your careers on the line."

She was right. No matter what I felt for Wes, I needed to think about more than myself.

Look at what had happened to Bryson. If I wasn't careful, I'd pull Wes down with me. It was going to kill me to see him with someone else, but we needed to be smart about this.

I turned to Wes. "Jen's right. Maybe a date is a good idea. I'll go with Tiff to the hotel." Every word was ash on my tongue.

"That's really what you want?" The heartbroken look in his eyes was torturous but only made it more obvious that this was the right decision. He couldn't see that yet, but I was sure of it.

"Fine." His mouth was a flat line, eyes dull and distant. The cold had reached my gut, sealing in the guilt.

As he stood, I reached out, catching his sleeve. "Wes." He pulled until the material slipped out of my fingers.

"I'm fine." My two least favorite words. "I need to find a date."

He said nothing as he walked toward the bedroom, phone already at his ear. Every step hurt. I didn't want him slipping behind that wall of his again.

But if Jen was right, if being together was going to jeopardize our roles on the show, how would we make this work?

Was being together worth the risk?

Jen walked to the door, then paused. "I wish I didn't have to say this, Olivia. Trust me, I do. But you pay me to look after your career, and unfortunately, that requires me to tell you that whatever is going on with you and Wesley needs to end. The public is fickle, and if this gets out—"

"I know."

"I don't like it any more than you do."

"Somehow I doubt that."

She blinked, and I could see her surprise. I didn't talk back to Jen, not very often. But my relationship with Wes was on the line. She could handle a little attitude. I only hoped she was wrong about the producers.

After Jen left, I waited for Wes. The adrenaline faded

away, leaving my fingers cold against the marble countertop. It had been the first thing I'd fallen in love with when I'd viewed the apartment, followed swiftly by the subway tile backsplash and farmhouse sink. The picture-perfect kitchen. Always pristine, never used. It all looked amazing. It also looked like someone else's life.

———

I couldn't believe it. How had I messed up so badly? Bryson, Jen, Wes. I was disappointing all of them.

When Wes finally emerged from the bedroom, I felt nervous in a way that I hadn't since the first time we'd kissed. I wanted to ask him if we were okay, but I wasn't sure we were, and I didn't know if I could handle hearing it.

"It's done. It's someone I've been seen with before, just a PR gig, and she's available on short notice."

Every word made me feel worse. This was what I'd asked him to do, but I hated this anonymous girl with every fiber of my being.

"I also gave Jackson the heads-up. To be honest, I was hoping he'd tell me where to shove it." Unlikely, knowing Jackson. "But he said they had room for one more."

"I can't believe I'm going to have to sit next to you and your date all night."

He closed the gap, walking over to me, and I sighed with relief. He was still here. Maybe this would be okay.

"I'm sorry."

He gently cupped my cheek. I turned into it, seeking the comfort.

"What are you sorry for? This is my fault."

"It's not. Don't say that."

"Of course it is, Wes." Once again, I'd gone with my gut, and it had backfired.

His thumb caressed my cheek. "I'll call her back, tell her not to come."

"No, you can't do that."

"Of course I can. You're upset. Nothing is worth that."

"No, no. As much as I hate it, Jen is right."

Gathering me close, he leaned in, gently kissing my forehead, then my cheek. "You deserve better than this, Liv. I don't know what you see in me, but I'll do everything I can to earn you, and I'll prove Jen wrong. We can have this without ruining everything."

Something in his tone told me it wasn't just me he was trying to convince.

I arched up to kiss him, his soft lips finally settling my nerves. "I missed you."

One, two, three soft kisses, and Wes pulled back. His hands were strong and steady, his eyes sure. I wish I had his confidence. "It'll be okay. I promise."

Usually, when Wes said that, it was easy to believe him. I wasn't so sure this time.

30

WES

LIV SPENT the night at the hotel with Audrey as part of her getting ready crew. I hadn't seen or touched her in hours, and I was slowly going out of my mind.

Maybe what we'd had in LA was an illusion. I'd told Liv I loved her, and I'd known she hadn't been ready to say it back. Maybe she'd never say it. Would it even matter? I'd spent the last six years loving her, knowing it was a one-way street.

Except it was different now. I'd let her in, given her the keys to the vault and shown her where the self-destruct button was. Liv had been holding my heart in her hands for years without knowing it. Now all it would take was one small squeeze, and it would shatter.

It was inevitable.

A car service picked me up, then stopped to collect India, the beauty guru makeup influencer who had agreed to be my date. Since it was only a work arrangement, there was no awkward flirting. But it didn't make it any easier. I was still sitting next to someone who wasn't Liv.

India was quiet beside me in the back seat, her black strapless dress pooled at her feet. Her hair wasn't the honeyed blond I wanted, and she didn't have the soft smile that made my heart melt, but she was doing me a favor, and I wasn't going to be a prick about it.

"Thank you for agreeing to do this. I appreciate it."

"Sure, no problem. I was only surprised you needed a date."

I picked at the seam on my suit pants. "It's complicated."

India let out a small snort, but when I turned my head, she was staring out the window, her features illuminated by the streetlights. She was definitely beautiful, although she looked pained. In the reflection, I saw her lips flatten into a straight line. "I know what that's like."

Five minutes of silence passed before she spoke again, eyes still trained out the window. "If you loved someone, but everything was working against it, would you stick it out?"

The chains of a long-held fear tightened around my chest. Experience told me no. That waiting in hopes of everything working out was a fool's errand.

People didn't change. They showed me their true colors, and if you ignored that, then you deserved to be hurt. I knew all of that, and it hadn't stopped me from pursuing Liv.

"I'm the wrong person to ask."

Her eyes were stormy when she finally turned to me. Whatever it was she was wrestling with, I felt an odd kinship with her. Even if I couldn't tell her that.

The car stopped, putting an end to anything she was going to say, and her sadness shifted into a bright smile. It was a mask I'd worn many times, one I'd be wearing tonight, but it was strange seeing it on someone else. I barely knew India beyond the basics, but I liked her a lot better when I was looking at the real her.

I wondered how many people felt the same way about me.

———

The room was smaller than I'd expected. I mean, it wasn't *small*, but it was a damn sight smaller than the marquee my parents had set up for their anniversary. What a different occasion. Jackson and Audrey were two people I thought might actually be perfect for each other. A world away from my parents and the constant productions they made of proclaiming their love for each other.

But this. This wasn't for show. This was real. Jackson and Audrey had found each other by chance—and a little of Tiff's handiwork—and now they'd gathered their nearest and dearest to share in their joy.

It was an indoor space, but only just—the ceilings were high, and a long table ran the length of the room, with a dance floor and stage set up at the opposite end. The decor was simple and soft and beautiful. I wondered what Lucas would think of it.

Standing beside Jackson at the altar was nerve-racking. I'd never given marriage much thought, but I was suddenly anxious. And I wasn't the one getting married. I patted Jackson on the shoulder and laughed when he startled. Poor guy looked ready to pass out. "You'll be fine, man. She loves you."

"I know that," he said, a little defensive. Nervous about being nervous. What a guy.

"It's not like you aren't in front of people all the time. This should be easy."

"I can't mess this up, you know? She's ... too important."

My heart rattled in my chest, my eyes instinctively searching for Liv. I breathed out a sigh of relief when I found her a few rows away. Her hair was down, and the light cast her skin in shades of gold, matching the color of her dress. A fresh wave of affection burned in my chest, leaving me temporarily speechless.

Liv looked up, and there was the smile I'd been craving. I savored it for as long as I could before turning back to the groom. "She's probably as nervous as you are."

He nodded, jerky movements that went on for a beat too long. "Maybe we should have eloped."

Jackson's sister appeared behind us, causing both of us to jump. "Uh, I heard that, and you are so damn lucky you didn't."

"What are you doing? You're supposed to be with Audrey," Jackson loudly whispered while Sarah's gaze raked over the crowd before us.

"I wanted to see how you were doing. You look great, by the way." She beamed. "You, too, Wes."

If it was possible, Jackson looked more nervous. "Get out of here before mom sees you."

Sarah rolled her eyes before she disappeared, then reappeared a few seconds later. "She looks incredible, by the way. And she's really excited."

Finally, Jackson's shoulders relaxed, having heard what he needed to. "Thanks, Sarah."

The ceremony was short but sweet. When Jackson choked up during his vows, I'd had to turn my head to blink away tears. And when the officiant pronounced them married and they'd kissed to the cheering of the room, I couldn't hide the tears that escaped.

———

Despite having a "date," I wasn't doing a great job of keeping my eyes off Liv. In six years, had I entered any room without looking for her first?

It was easy to see she was still stressed out about what Jen had said. Pinch to her brow, strain in her neck. The way she carried herself: tired and small. Jen had gotten in her head again.

It was exhausting to see Liv go through this, but what could I do? I'd tried. I'd gotten Liv that meeting with Sym, and it hadn't changed anything.

I was tired. And annoyed.

Liv should have pushed back. Should have fought harder.

She'd said she was falling for me, but it didn't mean a hell of a lot when she backtracked as soon as Jen told her to. And what happened if Jen said that we couldn't ever go public? Would Liv just accept that? How long could we pretend before it all became too much?

I should have taken it slower. Shit, why did I tell her I loved her? I meant it, but now I was standing on a tightrope without a safety net, and Liv was at the other end with a bolt cutter. Which I'd handed to her.

Watching her from across the room, so close but so far, was a special kind of torture. It was nothing like my parents and yet exactly the same.

"I saw those tears," Tiff said, sidling up beside me to hand me a tissue.

"You too," I said, indicating where her eyeliner had smudged in the corners. "Where's your man?"

"He was supposed to be getting us drinks, but the last I checked, he was discussing marketing strategies with Jackson's uncle." The eye roll she gave was affectionate. "So it'll be a while."

"You look happy," I said, because she did. In fact, she looked practically giddy.

Tiff nodded. "I really fucking am."

I was happy for her, and a bit jealous. I knew how she felt, but I couldn't say anything.

Tiff's grin slipped into something shrewd. "You two are cute together."

I jumped to correct her, until I realized she was looking at Liv, not India.

Trust Tiff to figure it out. "How did you know?"

"Please. You're as stealthy as a terminator." She smiled. "I always saw how you looked at her, but now she's looking back the same way. You two have been eyeing each other all night."

"It's scary how observant you are."

"It's what makes me so good at my job." She gestured with a hand. "Come on, spill."

But I couldn't. It was too new. And I hated to admit it, but part of me wondered how long this would last. Knowing Tiff had seen how long I'd wanted it, I couldn't face the idea of her pity when it went south. Of anyone's pity.

"She's something special," I said.

"So are you."

Sam arrived, sliding an arm around Tiff's waist. India appeared next to me as well, quietly making conversation and trying her best not to look like she didn't want to be here.

"I heard you're opening a new bar."

Sam nodded. "That's right. We're deciding on a location at the moment. It'll be in both our names, but Tiff will run it."

"God help us all," I joked, getting a middle finger from Tiff.

After dinner, I made my way to Jackson, catching him with his sister, Sarah, and wrapped him up in a hug. "Congratulations, man." Nerves now gone, he looked like a new person.

"Thanks. I, uh …" And he looked blissful. "Thanks."

Sarah cooed. "My brother, as eloquent as ever."

"I'd like to remind you that you weren't much better at your own wedding."

"I'm only teasing, Jace. Happy is a good look for you."

They shared a warm look. Sarah touched his shoulder. "Okay, well, I better get back on mom duty. She's already told the Mrs. Claus story like, five times."

"Oh god."

"It's fine! Everyone thinks it's cute."

"I'm assuming she means you," Audrey said, slipping her arms around Jackson's waist.

"Sarah, stop her, please."

"What? I said I'm on it!" Sarah rolled her eyes. "Audrey, please help him calm down. I'm pretty sure the bathroom locks."

She scurried away as I laughed, missing what Jackson said to Audrey as India tugged on my sleeve, speaking low enough that we wouldn't be heard. "Hey, uh. Something has come up. Is it going to be an issue if I leave?"

"Everything okay?"

"Fine." She sighed, and I almost laughed. Is this what I sounded like when asked the same question? "It's complicated. I can stay if you need me to, but I—"

I shook my head. We'd taken the requisite photos. Mingled. Been seen. There was nothing else to stay for. "No, don't worry about that. Just take care of yourself."

"Thanks."

"Is she okay?" Audrey asked after India had left.

"Of course. Nothing to worry about."

She unwrapped herself from Jackson to give me a hug. "You clean up good, Wes."

"Not even married for five minutes and already looking around?" I joked. "You gotta do a better job, J, if I'm looking good to her."

He laughed, pulling her against him again. "She was trying to make you feel better."

"Might not be all she wants to feel." I winked.

"Hitting on a bride at her own wedding, Wes? Now I've seen everything." And finally, I felt the ache in my chest lighten as Liv came into view beside me. "Don't you already have a date?"

The *t* hit sharply, and I realized Liv was *jealous*. Actually jealous. Of my fake date.

"Where is little miss tall, dark, and gorgeous?" Came a voice to my left.

Liv grimaced at the mention of India, and I narrowed my eyes at Tiff, who didn't look sorry at all. She meant well, but she was a menace. Sam certainly had his hands full.

"She had to go," I said, and watched the darkness clear from Liv's expression.

———

The noise had finally ground to a light murmur as Jackson's dad walked to the front of the room, mic in hand. The rest of us had gathered in a pack around the dance floor, our drinks ready to toast the happy couple.

It was a great speech. Heartfelt, kind. Loving. Jackson was a lucky guy to have grown up with a dad like that. With a family like that.

My gut clenched. I realized that even if my father gave a speech at my wedding, it wouldn't be anything close to this.

I'd already started to inch my way toward the back of the crowd when Audrey got up and started talking about how she'd found her place in a new family. "I've never had siblings, but now I feel blessed to have not one, but two sisters." She gestured toward Tiff and Sarah. "It's just so incredible to stand here, surrounded by the love of everyone in this room."

From where I was standing at the back of the group, I took in the collection of family and friends that had gathered. Their faces mirroring the happiness of the bride and groom. Suddenly, my chest felt heavy and constricted.

Outside was a small terrace with a tall trellis covered in snaking vines. A wooden bench seat and a basket of blankets welcomed guests who needed a break from the festivities. The glass door didn't close out much of the sound, but I didn't care. I was just glad to get a moment alone.

Because wasn't that what I'd always done? Run whenever it got bad enough?

I'd never have this. It was something I'd known—my parents had been privately supportive of my career—but this? A public display of love, one that was born from years of emotional support? Not possible. Maybe for Lucas, now that he was the golden child.

I couldn't imagine something like this for me. Half the guest list would be Dad's professional connections or Mom's luncheon friends. Just another networking opportunity. Who the hell would want to marry into that?

"Wes? Are you okay?"

"I missed you today."

"Me, too. I wish we didn't need to lie. But once the spin-off is secured, it'll be different. We just need to wait a little longer. Be careful."

Years of practice kept my disappointment from showing. I focused on the positives. She wasn't saying no. Just not now.

"I want this, Wes, I really do."

"I believe you." And I did.

"If I hadn't already fucked it up with Bryson, this wouldn't be a problem."

Or we might not be together.

Her face crumpled. "I wish I could kiss you right now."

I gave her a sad smile. "Same here, doll."

Before I could react, she stepped in, hands in my jacket, pulling me into a passionate kiss. My heart skipped so suddenly I wondered if I'd been shocked. But I didn't stop kissing her. It was all I'd wanted to do all night. It was lucky we were hidden by the alcove, but I knew I wouldn't care if we weren't.

When we parted, she stayed close. "I don't want you to doubt how I feel about you. I love you, Wes. More than anything."

And dammit if those weren't the magic words.

Her eyes, dark in the moonlight, stared at me, deep with

devotion. She was looking at me like I mattered. That look made it impossible to not want to dive in, to let my love for her wash over me in waves.

I stroked her cheek. "I won't ever feel this way about anyone else as long as I live. My whole heart belongs to you and only you."

The words weren't enough. My feelings for her were too vast to explain. It was her unending faith in me, her compassion, her strength. The way she felt in my arms, the taste of her lips. Early morning texts and movie facts and how making her smile made me feel like the most powerful man on earth.

"Can we get out of here?" I asked.

I knew Liv would want to stay, but I didn't want to go without her, and I didn't know how much longer I could keep pretending I was fine.

It was a shit thing to do, leaving before the end of the night. And maybe Jackson would understand if I'd ever told him about my parents or my past. But it was more likely that he'd realize how much of a lost cause I was.

I avoided his eye as we snuck out, but couldn't miss the look of concern on Tiff's face. I pushed the guilt down, out of sight.

31

LIV

BEFORE I EVEN OPENED MY eyes, I was aware of Wes'
arms around me, the steady beat of his pulse under my
cheek. My body felt heavy from sleep, last night's orgasm
leaving a lingering buzz under my skin.

Slowly, I lifted my head, wanting to see Wes but not
wanting to wake him.

The sun streamed into the room, highlighting the halo
of hair framing his strong cheekbones, last night's perfect
waves no longer styled but disheveled. He looked so
heartbreakingly real that I couldn't breathe.

Wow.

Time stopped for a moment.

He's beautiful.

It was as if I was seeing him in 4K—every fear he'd
trusted me with, every whispered confession. He had shown
me each smile, real and faked, and let me see what lay
behind them. It was impossible to not want to bundle him
up. Keep him to myself. Keep him safe.

I never thought I could love someone so much.

Lying here, naked and tangled with him, I felt insatiable. Years of making myself not think about Wes had accumulated until I was swept away by a tsunami of never-ending need to be near him. Touch him. Tease him. Taste him.

And in the early morning quiet, I knew exactly how I wanted to wake him up.

My fingers skimmed his skin, feeling the indents of sinewy muscle. His nipples, so pink, so hard, called out to me. I couldn't get enough of how rough his breathing got when I nibbled and licked at them.

He made a gruff attempt at a word, his voice rough with sleep. I smiled against his skin. Slowly traced a circle around his nipple. He tried again. "It's too early. Go back to sleep."

"What if I told you I had coffee?"

I looked up in time to see one eye crack open. He was trying so hard not to wake; it was adorable. I pressed a kiss along his sternum. His eye slid shut again. "Not even for coffee."

"What if I brought you breakfast in bed?" I raised myself up off his chest.

Without looking, his fingers curled around my elbow, pulling me back in. "Nope, you're not allowed to leave."

"But I'm hungry," I said, moving over to kiss his pec, not thinking about food at all.

I felt his contented hum through his chest. His eyes were still closed, his voice rough with sleep. "That is a problem."

"I think I have a solution." I felt myself grow wetter at the thought and was glad that Wes couldn't see the shit-eating grin I was sporting. He'd discover my intentions soon enough, but I was definitely going to enjoy the reveal.

His fingers traced a gentle line up and down my bicep. "As long as I don't have to move."

Don't worry, you won't have to do a thing.

When I pulled away, Wes made a murmur of protest. But the small crease between his brows disappeared when I slipped the sheet the rest of the way off, revealing every inch of his naked body to the air. Carefully, I spun around, positioning myself above him, my knees above his shoulders, facing his legs.

I leaned down, kissing the V of his hipbone, waiting for him to realize.

His extremely interested—and more awake—"Oh" was music to my ears.

I nosed the lines of his body, breathing in his natural scent, the clinging remnants of his late-night shower, and the sex we'd had before we'd fallen asleep. It wasn't the clean, sophisticated way he usually smelled when he was dressed, which made me immediately want to strip down and let him have me. It was real and a little dirty. This was everything beneath the showy exterior. It was the Wes that existed before hair and makeup and sass (okay, probably not sass).

And I loved this Wes just as much as every other version of him.

He wasn't bulky, not like Jackson, but he was lean—bones and muscles and length—everywhere. His cock was satin heat in my hand, long and darkened at the tip. The reddened head already shiny with precum. My tongue curled in my mouth, aching to taste him.

"I didn't realize you delivered," Wes said playfully.

Giggles bubbled up inside me until I was silently laughing, my nose jammed into Wes' hip. "You can't say something like that when I'm about to blow you."

"Why not?" I could hear the amusement in his voice. Slowly, his hands slid up my thighs to massage my hips and butt. I trembled and breathed out a soft moan into his skin.

"Because" was all I could manage when Wes started kissing the sensitive area of my inner thigh.

Deliberately, he exhaled a slow, hot breath over me, and I dug my nails into the mattress. I could feel myself clenching around nothing.

"Because why?" Good god, he sounded smug.

"Oh—"

His fingers trailed the gentlest of touches along my pussy, and I felt myself getting wetter. I wondered what it looked like, and suddenly I could picture Wes licking his lips, eager at the sight. I sighed out another moan, louder this time.

Well. *Two can play at this game.* Bracing myself on one arm, I guided his hardening cock to my lips, keeping my grip light. I pressed an open kiss to the tip, then dragged my tongue down the entire length, smiling when I heard Wes' head hit the pillow.

"Fuck," he whispered, dragging the word out.

Oh, yes.

From there, we took each other apart, abandoning the teasing quickly as our tongues worked each other over. I could feel my elbows and jaw aching, but I didn't care, breathing through my nose and minding my teeth as I licked and sucked.

When Wes slid his fingers inside me and sucked on my clit, I came hard, letting his dick fall out of my mouth while my orgasm echoed in the room. My thighs trembled through the aftershocks, and Wes never gave up, wrecking my body with his teeth and tongue until I was shaking.

The first hot spurts of his release hit my neck and chest

seconds later, making every primitive fiber of my body light up at being marked.

With what little energy I had left, I rolled off him, dropping onto my back and panting. I felt a drop of his cum roll down my breast and had the passing thought to dip my finger into it, bring it to my lips. But that required movement, which required energy. And Wes had definitely fucked both of those out of me.

The bed shifted as Wes moved, and from the corner of my eye I caught the pert shape of his ass as he entered the en suite, only gone for a moment before he brought a damp washcloth back to clean my chest and throat.

I opened my eyes when he had finished, watching as he tossed the cloth aside and lay down next to me.

I felt so light, like he'd reversed gravity. How could I possibly still be on the ground when it felt like every cell in my body was bubbling upward? I was helpless to stop the giggles, overwhelmed by the joy that had overtaken me.

"What?" Wes asked, amused and looking slightly worried for my breathing. To be fair, I was having trouble getting air.

"I just thought—" I broke off into more laughter "—I just—"

"Any time now."

"Sorry." I forced a deep breath, my cheeks sore. Wes was propped up on one arm, his chiseled features gorgeous enough to carve into marble. Damn, I was lucky. But as I opened my mouth to explain myself, the giggles took over again.

"A guy could get a complex," he teased. I'd curled into him, and his thumb was patiently stroking my hip.

"Sorry, sorry. It's not you." I finally pulled myself together, heart beating fast, face flushed from laughing. Wes was watching me lovingly. I suspected I had the same dopey look. He pulled me closer. "I'm just so happy. I can't help it."

He pulled me in for a deep kiss.

"I love you," I said between kisses. "I'm so completely head over heels in love with you."

When Wes pulled back, his eyes were intense, the look of pure adoration making my chest seize in the best way. I felt a rush of affection roll over me.

And I knew there would never be room in my heart for anyone else.

32

WES

I WAS CONVINCED Liv's hair was magic. I'd seen what she went through for the show, having to wear wigs or extensions, sometimes getting covered in fake mud or blood or unidentified goo. And yet her hair always felt so damn soft.

What in the hell had I done to deserve this woman? Maybe I was a better man in a previous life, one of those saints or sirs knighted by the queen, with so much cosmic goodwill saved up that I managed to bless my next life as well.

Because this? This goofy, gorgeous, incredibly talented woman who could make dirty jokes and quote her favorite movies and was so inexplicably into me? She was more than I deserved.

In a week, we'd be back in LA, a quick trip to present at the MTV Movie Awards. Two nights. In and out. Liv and I hadn't talked about it yet, but I was already planning on christening at least four different rooms at my place, five if we got creative.

We lay together on the couch, her cheek on my chest, our legs tangled. A tall, buff guy battled a CGI monster on the TV, but we were both ignoring it. Probably one of the many Chrises that always ended up in those movies.

She toyed with the neckline of my shirt, spreading fire where her fingers grazed the skin underneath. Her smile was tender, and I couldn't think of anything more beautiful.

"I know I've already said this, but you should let more people in. Let them see the Wes I know. He's a pretty great guy."

"I don't know about that. I have it on good authority he's a mess."

She pressed a kiss to my lips. "He really isn't. And I'm not the only one who thinks that."

"Most people only know the fun, jokey me."

"That's because you don't show them who you really are."

"No one wants the me underneath it all."

"I do." Her tone was unwavering. "I'm in love with all of you, Wes. The hidden parts most of all. And everyone else would be, too, if you trusted them enough to show them."

And god help me, but she was actually making me believe it.

She caught my expression and sat up. "What are you thinking about?" Liv asked.

"It's stupid."

"I'm sure it's not."

My mouth twisted, and I debated even saying anything. But it had been nagging me since we'd gotten back to Chicago, and Liv had a way of making the truth come spilling out of me.

"I keep thinking about what Lucas said at the party. I just wish I knew what I did or didn't do to make him hate me."

"He doesn't hate you, Wes."

I had a snowball's chance in hell of that being true.

Liv sat up, and I followed suit. "You should talk to him. Be honest. He won't know you're upset until you tell him."

God, how I wanted to. It seemed ridiculous to still be holding out hope for something that hadn't changed in more than four years, but I'd had that same thought about Liv, and look how that had worked out. Maybe it was worth the risk to put myself out there.

If only the divide between us didn't feel like an ocean.

"It's not that easy, Liv."

I'd built up those walls for a reason. Because shit hurt. Growing up with two parents who didn't give a shit about me hurt. My brother turning his back on me hurt. And when Liv decided to leave, that would hurt, too. Actually, it might destroy me. But I'd do what I always did. I'd pack up what was left of my heart, lock it away, and keep going.

Lonely I could deal with. I'd done lonely. A lot. The problem was rejection.

Lucas used to understand. Used to feel the same way. Before he jumped the fence and signed up to follow in dear ol' Dad's footsteps. I wondered what he would say now. If he would even take my call.

"I'll think about it. Right now," I said, pulling Liv over to straddle me, "all I want is you, naked in my bed for the next month."

But as I leaned in to kiss her, her phone beeped with a message. It was Jen. Who else would it be?

Liv's face fell at the text.

"What is it?"

And the look of fear she was wearing told me I wouldn't like what came next.

"Mike and Alicia are here."

33

WES

PISSED DIDN'T BEGIN to cover it.

Ever since this meeting had been confirmed, I'd been on pins and needles. I needed Jen to be wrong. There was no way I would give up Liv. Or my job. I'd left behind being told what to do and how to live my life when I moved out.

We'd been summoned to the hotel where Mike and Alicia were staying and stuffed into a lifeless conference room. Everything in the room was cold, from the greeting to the colorless furniture. Like the interior decorator had googled "office furniture" and bought everything they saw.

Liv and I sat facing Jen and *The Guild's* two executive producers. It was obvious they were EPs because they had wardrobes full of clothes one size too big and thousand-dollar haircuts that looked like they'd let a kid loose with a pair of tiny scissors.

"Thank you for joining us," Mike started. Like we had a choice. *It's only our careers, you dipshit.*

I'd never liked Mike. Bit of a wet blanket, if that

blanket thought it was hot shit with a stick up its ass. Was that too many metaphors?

I chanced a look at Liv. Her face was calm, but the line of her shoulders was set so straight I could have used them to measure my cabinets. Her elbow was resting on the table, a lock of hair tightly coiled around her finger. I knew this look. She was bracing herself for bad news.

Jen, as predicted, did fuck all.

"I think it's best if we rip the Band-Aid off as quickly as possible," Mike said. "The spin-off is happening. An official statement announcing *The Twelve* will be released in a week so that we can build excitement over the last season of *The Guild*. It will be a standard press release, including details about the showrunner, main cast, and airing date. We thought it was best to let you both know before the news comes out."

He waited, but if he thought he was getting a thank-you, he was mistaken. We'd been strung along for months, waiting for this news. And there wasn't a strong enough word to describe how fucking frustrating this was, but Jen's warning had gotten into my head. If they really were here to say Liv and I couldn't be together, it was going to be difficult to not throw one of these plain-ass chairs at him.

The silence stretched out, and I reached under the table to capture Liv's hand in mine. She squeezed lightly in thanks.

"So the spin-off is still going ahead?" Jen asked, and I fought the urge to congratulate her for finally doing her job.

"Yes," Alicia said slowly, but one didn't have to be a genius to hear the apprehension in her voice. "At this point, we see no reason it shouldn't continue. Although …" she trailed off, her eyes flickering toward Liv.

Mike had no such issues, the asshole. "There's

something we need to discuss. There's been a shift in the direction we'd like to take the show. Instead of following Meira and Ares as they travel to locate the medallion like we'd originally planned, we thought it would be more interesting to delve further into the god's realm. Follow Ares home and see the other side."

Alicia doubled down. "We've deviated enough from the source material now that this would be a wholly new concept, and it would allow us to introduce a slew of new characters."

Jen finally seemed to sense her commission was on the line and turned to Mike, all business. "But Liv will still be co-starring. That was what we agreed."

When Mike hesitated, I couldn't hold my tongue any longer. "People watch the show for Meira more than anything else."

Mike looked like he wanted to argue that point, and I knew in that second that if he did, I'd have no qualms punching him in the face, career be damned. "Now," he looked directly at Liv, and if I could have, I would have stepped between them, "I want to preface this by saying that we're both big fans of your work on the show, Olivia. It's been an absolute delight, and you've really surprised us over the last four years."

None of this sounded good. Liv squeezed my hand again. What this must be doing to her.

"But there have been some concerning whispers that we felt best to discuss in person. I didn't want there to be any room for misunderstanding. Is there anything going on here beyond a working relationship?"

"Yes," I answered, but stilled when I heard Liv's stuttered response.

Mike's frown deepened. I hoped the wind changed and

he was stuck that way. "I was hoping you wouldn't say that."

Do you think Superman has ever wanted to laser someone? Probably not; that guy's a saint. Ares, however, wouldn't hesitate to jettison a spear directly between Mike's legs. Rebekah probably wouldn't either.

"I'm sorry to say this," he started, and my eyes narrowed. Yeah, he looked really cut up about it. Practically beside himself.

"The Network has been very concerned over the recent situation with Bryson. It was an unfortunate oversight that we weren't aware of, which is why we'll be taking a more hands-on approach with the spin-off." Liar. It was the worst kept secret on set. There was no way in hell Mike and Alicia hadn't known. Saving his own ass as usual. "You should also be aware of the effect the incident has had on the reputation of the show. As you know, *The Guild* is a family-friendly program, and that is something we're very proud of. Recent events have alienated certain viewers, and we can't risk any further scandal affecting the future of what has been, to date, a very successful property."

This chair was pretty flimsy. I wondered if it would break before or after it punctured his nose.

"If you were prepared to break it off, quietly, of course, we could possibly consider a different route."

"No," I said.

Liv turned. "Wes—"

"No." How could she even consider it?

"In that case, my hands are tied. The network is prepared to let you stay on, Wesley, but Olivia, if you're determined to conduct a public relationship with your co-star, the network has made it clear that we cannot offer you a role in the new show."

Liv was still beside me. I hated this. I didn't want to do the show without her. But whose fault was this really? I'd spent the last week convincing her this exact situation wasn't going to happen. One look at Jen confirmed it. Her face was dark, her gaze bearing down on me with accusation. *Fuck.* I needed to fix this. I needed to figure out some way to turn this around. Without losing her.

Alicia was smiling sweetly. "Absolutely. And we love the possibility of having you on in a guest role in future if the schedules allow for it." She couldn't have added more loopholes to that flimsy excuse of an offer. If, maybe, possibly, we hope. It was the same bullshit they always used.

My mouth was open before I could think better of it. "What?"

"But we think, for the moment," Mike started, but I'd stopped listening. *How dare they?*

"This is bullshit. Is this because of the photos? That wasn't her fault."

"Wes," Liv said, but it was lost in the fray.

Mike straightened. "It's an unfortunate coincidence, but no. This was already in motion before that."

"Mike, I don't appreciate being blindsided like this." Jen sounded as angry as I felt. "Olivia has been crucial to the success of the show, and you'll lose a large part of the fan base by not including her in the spin-off."

"I'm not denying her appeal, but we truly believe, and the network agrees, that this is a better direction."

Bullshit. Fine. If it was so easy without one of us, then they could do it without either of us. But before I could say anything, Liv tugged sharply on my hand. When my eyes met hers, I saw the same pleading look she'd given me before LA. She shook her head.

I returned my gaze to Mike, who looked about ready to sweat. *Good.*

Jen stood, the sound of her chair scraping the ground harshly. No doubt she'd done that on purpose. "If that's everything, then we'll leave."

Liv stood as well, and the slow slip of her hand out of mine cut through me.

Alicia placed a contract and pen before me. I wanted to throw it back and tell them to shove it, but the part of my brain that was still rational knew I'd regret it. And Liv would kill me if I did. So I signed. Because I loved playing Ares, and I wanted to do it for as long as possible. But I also knew that I wouldn't rest until I got Liv back on the show.

34

LIV

THEY SAID bad omens came in threes, or in some cases, the body of a pale, dark-haired boy named Damian, but it seemed I didn't need omens. I was fully capable of destroying my own life.

Jen and I had just left the meeting with Mike and Alicia, and I was still reeling.

"What do I do?"

"I was worried this would happen, so I've spent the week making some calls. I've gotten you an audition, but you'll have to fly to LA tomorrow. You were already due back for the awards, so this will just mean getting there early and extending your trip."

"Oh. Why so soon?" The thought of being away from Wes in the middle of this mess only made me feel worse.

"Olivia, this is the best you could have hoped for. Considering the hit your reputation has taken lately, you're lucky I could get this much. Not to mention what will happen when word gets around that you haven't been signed for the spin-off."

How had I screwed up so badly? It felt like I'd done nothing but pull my future apart, one decision at a time.

"You're right, I'm sorry."

She paused, appearing to choose her words carefully. "You might want to consider moving back after this season wraps."

And leave Wes? My heart sank.

"What's the audition?" I asked because thinking about work was much easier.

"It's a new drama thriller series. You wouldn't be top billing, but you would be regular ensemble, and when I mentioned the possibility of directing, they said they'd be open to that if it gets picked up."

I was torn. On the one hand, it was a good sign that Jen was finally listening to what I wanted. The opportunity to direct even one episode of television meant opening the door to similar opportunities. On the other hand, I knew absolutely nothing about the show, and I'd be leaving Wes.

If the audition was in LA, it likely meant filming there, and the idea of being separated by thousands of miles made me want to cry.

Jen seemed to sense my reluctance. "If you don't want it, I'll turn them down, but I need you to tell me if this is a priority for you or not because I'm getting mixed signals."

"No, I'll be there." It was just an audition, right? No harm ever came from going to an audition …

"Great. I'll send through your flight details and have a car pick you up first thing. Since you're booked to present at the MTV Movie Awards on Saturday, I've booked you a hotel as well. That'll give you six days at the Chateau Marmont."

"Actually, I was hoping to see my dad this time."

There was a non-committal hum. "We'll talk about it once you're in LA." She left.

A restless energy simmered under my skin. This was what I wanted. I'd finally be taking a step forward in my career. So why didn't I feel like celebrating?

Something about Jen's tone bothered me. Had I ever noticed that before? Maybe it was simply the stress of the last few weeks straining our relationship. I'd also made her work life miserable since those photos of Bryson dropped, and geez, that felt like a lifetime ago now.

My fingers hovered over my voicemails, wishing for some tried-and-true mom wisdom to help me untie the knots in my stomach. Instead, I tried the next closest thing. My dad.

"What a surprise! How's my superstar doing?"

"Good," I said on instinct, then mentioned the audition.

"That's great news. Are you excited?"

"I think so?" That was a stretch. I'd have to work on that before the audition.

When I told him I hoped to see him this time around, he said, "It's okay if you can't. I know how busy you are."

"I just need to clear it with Jen first."

He made a disapproving noise.

"Don't you start. I already get enough of this from Wes."

"Maybe you should listen to him."

"I'm not having this argument again. Jen has done a lot for me. You don't know what it was like."

"Don't I?"

My heart sank. Of course he knew.

"I know I wasn't as involved in that side of things as your mother was, but we did talk. She agreed that Jen was the best choice at the time because she would be the most hands-on, but your mom always wondered if she had your best interests at heart."

This was territory we rarely traveled. And I didn't enjoy him bringing Mom up as leverage.

"Why didn't she ever tell me that?"

"Because she didn't want to make you worry. And back then, everything Jen did was helping you. Why do you think your mother was so adamant about being involved in every meeting you had? She didn't want Jen overstepping."

His words were a blow. Why didn't Mom ever tell me she felt this way?

Suddenly, I was angry. I didn't want to hear anyone else's opinion of Jen. Out of everyone, she was the one trying to help me. I'd followed Mom's advice—and Wes'—and look where that got me.

Fired. My reputation hanging by a thread.

Jen should have seen the disaster coming after the photos with Bryson came out and jumped ship while she had the chance, but she hadn't. Once again, she'd stuck with me.

A long time ago, I'd promised her I'd do the same. It had just taken my life blowing up for me to remember it.

35

LIV

PAIN WAS ETCHED INTO WES' face. It was hard to look at, but I also couldn't look away.

"Do you want this role? Or to move back to LA?" he asked.

No. But ... "What choice do I have?"

"There's still another season of *The Guild*. Plus the spin-off. I don't care what Mike said today, we can talk to him, convince him."

Oh yeah, that show the network was currently writing me out of. The consequence Jen warned me would happen if Wes and I got together. The same warning that Wes had repeatedly told me meant nothing. Except it did mean something. It meant the end of my employment. "Wes, stop. We both know I'm not going to be on that spin-off."

"Bullshit. We don't know that," he said angrily, taking a step away from me to pace.

"If we'd just listened to Jen." As soon as I said the words, I wanted to take them back.

He spun to face me. "Oh, here we go. Fuck. Is there

anything Jen doesn't know? Maybe she could tell me what the next winning lottery numbers are."

"I know you don't want to hear it, but it's the truth. If I'd listened to her and laid low, we wouldn't be in this position."

"This is ridiculous. Mike is an idiot. You're half that show. The network won't let them do this."

"Wes, stop." Couldn't he see he was only making this harder?

"Why aren't you fighting this?"

"Because I know it's a losing battle. They've made their decision, and now I have to plan for what comes after this season is over. I can't just avoid reality."

"What does that mean?"

Shit. This wasn't how I'd wanted this conversation to go. I'd known Wes would be upset that I was leaving, but it was only for a few days, and after the meeting with the producers, I'd thought he'd realize how important getting another job would be.

"It means that while our escape to LA was nice, it was just that. An escape. We weren't thinking about what would happen when we got back."

He flinched like I'd hit him. "You're the one who kissed me. Who pursued me."

"Yes. Because you weren't ever going to." How long would he have waited? Forever? "You knew I was worried, and you treated it like it was nothing. You said Mike and Alicia wouldn't do it. And look what happened."

He had avoided his feelings for me, just like he avoided every difficult conversation. Like he'd avoided Jen's warnings. He'd been so convincing. And I'd listened. Because I hadn't wanted to believe it any more than he did.

But we couldn't avoid it anymore.

"You're blaming me? You invited yourself to LA, Liv. You posted those videos. You kissed me." It bared repeating. *You chose this*, he was saying. We were equally at fault here.

He was right.

"I know, and I'm sorry."

"Don't. Don't say you're sorry. Like you wish it never happened."

I didn't. Being with Wes was one of the greatest things to ever happen to me. I'd never regret a single second of it.

But I couldn't help wishing the timing had been better. Maybe if we'd waited. Just a year, once the spin-off was in play. The press would have died down, and we could have started something without Bryson hanging over our heads.

Unfortunately, Wes misread my hesitation. His face crumpled.

"Wes." I reached for his hands, desperate for the connection, the baseline, his touch provided.

The sound of a text notification pierced through the tension between us. I pulled my phone from my pocket, already knowing who it would be. What it would be.

Jen: Your flight details are attached. Driver will pick you up at 7am.

Wes scoffed. "Is that her? What does the senator want now? Is she finally telling you to murder innocent Jedi babies?"

I stepped back. "Don't call her that."

"Why can't you see that she's manipulating you?"

The implication being that I was weak. Incapable. Unable to make my own decisions. Based on the last few months, he might not be far off. I huffed a humorless laugh. "Good to know you think so little of me."

"That's not what I meant." He ran a hand down his face. "I know you think you owe her."

"You think you know a lot of things, but I don't need you to fix this for me. I know you don't like her—"

He interrupted. "I don't like her, you're right. But this isn't about me. It's about the fact that she has done nothing but scare you with losing this role for weeks now. She hides the fact that you've lost work over this but still constantly mentions it and sends you headlines?

"There was a reason you wanted to escape to LA, and I don't believe it only had to do with me. Tell me, what part of your life is yours? You stay in when she tells you. Date who she lets you. Wear only what she approves. You don't have a life. You have a schedule."

He laid them like facts at my feet, but he was wrong. He wasn't the one who had to deal with the backlash. He and Jackson had been able to hook up with whoever they wanted. Their virtue was never questioned. If anything, it made them more attractive.

"That's not fair."

I didn't want to hear it. It was the same thing he'd been saying on repeat. I was done. It didn't matter that there were nagging thoughts in the back of my mind, my mom's voice, Wes' voice, my own fears.

Did I want to have every part of my life controlled? No. I wanted to live in an apartment that didn't feel like a show home. I wanted to be free to love who I wanted and tell the whole fucking world about it. I wanted my mother to still be alive.

But just because I wanted it didn't mean it I could have it.

"That's what I'm trying to tell you. You left modeling because you felt like a puppet. How is this any different?"

I didn't have an answer that would make sense. How could I explain that Jen had been there when I needed someone? That I had relied on her at a time when I'd lost my most trusted person? How could Wes understand it when he'd never had anything to compare it to?

"It's different because—" and I stopped, because I couldn't work out how it was different, just that it was.

"You're letting someone else dictate how you live. I've been there, Liv. That's not a life."

LIV STARED AT THE FLOOR. I felt worse than useless. Six years of keeping myself away from her, and now I'd ruined everything.

"I don't need you to understand my reasons. I need you to support me," she said.

"I do support you."

"Then you need to let me make my own decisions. If it's a mistake, let it be my mistake."

I reached for her, thumb caressing her jaw. Why couldn't she see? I'd been there. I'd grown up under the rule of someone who didn't truly care about me. The second most important day of my life was the day I left that behind. The first was the day I'd met Liv.

"I know what it's like to be seen but not heard. To be used for what you can offer a person but not wanted for who you are. That's what I'm trying to save you from."

Liv shook her head; the smallest movement. She felt fragile under my palms, so incompatible with how strong she was. Stronger than me. Fearless. Watching her be held back was a dagger to my heart.

"And what about saving yourself, Wes? You've got all this time to fix what's apparently wrong in my life, but you can't pick up the phone and call your brother? You talk about wanting love and feeling connected, but you're the one pushing people away."

The words cut deep. "I've tried talking to Lucas."

"No. You haven't. You've closed the door on him like you have with everybody else."

"What's that supposed to mean?"

"You never let anyone get close enough! You were in love with me for six years, and I had no clue. Would I have ever known if I hadn't kissed you first?" It was something I'd only just started to wonder. If I'd never taken that first risk, would we have gone our whole lives never knowing?

"That's different."

"No, it's not. There are people in your life who love you, and you can't even see it."

"What good would it do? Lucas only cared until I wasn't around anymore; you don't care enough to fight for us."

"Wes, of course I care enough! I'm still here, aren't I? But I know how much the show means to you, and I won't be the reason you lose that."

"I don't care about the show. I'd rather have you, but I guess I'm the only one who feels that way. Jen will be happy. She's getting what she wanted."

"That's unfair."

"It's true. She already makes all of your other decisions for you. Why not this one as well?" I'd known Jen had her hand in every part of Liv's work, but to have her get between us was the last straw. "She won't be happy until she's the only one you have left."

"At least I'll have someone. Who do you have, Wes? Your family? Friends? You're so busy thinking people will hurt you, you never let them get close enough to know you. You're alone, and you're miserable, and you have no one to blame but yourself."

The room went deadly silent.

A hollow ache filled my chest. I almost expected to look up and see a reflection of my failures staring back at me. Instead, I saw Liv, eyes wide, shocked.

"Wes, I'm so sorry."

She shouldn't apologize. She'd only told the truth, after all.

"Anyone ever tell you you're a crack shot, doll?" A bull's-eye, right to the heart.

She rushed over, her hands hovering, unsure if she could touch. "I can't believe I said that. I'm sorry."

It was a heavy pill to swallow, but I wasn't naïve. Of course I'd known what I was doing. Because the closer you invited people, the easier it was for them to get to all of your soft places. And those wounds hardly ever healed.

"Please, Wes." Her hands slid into mine. "I've already lost the show. I can't lose you, too. Your friendship means too much to me."

"You could never lose me." It was the immutable core of my being.

She squeezed my hands tight, digging in. Her eyes large and stormy. "I love you." And the pained way she said it only twisted my gut further. Because loving me had meant losing her job, and I should have known I couldn't have everything I wanted.

"Then why does this feel like goodbye?"

"It's not."

But how could it not be? She was about to leave, and if she got this role—more like when, because, let's face it, she would. She was amazing—she'd be gone. Not permanently, but she'd be far enough.

And then who would I have?

Despite my best efforts, I didn't like being alone. I hated it. Spending so much time with Liv these last few months had reminded me of how much I'd missed having someone in my life.

"Wes." She tugged on my shirt, bringing my attention back to her. "This doesn't change how I feel. I love you. So, *so* much. But ..."

My gaze snapped to hers. *But.* Said with the force of a final blow.

"But this isn't about how I feel. It's about my career. And yours."

"We can have both."

"Maybe." But it didn't sound like maybe. It sounded like no. And the worst part was that I thought she might be right about that, too.

I'd always known it would end; I just hadn't realized it would be so soon.

"I don't regret this. I want you to know that. It's the best thing that's ever happened to me. And you'll always have me as a friend. If you want me."

"I'll always want you."

"You should think about what I said. I'm not the only one who cares about you. You're amazing, Wes. People see that, and they want to get to know you. Stop shutting them out."

I pulled her to me, pressing a kiss to her forehead. "I

love you," I said, one last time. Because it was true. It would always be true.

She slid her hands around my neck. The nerve endings across my scalp lit up as she ran a hand through my hair, pulling at an errant curl or two. I savored every detail, every touch, the gentle curve of her mouth. Locked it away to remind myself.

It had been real.

When her arms slipped away, I smiled. I didn't want to make this any harder on her. "I'll see you soon."

She blinked, nodded.

I didn't tell her that it would be okay. It didn't feel right to have the last words I said be a lie.

37

LIV

MY HEART HAD TAKEN up permanent residence in my stomach.

The audition had gone ... not great. I'd said my lines; they'd smiled and thanked me, but I could tell they weren't happy. They'd probably already forgotten my name, which was why they'd gone out of their way to not say it, throwing out the usual "we appreciate you coming in" and "we'll be in touch." They wouldn't.

I didn't blame them.

I missed Wes like crazy. I wanted to call, hear his voice, a dick joke, anything.

Jen shouldn't have wasted the money on this suite. My mind and my heart were still two thousand miles away.

"Olivia?" Jen's voice pulled me back to reality.

"I'm here." Barely. "Actually, I wanted to tell you that I'm going to check out of the hotel today. I'm going to stay with my dad."

"You can't. That's what I was explaining. I've booked a

meeting for you at the hotel. I'll need you to be in the lobby to meet them in an hour."

"What meeting?"

"A short meet and greet. It'll be a good brand builder."

I sighed. "Okay. But then I really want to see my dad."

"We can talk about that later. I have a thing right now, but I'll call you after the meeting. Remember. The lobby in an hour."

"I remember," I said, a little petulantly. It had been like this all day. Phone calls, messages, reminders. Like I was a child.

I wondered what was so important that she'd arrange the meeting at the hotel. I'd already had two separate conversations with reps from LVMH, made especially awkward when I declined their offer for an ambassador contract only to find out that Jen had already signed it on my behalf. Based on the astronomical number they gave me, her cut would end up in the six-figure range.

I'd be impressed if I wasn't so pissed about it.

After I hung up, I checked my messages again. Nothing from Wes.

I hated the way we'd left things. All I wanted to do was call him, but what would I say? I would still be here, and he'd still be all the way over there, and nothing else had changed.

The hardest part was that I didn't know that I disagreed with him. Now that I'd had time to think, I couldn't stop picking at it. Hell, even my dad had agreed with him. And Mom.

My phone stared back at me, taunting me with its silence.

Without Wes to talk to, I turned to the only other

person I wanted to hear from, opening the familiar folder of voicemails.

"Happy New Year, sweetheart! Sorry about the noise. Yes, Joe, I know it's past midnight. I was here for the countdown."

"What happened to your resolution to be nicer to me?"

"Did I make that resolution? That doesn't sound like me." Mom laughed. I missed that sound more than anything.

"Did you hear that, Olivia? Your mother —" Dad's voice became muffled, like there was a hand over his mouth.

"Shush, Joe, I'm trying to talk to our daughter and wish her a happy new year. Olivia, sweetheart, you're probably sleeping, but I wanted to make sure you woke up and knew how much we love you."

My heart clenched.

"Shit, I couldn't be more proud of you. Don't give me that look, Joe. Our daughter is incredible. You keep it up, sweetheart. Joe! Joe, give me the phone back—"

The voicemail ended, taking their laughter with it. They sounded so happy. Drunk and full of life. Mom had always called Dad her best friend. That she'd had no choice but to fall in love with him. Because he'd understood her like no one else had.

I'd always wondered what it would feel like to love someone like that. Now I knew.

My phone buzzed, spiking my heart rate. But it wasn't Wes.

Jen had sent me instructions on which outfit to wear to the meeting. It wasn't the first time she'd done it, so why did it make me so mad? I was tempted to go in my sweats, just to spite her.

Was she really overstepping or had Wes' words gotten caught in my head? Sure, I didn't like everything about the way Jen managed me. And yes, I was beginning to feel stifled.

But was that enough to outweigh all the good she'd done?

I eyed myself in the mirror as I braided my hair, hoping something on the outside would explain what was going on inside. Like my reflection might gain sentience and tell me *what the hell to do*. But there was nothing.

Just a confused mess of a woman who still felt like a girl.

———

Jen's instructions were to wait in the courtyard. It wasn't as private as I'd like, too accessible from the lobby to stop curious tourists from snapping a candid of their favorite celebrity. I couldn't shake the feeling of being watched.

I took up a seat at a table facing the open doorway, hoping I'd know who I was meeting when I saw them enter.

Two businessmen sat nearby, in matching uniforms of blue button downs, jeans, and tan loafers. They were simultaneously sporting power poses, and I wondered if they'd end up fighting over the check. I pictured them locked in a Patrick Bateman-style business card stand-off.

When I sensed someone walking toward me, I looked up, smile in place, ready to greet whomever I was meeting.

No. No, no, no.

Had I known Bryson was in LA?

The urge to run was high, but we'd already made eye contact, and he was walking straight for me.

I stood as he approached. It felt like an out-of-body experience. Why was he here? What could we possibly have to say to each other?

The last time we'd talked, he'd been angry. I'd expected that if we ever saw each other again, the most I'd get from him was polite avoidance. Not the big grin and warm greeting he was giving me.

Nothing about this felt right.

"Hi, Liv."

Awkwardly, I forced my limbs to return the hug he gave me. Everything about it felt wrong. He was bulky where I wanted slim. A gruff beard where I wanted smooth skin. The strength of his cologne, a strong musk that I used to enjoy, overwhelmed me. I tried not to flinch when he moved his lips to my ear.

"Act natural," he said, his voice flat, proving that the smile and hug were for show.

I kept my smile in place. "What is happening?" I whispered back. Then I heard the telltale clicks. Cameras. Multiple.

What the hell?

"Jen thought—" and he didn't need to say more than that.

My gut twisted. Wes had been right. Whatever inch I'd given Jen in the beginning had turned into more than a mile. I'd simply been too lost in my grief to notice.

Of course.

I wanted to scream at her. I'd already run the gamut, done everything the way she'd asked like a damn gladiator —without all the blood, although even that was debatable. I'd thought that Jen was in my corner. She'd gone above and beyond when Mom passed, and I'd been grateful.

I'd also felt guilty, and she'd turned that guilt into a weapon, wielding it with cold precision.

Everything became clear.

The apartment that wasn't mine. The clothes that I'd never picked out. The food I never bought myself. The interviews I didn't give.

I thought about how free I'd felt with Wes in LA. How happy a simple stack of pancakes had made me. How rebellious I'd felt when we'd taken a drive and talked under the stars. How protective I'd been of him when his brother had called him selfish.

And I knew it was the same feeling of protectiveness that Wes had for me. The same fuel that kept him so critical of Jen. He'd been looking out for me, and I'd hurt him.

Bryson was still talking, but I'd stopped listening. I kissed the air by his cheek, acting like this had been the plan all along.

"Goodbye, Bryson."

Something real flashed in his eyes for a second. Until he remembered we weren't alone. He schooled his expression into something suitably fond. "Take care, Liv."

The walk back to my suite was a blur, and before I knew it, I'd packed a bag, left a note for the rest to be delivered to Jen's office, and checked out of the hotel.

When Mom had first gotten sick, I'd been frustrated that she hadn't slowed down. She should have been resting, but she wouldn't. Said that if she only had a short amount of time left to do all the things she enjoyed, then she was damn well gonna do them. When she no longer had enough energy to go out, we stayed in. I'd promised her— hell, I'd promised myself—that I'd try to remember that. To keep living.

The first summer after she died, Jen had pressured me to go to Hawaii with some friends. She'd said it was important for me to look like I was doing okay, and at the time, I'd agreed. I thought it might help. But I'd spent every day crying into my pillow.

Even now, four years later, I knew I wasn't doing it

right. Mom wouldn't have wanted this for me. And I didn't want it for me, either.

I was twenty-five. Four years younger than she'd been when she'd had me. And now she wouldn't be around to see me reach that age. Watch me walk down the aisle, be my plus-one to the Oscars, or any of the rest of the long list of things I knew I wanted for my future.

All these years, I'd been trying to fit in a box that I'd been told I should be in. I'd followed all the advice. Jen's advice. I'd heard so many horror stories of managers who took advantage, who pressed their own agenda. But Jen's compassion early on had stood out, and I'd felt compelled to continue working with her, both to distract myself from my pain and because I knew it would help her.

I had assumed Jen had my best interests at heart. Now I knew I was simply a means to her own ends.

It was the last straw.

I'd expected Sym's assistant. Or voicemail. But, instead, they answered the phone like we were old friends. "Olivia, what a pleasure. I was just thinking about you. How are you?"

"I'd like to know if your offer is still on the table." Now that I'd checked out, I was hovering in the lobby, trying to calculate my next move, knowing the decision was entirely my own. It was equal parts freeing and frightening.

"Absolutely. Effective immediately, if you'd like."

I breathed a sigh of relief. "Great. Also, I need to ask for a favor."

"Anything."

"I'd like to stay with my dad for the next few days. I can be back by Saturday to present at the awards, but I'd like to be with him until then."

"Oh, sweetie." They sounded surprised. "You don't need to ask me to do that. Of course you can see him."

Oh. My brain stuttered, so unprepared for the agreement. It suddenly hit me. I didn't have to ask permission anymore. I was in charge. "Yes, right. Great."

I held down an irrational laugh. Was it really this easy?

"Okay. And don't you worry about the other details. That's for me to sort out. I'll even have a courier bring the paperwork to your father's house."

There would be more to work out, of course. I wasn't looking forward to talking to Jen, but I had the sneaking suspicion that Sym would be there with me if I asked them to.

"Thank you." I could have jumped for joy, right in the middle of the hotel lobby. It must have shown on my face because the concierge was watching me curiously. Over by the check-in desk, the teenage daughter of a family of four was taking my photo, not even attempting to be subtle. I was so happy that I gave her a little wave. She jumped and hid her phone in her pocket. I wondered how long it would take before I was trending somewhere.

Actually, it didn't matter. I wasn't going to check anyway.

I passed Sym the details of where I'd be for the next few days in case they needed to contact me. Then, in a fit of inspiration, I added, "There's one other thing."

"Name it."

"I want to redecorate my apartment."

Sym laughed. "I think that's a great idea."

———

"Look at these spoons." I held up a vintage teaspoon that ended in a heart shape, a tiny Statue of Liberty dangling from its center. "Mom would have loved these."

"She would." Dad looked up from his cappuccino. His smile was fond but sad, and I opened my mouth to apologize, but he shook his head and reached over the small table to squeeze my hand. Usually, that was my move.

"You know you can talk to me about anything. I'm not your mother, but I'm still here for you, and I love you."

I blinked slowly as my throat constricted. Dammit, I wouldn't cry in this antique café. He really was an amazing dad. When my eyes cleared, I squeezed back. "Sorry. I didn't want to upset you. We've never really talked about any of that stuff before. It always came so easy with her."

"I know. For me, too. But I'm happy to stumble our way through it if you are. She'd want that, I think."

I could only nod, not trusting my voice. After another light squeeze, he released my hand and took a drink of his coffee, giving me time to collect myself.

"I don't really know how to …" His hand gestured aimlessly. "Your mother was better at this."

"She really was," I teased.

"Yeah, all right, take it easy on your old man."

He could have been cast as the quintessential dad in every nineties sitcom—faded jeans, knit sweater, kind eyes. I was fairly sure he hadn't bought new clothes in at least a decade. It made me endlessly happy.

What surprised me was how good he looked. Better than I'd seen him in a really long time. A few less hairs and a few more wrinkles, but with a lightness that hadn't been there before.

"You're not that old."

"That's what I've been trying to tell you."

I stared down at my hot chocolate, looking at the spoon in my hand. I wanted to talk to him. We still had each other, and that meant so much to me. So why was I finding it so hard to tell him that?

"She was so easy to talk to, I never ..." There was a soft pat on my hand when I trailed off.

"I know," he said, full of understanding.

"But I still love you."

He laughed. "I'm glad to hear it."

I took a deep breath and found that the words came easy once I let them. "I want to talk to you about her. There aren't many people in my life who knew her, and I —" my throat constricted, heat prickling at my eyes. "—I'm scared I'll forget her."

"Oh, honey. You won't. Trust me. I see her every time I look at you. You might have my nose, but you have her spirit. Will some things fade over time? Maybe. But you can't live your life in the past. You know she wouldn't want that for you. You can love her and let her go."

The dam broke. Four years, and this felt like the last piece of a puzzle I'd been slowly completing. The words I'd known to be true but didn't want to admit. Dad's arms came around me, squeezing me tight and making me ten years old again.

"I miss her so much."

"Me too, sweetheart. It's okay. We'll be okay."

He hadn't needed to say it. I finally knew it to be true.

———

As we walked down the street, he pulled his hand out of his pocket and thrust it into mine like a spy. Confused, I looked down, then gaped. It was the spoon I had admired earlier. "Dad, what?" I asked, shocked. "Did you steal this?"

He pushed my hand closed, hurrying me down the street. You'd think we were in a heist film, the way he was playing it. "Just put it in your pocket before anyone sees."

Once it was hidden, I laughed. I laughed for so long I finally had to stop on the sidewalk to catch my breath. "This is how mom got all those spoons, isn't it? You stole them for her."

"From our very first date." He wasn't repentant at all.

Geez. How had I never known this about him?

"And your mother loved it. I mean, not the stealing. She always made sure we left a big enough tip to cover it."

"Oh my god." We continued along the sidewalk, my fingers curling around the spoon in my pocket. I felt closer to him, both of them, in a way that was overwhelming.

"You know, I kept her voicemails. Missed calls or voice notes she sent me. I've been listening to them a lot lately." Telling him lifted a weight off. "Sometimes I almost call her back... before I remember."

Dad's arm came around my shoulders. He smelled like freshly cut grass and memories.

"Did you know that your mother hand made me a card for every anniversary we had?" he asked, voice fond. "And not just the big ones. All kinds of 'em. Twenty years since our first kiss. One thousandth I love you." He chuckled. "I'm sure she made half of them up, but I didn't care." His arm tightened around me. "I've kept every damn one of those cards. Don't have half a clue what to do with them, but I kept 'em."

"I had no idea."

He brought us to a stop on the sidewalk, both hands

coming up to my shoulders, impressing upon me the seriousness of his words.

"Your mother was the love of my life. There was no one like her. I know you looked up to her, but she wouldn't want you to hold yourself back out of fear of living up to her." And in one sentence, he had pinpointed exactly what I had been afraid of. Typical.

He continued, more serious than I'd ever seen him. "You have your own adventures ahead of you. And she'd want you to have them."

My mind immediately went to Wes. To the heartbreak I'd seen when I'd told him I was leaving. The devotion in his eyes when he'd told me he loved me. The feel of his hand in mine every time I needed him.

And now he was probably seeing photos of me hugging Bryson.

Shit.

Fresh tears stung my eyes. "What if I mess up?"

He smiled and said, simple as anything, "Then I guess we'll need to find more spoons."

38

WES

THIS WAS SILLY. I shouldn't be this nervous.

I resisted the urge to drop the gift off and leave. I might not be used to letting people in, but I owed Jackson an apology, and if I didn't do it now, I might never do it.

Liv's point about me being afraid had been living rent free in my head since we'd talked. *Fought,* my wounded heart reminded me.

I needed to make this right.

I knocked again, the bottle of whiskey in my hand clinking against the door, whiskey stones in my other hand. I hoped he would see it as the "Hey, I'm sorry I've been a shit friend" gift it was meant to be.

Another minute passed before he answered the door, looking relaxed in sweats and the kind of bone-deep peace I didn't think I'd ever felt in my life.

Except maybe with Liv …

"Wes, hey. I wasn't expecting you."

"Yeah. Is it a bad time? You just got back from your honeymoon. I can go."

"What are you talking about? Come in. Audrey is working late."

I followed him inside, taking in the suitcases propped against the wall and a pile of mail stacked on the dining table.

He walked straight into the kitchen, reminding me that I was still holding my apology gifts.

"These are for you," I said, following him and putting them down on the counter.

"Thanks. Didn't you already get us a wedding present?" He took both items from me and eyed the label on the bottle, impressed.

"Actually, this is to apologize. For being a dick."

Jackson looked like he didn't know whether he should laugh. "Any particular time, or …?"

"All of it, I guess?" Shit, this was hard. "I don't think I've been a very good friend, and uh, I'm sorry."

"There's nothing to apologize for," he said, then saw my grimace. "But if it helps, then consider it forgiven."

I let that sink in for a long moment.

"Drink?" Jackson asked, and I nodded. "I just opened something new. Let me grab some glasses." He busied himself in the kitchen, pulling two thick tumblers from his cupboard. It reminded me of Liv. And LA, and that I was doing the right thing.

"Come on, sit down. Tell me what's going on with you." He held one out to me, and I finally felt something loosen in my chest. I nodded my thanks as I took it and followed him to the couch.

Normally, this would be when I'd crack a joke. I could even feel it, hanging on the tip of my tongue. Some crude joke about his honeymoon or a dig at how he'd soon be too busy to hang out with me.

But that was the exact habit I was trying to break, so I shoved down the instinct and readied myself to be honest with him.

Jackson said nothing, patiently waiting. I hated these awkward silences, and he knew that, and he knew that *I* knew that, but he waited anyway, probably hoping I'd crack and finally say more.

I did.

"I'm in love with Liv."

The corner of his mouth twitched. "I know."

Shit, that was right. I huffed a nervous laugh. "Right, yeah. I'd actually forgotten that." How long ago had that been now? So much had changed since then.

Jackson waited as I tried again.

"We've been …" I really should have put more thought into this conversation because I didn't actually know how to explain what we'd been doing.

Seeing me struggle, Jackson offered, "Dating?"

"Yeah." And now that the door was open, the rest became strangely easy. "It happened while we were in LA. Best week of my life. Just the two of us. And Baxter." I pulled my phone out, showing Jackson a photo of him for clarity. "I kind of dognapped him from my parents' house."

"You don't talk about your family much."

"Uh, it's a whole thing. We're nothing like your family." I waved off his concern. "It's fine. I mean, it's not, but it doesn't really bother me much anymore."

"And your brother? Are you still close with him?"

I stopped, glass midway to my mouth. I didn't realize he even knew about Lucas.

Jackson continued, "The first day you were on set, we were joking about our costumes—you remember those tights I used to have to wear?" He shuddered, and I didn't blame him. Those pants had been god-awful. "Anyway, you said that he'd get a kick out of seeing you like that because of the shows you'd watched as kids."

Shit. He remembered that? A throwaway comment from four years ago from someone he'd just met. Jackson really was a good guy.

And I really had been a shit friend.

Touched, I sipped at the whiskey, letting the thick, smoky taste and warm burn distract me from the surge of emotion I felt.

"His name is Lucas. He's two years younger than me, and we used to be really close. My parents weren't around much. Dad spent all his time working, and Mom spent all her time socializing, so Lucas and I kept each other company. We played a lot of board games, mostly."

"I can relate. My parents worked a lot, too, leaving me on babysitting duty. I used to read to my baby sister a lot."

"What was your favorite?"

"The Twits. Or really, anything by Roald Dahl."

"Really?" Not what I'd expected.

Jackson nodded.

"I don't think I've read it." And since he'd trusted me, I repaid the favor. "Mine was Pride and Prejudice."

"Seriously?" he asked, curious.

I shrugged. "I'm a big Austen fan."

"You know, I can see that."

A laugh escaped, and I finally relaxed. It felt good to get out of my own way and talk to Jackson freely. "Anyway, we hated living at home. Talked all the time about moving out, getting a place together, finally having our freedom. After I signed for Ares, I was going to ask him if he wanted to move over here, get a fresh start, but by the time we finished that first season, he'd already stopped talking to me."

"Sorry to hear that, man. If it's anything like Sarah and me, I'd be devastated if we weren't close anymore."

Instead of answering, I took another sip of whiskey. It was good. Jackson had great taste. Although it occurred to me at that moment that perhaps it was his wife's taste. He laughed when I asked him.

"Oh, it is absolutely all Audrey. She's been teaching me a few things."

"I don't need to hear about your sex life, J."

Jackson tipped his head back, laughing harder now. "I'm not touching that one." He topped off our drinks, then sat back, gearing up to ask me something. I waited.

"Will you see your brother while you're in LA?"

I shrugged. I hadn't decided yet. "I don't know."

"For what it's worth, I think you should. I think if you told him what you just told me, you might be surprised by his reaction."

Liv had said the same thing. It's how I knew he was probably right. "Maybe," I said.

"What's the worst that could happen? He could tell you he hates you and wants nothing to do with you, which I doubt. Or, he could tell you he's hurting, too. But you won't know until you talk to him."

Already, I knew where he was headed with this but could feel the fight against it spark inside me. The idea that I could finally have an answer felt immense. This weight pressing on my chest might finally be lifted, and I could finally know *why*. And that was the whole point. I wanted the answer, but first I needed to ask the damn question.

Which I'd been running away from.

"How'd you get to be so wise, man?"

He let out a surprised laugh, shaking his head as he looked down at his glass. "I'm definitely not that. But I'm getting better. Mostly, I try to be honest about what I'm feeling and go from there."

How did I know he'd say that? "Yeah, yeah. Try not to kick a man when he's down, doc."

Jackson laughed, then sobered. "I'm really glad you came over. We should do this more often."

"Sounds good, man." I reached over and clinked my glass with his. It wasn't much, but it felt important. I'd done the right thing, taken the first step.

And I knew what I needed to do next.

39

WES

"YOU SIGNED A CONTRACT."

I could almost see the spit fly through the phone. See, this was why I hadn't gone to see Mike in person. Also, he hated phone meetings. So even though I was in LA and I could have driven over to his office, I'd called. Because fuck him, that's why.

"I don't care. I'll find a way. Creative differences, a scheduling conflict, whatever. Either way, I quit."

"Wesley," Alicia said, her tone too tight to sell the casual vibe she was going for. "Don't make any rash decisions. The fans love Ares, and this is your opportunity to take center stage."

I looked down at the script that had been delivered to me this morning. The first episode of *The Twelve*. I threw it in the trash. Back to the drawing board, boys.

"Did you even look at what I sent you?" I asked.

A pause.

I smiled. They'd looked at it. They didn't like it, but they'd looked at it.

I almost wished I'd gone in person just to see their faces. "If anyone should be on the show, it's Liv. The fans love Meira more than they love Ares."

"What do you think you're doing, Wesley? You don't have any power. We can film this show without either of you."

Ouch. I couldn't see him, but I'd bet ten to one Mike's face was really red right now. Dude had the complexion of a mood ring. He'd be shit at poker.

"Sure, go ahead. Good luck trying to get your show off the ground without any of the original cast. That's worked really well in the past."

A series of scuffled sounds came next, until a door slammed and Alicia took over, losing any pretence of calm. "You'd seriously give up this role for her? We know how much you've invested in this."

"Doesn't matter. She's more important to me." It didn't matter what Mike or Alicia thought. They weren't changing my mind.

———

The house was too empty without Liv, and still, I felt surrounded by her. The memory of her curled up on the couch or barefoot in the kitchen comfortable and familiar. The bright sound of her laughter echoing in every room.

I could still hear what she'd said about Lucas. It was nagging at me, making me question myself. Worst of all, it was giving me hope. Hope that Lucas and I could fix whatever had broken between us.

I set off in the direction of the house I remember seeing my brother at last time. When I got there, I found a Sold sign and an offensively large Hummer parked in the drive.

Disappointed, I kept walking, enjoying the fresh air and novelty of anonymity. A few houses down, I spied a For Sale sign with my brother's name listed. He really was keeping busy. I wondered if he really did enjoy what he was doing. I didn't know how to feel if the answer was yes.

The house itself was an eyesore. A looming mass of characterless black concrete that you couldn't look away from. Like someone had looked at a picture of a black box and thought: "I'd live there."

"If you're thinking of buying it, you're too late. The new owners just signed for it."

I turned at my brother's voice, and he tipped his head toward the house. "What do you think?"

It's the ugliest thing I've ever seen. "It's interesting."

"It's monstrous."

I laughed, raw and real, the tension cracking just enough to be honest. "Thank god. I thought it was just me."

"I tried to tell them, but I'm just the help. Too young to know anything."

"Idiots."

Lucas shook his head in amusement, his eyes still trained on the house.

This was my opportunity. "Hey, you, uh, want to grab a beer? If you're free." I expected him to brush me off. It really shouldn't be this hard to talk to my own brother, but here we were.

"Only if it's not that watered-down stuff you like."

The relief was instantaneous. "Nah, man. I finally upgraded to that fancy swill you're always posting about." It was a small thing that felt huge, to admit that. Another brick removed, another branch extended.

"Lead the way," he said, and I felt the beginnings of hope stir in my chest.

———

Everything between us felt tentative. As Lucas followed me into the house, neither of us said much, and the familiar urge to just give up, forget it and save myself the hurt, bubbled beneath the surface.

I pushed it away. I wanted to do this.

When I opened the bar fridge and found what I was after, I let out a sigh of relief. Lucas was sitting in the living room, back a little too straight to be comfortable. I wondered if it was out of habit or if he couldn't relax.

I knew the feeling.

The tops clinked against the counter, highlighting just how quiet it was. I kept cycling through different openers and then chickening out. Everything was either too casual or too serious.

In the end, I said nothing, walking back and holding the beer out to him before sitting down.

"Thanks. I probably shouldn't have too many of these. Not all of us can get to the gym as much as you do," he said, taking the bottle from me and settling back on the couch.

"Don't you haul furniture around for your houses?" Honestly, I had no idea what he did. What the hell did I know about real estate?

"Smoke and mirrors, dude. Half the beds are just tables with quilts thrown over them."

"No shit?"

"Staging tricks." He shrugged. We were talking without talking, but it was something. A start.

Lucas looked around. "No Baxter?"

I had the good sense to look guilty, even if I didn't feel it. "No. Not this time."

"And no Liv this time?"

"No. We're, uh, we had a fight."

His response was genuine. "I'm sorry to hear that."

"Thanks. Sorry for being a dick about all that 'friend' stuff last time. I may have completely fucked it up, but you were right, we were seeing each other."

"I kind of guessed. I knew something more was going on when she cornered me at the party."

"She cornered you?"

"Oh yeah, read me the riot act and everything. You didn't know?"

"No," I said, surprised. Liv hadn't mentioned anything.

"Yeah. Told me to get my head out of my ass. Said you missed me and that I should talk to you about it. Made me feel like an asshole."

I drank instead of responding, not sure what to say. This might be the longest we'd gone without fighting in years, and I wanted to keep it that way.

I could see the tension in the lines of Lucas' shoulders, his grip on the bottle. My body kept wanting to twitch, expend the energy somehow. I didn't have the first clue about how to have this conversation. So I stared at the floor instead. I'd never found wood grain patterns so interesting before, but now I couldn't look away from it.

When it finally got to be too much, I dove into the deep end. Anything was better than this. One deep breath, and then: "What happened to us, man?"

I hadn't realized it was possible for Lucas to sit any straighter.

He spoke quietly, but I could still hear the pain. "You

tell me. You're the one who moved to the other side of the country. Couldn't get away fast enough."

It would be so easy to bite back. I wanted to, dammit. But that wasn't why I'd sought him out, and getting angry at him now would derail everything.

I dug deep. He'd been honest. I owed him the same. "I needed to get away from them, feel like I was my own person. I didn't think we'd stop talking."

Lucas said nothing.

"It wasn't ever about you." I added.

"Hard to not feel like it when you never had time for me."

"Work was crazy, you know."

"I don't, actually."

"Sorry. I thought you were happier. I mean, look at you now, taking over the family business. You guys are … close. I didn't fit in."

"Are you serious? You're their favorite."

"Bullshit."

"I'm serious. You think I wanted to get into real estate? It's the only way I could get Dad to even talk to me."

"But you're all …" I waved a hand around. "Buddy-buddy with him now."

"You think that's real? He's the same as he ever was, but at least he's stopped comparing me to you."

I mentally facepalmed. This whole time, I'd hated the way my parents had lauded Lucas' choices above my own, when the whole time, they'd been playing the same game with both of us.

And if I'd made the effort sooner, I would have known that.

The words came before I could stop them. "I've missed you. When we stopped talking, it felt like I lost the only person who loved me. I thought it was us against them, you know? Then you stopped texting me back, and then I heard you'd started working for Dad, and ... it felt like you were choosing them over me."

Lucas shook his head slowly. "I was alone after you left. And angry. Really angry." He picked at the label on the beer. "You left me alone with them, and I hated you for it. It was already hard enough dealing with them, but at least there was someone else who understood. But then you disappeared. Took off to the other side of the country at the first chance you got. What else was I supposed to do? Dad always comparing me to you—*at least Wesley knows what he wants in life. Why can't you be more ambitious, like your brother?*"

"You could have called."

"You could have stayed."

"No, I couldn't." Even though it had been a difficult decision, I would never regret choosing to accept the role of Ares. "I didn't want to leave you. You have to know that. But I couldn't stay there. I needed something of my own. I needed to get them out of my head."

"I know."

"I'm sorry."

Lucas looked away, his jaw working. I wanted to reach out to him, but everything still felt tentative between us. Eventually, he nodded. "I'm sorry, too. I get why you needed to leave. I just wish you'd taken me with you."

Taking a chance, I leaned over and hugged him, relieved when he returned it.

———

Now that I was really looking, I could see how tired Lucas was, how hard he must be working himself. But I could also still see the kid underneath, the glint in his eyes he always got before suggesting something that usually got me in trouble.

"What you said before, about Liv telling you to talk to me. Why didn't you?"

"I was still mad at you. You're here for all of two seconds, and it's all Mom and Dad could talk about. You swoop in, take Baxter, disappear, act like a dick about the party, and then I'm the one getting told off?" He rubbed his jaw. "Can I tell you something?"

"Go for it."

"I made you do that video because I knew how much it would annoy you. I could have paid someone to do it, but I wanted to get back at you for leaving."

"It worked."

"I'm sorry. It was a dick move."

"Yeah, but I get why you did it." I reached over and gripped his shoulder. "I don't want to fight anymore."

"Me either. I get enough of that from Dad. It'd be nice to have someone to vent to again."

"What about your friends? Or girlfriend?"

"No girlfriend right now." He paused. "Or boyfriend."

My heart squeezed at this new information, and the trust Lucas was showing me by sharing it. "Handsome guy like you? They're missing out."

I saw the relief on his face.

"And friends?" I asked.

He shrugged. "A few, but you know what it's like here. Hard to know who your real friends are. Most of them are okay to hang with, but I don't know that I can trust them with my secrets, you know?"

"I do." Man, did I know.

I placed my empty bottle next to his and asked if he wanted another, but he shook his head. To my amazement, he didn't immediately take off, instead reaching up to unbutton his collar and stretch his neck. When he relaxed back into the cushions, he finally looked like the Lucas I remembered. The nostalgia of it took me a moment to process.

"You know, Dad's been talking about taking a break. Now that I'm running things, they're gonna travel."

"Oh?" I said, not putting in the effort to hide my disinterest. I honestly had no idea why he was telling me.

"Yep. They'll be gone six months to a year, at least."

I still wasn't sure why he thought I'd want to know. "Guess that'll be nice for you."

"Dude," he said, finally annoyed that I wasn't following along. "I'm trying to tell you that Bax will need a place to stay. Jesus, were you always this slow, or has your celebrity status killed all your brain cells?" He was exasperated, but smiling, and I couldn't help but return it.

"For shit's sake, Lucas, you could have just said that. I'm not a mind reader."

"No, just a dumbass."

"Cool it, punk. I'm still older than you, and I work out now. I could definitely kick your ass if I needed to."

He barked out a laugh. "Sure."

I felt lighter than I had in years. There was more to say, but I knew we had time to work through it all. That we'd be okay. It might take a while to get back to where we were, but I finally believed it was possible. I might be jumping the gun, but I felt like I had my brother back, and that meant more to me than almost anything.

He shifted, draping a foot over one knee and tapping it to a silent beat. I felt a smile tugging at my lips. He only ever did that when he was gearing up to badger me about something.

"So," he slowly drawled. "Finally got yourself a girl, and you're already fucking it up. Gotta say, that might be a record. I'd be happy to help you out with some advice."

The tone was so familiar, sarcastic yet friendly, that I acted on instinct, punching him none too gently in the shoulder. "You dick."

He laughed even as he rubbed at his arm. "Just stating facts, brother."

I felt another knot loosen within me. Man, it was good to have this back again.

Lucas continued, "Whatever it is, I'm sure you'll be fine. From what I saw at the party, she's as gone for you as you are for her. I can't say I've had that yet, and I know you and I are both some kind of messed up from Mom and Dad."

I snorted in agreement.

"But you've never been one to shy away when you really want something. You're all heart, you know? All heart and no brains."

This time when I went to hit him, he dodged it.

40

LIV

Fact or Fiction? Olivia Davis spotted with ex (?) Bryson Green, fueling rumors of a reunion, laying doubt on fan theories that she and co-star Wesley Owens are secretly dating.

MIKE AND ALICIA looked uncharactcristically strained as I stood in their office. Mike's face was ashen, his sideburns dark with sweat. And Alicia was massaging circles into her temple.

Any other day, I would have taken pity on them, but I'd come here with something to say, and no matter how stressed they looked, I refused to leave until I'd said it.

"Meira is a huge part of the reason *The Guild* has been so popular, and it's a mistake to write her out of the spin-off. If you won't reconsider, then I'll have to rethink my commitment to the final season."

Mike started laughing, shocking me. He sounded out of

breath, and not to be mean about it, but a little hysterical. "Ridiculous," he finally said when he'd stopped. "Did you and Wesley plan this?"

"What? No." What did this have to do with Wes?

Mike and Alicia shared a glance that, in turn, caused me to look to Sym for a translation. A small twitch in their lips indicated they knew as little as I did. What was Mike talking about?

"Wesley quit the show yesterday. After he showed us this," Alicia said, holding up a tablet.

But I was stuck on what she'd said. I couldn't believe it. Wes quit the show?

"He told us that you mattered more to him."

Sym took the tablet from Alicia, reviewing it silently. Their brows raised, and they looked straight at me, impressed. I huffed with impatience, ready to ask for someone to spell it out for me, when Sym passed the tablet over.

On the screen was a petition. My eyes narrowed in on a photo of me in costume as Meira. It was a shot from the last season. I stood at the edge of a lake, hands outstretched, bright white tendrils of magic igniting outward, emanating from the tips of my fingers.

I looked at the image for a long moment before I read the heading. *Save Meres! Petition for Olivia Davis to be series regular on* The Twelve. Immediately, I scrolled down to read further.

After a year of teasing us with a show that would finally dive deeper into the lives of TV's most popular couple, Meres, from The Guild, *details now show that the planned spin-off,* The Twelve, *will only focus on Ares, with barely a mention of Meira at all. As the only lead female character on the show, Meira has been a huge inspiration for me. She has incredible power, but she still gets scared, still finds ways to help people without using magic, and is the true heart of the entire show. If the network really thinks what we want is another show about a reformed villain going on adventures when we've been telling them that we want* more Meira, *they are dumber than I thought. I like Meira and Ares together, don't get me wrong, but if I had to choose one of them, it would be the badass witch,* not *the cocky war god.*

Sign if you agree! If you love Meira as much as I do, please *retweet and share. Help save Meres!*

"Look at the number of signatures it has," Sym said gently.

I scrolled back up. Felt my heart skip. Almost 600,000 people. And counting. On a bad day, *The Guild's* viewership was only a few hundred thousand more than that. This was amazing.

Wes had sent them this?

That sly, sexy sweetheart.

"He's being childish." Mike, it seemed, was done with formalities. "Maybe you can convince your boyfriend that he's making a huge mistake."

Sym studied the numbers. "He is right, though. Olivia's value on the show outweighs his own, no matter what you or the network want to believe."

He visibly shifted. I could tell he wanted to argue, but he held back. Maybe in deference to Sym? Having them in my corner was working out better than I'd expected.

They placed the tablet back on the desk, calm but authoritative. "Do you really want to have to explain why you dropped the only lead female character from the show? Are you prepared to face that backlash after the network so publicly promised to raise the profile of female voices in its media? Because this won't look favorably on either of you. I'll make sure of that."

"It's out of our hands, the network —"

"Oh? You mean William?" Sym asked, referring to the network president. "I've already spoken with him about this, and he was as disappointed as I am that you would jeopardize the show's success by continuing without its leading actress."

For a moment, neither Mike nor Alicia said anything, and I knew if I wanted to speak, now was the time. Be brave. Raise hell.

"I'll consider signing back on to the show with two conditions. One, the role is co-lead with Wes. Same screen time, same pay. Two, I want a guaranteed director spot every season."

Alicia opened her mouth, looking like she wanted to object, but Sym ever so casually added, "William has been very supportive of encouraging new talent. Did I tell you he was one of my biggest financiers when I started?"

Silently, Mike stood, his movements slow and defeated. He cracked the door and called out for someone, then returned. "Let's get this over with. But I want your promise that once this is signed, these theatrics are over."

I shared a smile with Sym. "Give me this, and I promise I won't ask for anything else."

Alicia sighed. "And I don't suppose we could ask you to keep your relationship a secret in the meantime."

My smile widened. "Not a chance."

———

Sym tipped the attendant for the room service before pushing the trolley over to the table in front of the window. They'd lit up when I'd asked for a hot chocolate with extra marshmallows. Sym immediately declared they'd have the same, plus a serving of pastries. If I hadn't already decided to hire them, that would have cemented my decision.

A quick glance at my phone showed we had ten minutes before Jen arrived. Sym reached over the table to pat my wrist, offering a smile before they lifted their cup to their lips. "Oh," they said, pleased. "That's good. Just the way I like it."

The differences between Sym and Jen were small but glaring. Both were strong people, but Sym's strength felt lived in. Maybe it was because they were older, or maybe they felt they had less to prove. I couldn't tell. There was also a much more welcoming quality about them, not as readily defensive as Jen always was.

I understood why Jen felt the need to have her guard up, the need to fight for space in rooms where she wasn't being respected. It was why I had appreciated having her on my side. But now I needed something new.

It shouldn't have had to end this way.

Holding my cup in both hands, I watched as the marshmallows bobbed and bubbled, a white cloud expanding over the rich drink as they melted. The sight and the smell comforted me, even as I could feel my nerves rising.

I wasn't having regrets, but I wasn't kidding myself. Telling Jen would be hard.

Sym continued to surprise me. When I'd thanked them for taking time out of their day to be here, they'd said, "If you ever want for something, you tell me. I'll make it my personal mission to sort it out. If there's anything I want from you, we'll sit down and discuss it like adults. I might be your manager, but this is still *your* career."

Despite not knowing Sym very long, I trusted them. My gut told me that this was the right decision. Jen had convinced me that I couldn't trust my instincts, but I finally realized she'd been wrong. How could I not follow my gut when, the last time I'd listened to it, I'd kissed Wes? I figured it knew what it was talking about.

After that, I'd made two things clear. I wanted to be considered for the show she was producing and that Wes and I were non-negotiable.

"If you have a problem with our relationship or you can't help us make this work, I won't hesitate to find new representation. If it's a choice between Wes and you, or between Wes and anyone, it will be him, every time."

Telling them had scared me. Who was I to make that kind of demand? But Sym had taken it in stride, looking delighted. "I'm going to like working with you."

With me. I liked the sound of that.

Jen's knock rang throughout the room, and my pulse jumped. Sym's tone was gentle. "Breathe. It's going to be okay."

When Sym swung the door open, Jen's mouth flapped a few times, then slammed shut, her eyes cutting across the room to me. I'd never seen her this flustered.

"Olivia, what's going on?"

Sym shut the door, closing all three of us in the small suite.

I stood. Straightened my shoulders. "Jen, you're fired."

Jen's voice was dark. "Cut the crap, Liv. And why is Sym here?" She turned to face Sym. "What false promises did you sell her, huh? Or did you convince her to throw away her career for your pet project?"

I couldn't see Sym's face, but their voice was smooth

like honey when they responded. "The choice was entirely Olivia's, although I'm grateful she felt me worthy to represent her."

I bit my lip to stifle a smile. It was a shame Wes wasn't here right now. He would absolutely love this.

Ignoring Sym, Jen redirected her attention to me. I couldn't help but admire her outfit, as per usual. Red leopard print silk skirt layered under a shorter block red dress, paired with black ankle boots. Her hair was barrel curled, not a strand out of place.

"So that's it? After all I've done for you?"

"I'm sorry," and I really was. I took a stabilizing breath. I could do this. I'd practiced, "but I think it's better for both of us if we move on."

"Unbelievable." She tilted her head up, blinking at the ceiling, and I realized that I had genuinely hurt her. My mouth went dry, not having anticipated this as an outcome.

Sym remained where they stood, watching. I put myself in Jen's place, being let go while a rival watched. I'd wanted Sym's strength, but now I realized I'd hoped to make Jen feel a little of what I had when Bryson had shown up.

My stomach turned. This wasn't me.

"Sym, could you wait outside?"

They nodded. "Of course."

Once the door clicked closed, Jen's gaze returned to me, her voice steady. "You've really come into your own, Olivia. But it wasn't a solitary effort. No one succeeds on their own, not in Hollywood. Not anywhere. I've been just as crucial to your success as you have. Do you really want to burn this bridge? Because that isn't something you can come back from, and I'm not sure you have many left."

I stood my ground. I wouldn't let her pressure me. "I appreciate what you're saying, and I'm grateful for everything you've done for me. But I've told you repeatedly what I want for my career, and if you aren't going to support me in that, you can, respectfully, shove it."

"That's very disappointing to hear." She smirked then, smug and ugly. "You wouldn't be where you are if it wasn't for me. I hope you remember that. If I've been hard on you, it's because I believed you could do better than this. I won't let you go."

"Let me? That isn't a choice you get to make, Jen. For once, this is something you don't have any say in."

Jen was fighting for the same things I was, to find a place in an industry that thrived on working against you. But understanding her didn't mean I wanted to be a rung on the ladder she used to get where she was going.

I had my own places to be.

"I clearly underestimated your loyalties," Jen said. "Your mother would be so disappointed."

That was it. "Do you ever shut up?" I said, feeling the zing of adrenaline racing in my blood. Forget what I said earlier. This was what Wes would kill to witness. "I know what you're trying to do, and I don't want to hear it.

"I've looked up to you since we met, and you've taught me a lot. But I've grown up now. I don't need a manager to make every decision for me anymore. I won't always make perfect choices, but at least the mistakes I make will be my own. I want to own them, grow from them, discover who I am. I want to go after what I really want, and if I fail, then at least I'll know I've tried."

"How tragically romantic. You already blew up your reputation after that stunt with Bryson. If you go ahead with Wesley, you're going to sink it."

"I'm smart. Resourceful. I'll figure it out." I ripped the door open so quickly it bounced against the wall with a bang. Adrenaline zinged through me. I'd never felt more like my mother. "Now get out."

"Actors," she muttered with an eye roll.

There was an audible whoosh as the door closed behind her. I sank against it with a smile, my heart pounding under my hand.

I was still smiling when Sym re-entered the room, gracefully returning to her drink as if nothing had happened. "How did it go?"

"That," I said, joining them, "was the second-best moment of today."

"Only second?" They teased knowingly. I laughed into my hot chocolate. "I guess we better finish getting you ready for number one!"

A whole world of opportunities now felt in my reach, like Charlie holding the golden ticket. The future felt exciting. I couldn't wait to work with Sym and finally get my chance to see where directing could take me.

I couldn't be happier.

I was irrevocably, unerringly in love with Wes. Consumed. Besotted. Bewildered.

And ready to shout it out to the entire world.

———

41

LIV

A vision in pink! The Guild's *Olivia Davis stuns in Dior,* choosing to accessorize the gorgeous two-piece ensemble with fan-made jewelry.

"HI, *sweetie, it's Mom. I was thinking about what you said earlier, about being worried you wouldn't be good enough. I just need you to know that no matter what happens with this part, you will always be good enough. You're amazing. I know this is all so new and scary, but remember that being strong can be as simple as following your heart. I know people say gut rather than heart these days, but I don't. It was my heart that lead me to your father, and to you, and you're my two favorite people in the world. There's no one I know with more heart than you. Trust it and continue to be amazing. I love you."*

"I love you, too," I whispered, holding her words close to my heart.

I stepped out of the car and was immediately corralled into place on the red carpet by a series of assistants. I'd arrived in the thick of things, not quite early, not quite late, and so I was now behind at least two dozen other attendees, staggered at even distances until we reached an apex of cameras and interviewers.

There was noise everywhere. A steady stream of shouts came from both the crowd and the photographers. The buzz of instructions passed from organizers to assistants. Occasionally, I would catch the eye of someone I knew, and we'd share a wordless wave. So far, no Wes. I was trying not to look like I was searching for him, but considering I couldn't think of anything else, I probably wasn't hiding it well.

I followed the directions I was given, feeling far more experienced than the first time I'd attended a night like this.

A few interviewers called me over, and I answered the usual questions: who I was wearing, how excited I was about tonight, what I was most looking forward to.

Eventually, I was out in front of the bulk of the cameras, lights burning into my eyes, trying to look in the right direction as a dozen different photographers all called out to me.

There was still no sign of Wes.

It wasn't until I had finally posed and smiled, then turned and posed again, that I was ushered inside. I took a deep breath. It didn't help; my chest felt tight and my legs felt shaky.

Here went nothing.

Even in the darkened room, there was movement everywhere. A large, elevated platform shone brightly in the center, the space around it divided between a public mosh pit behind it and the attendant tables in front. I was handed off to yet another assistant who was busy talking into an earpiece as they guided me to my table.

It was only then that I spotted him, head and shoulders above the person next to him, looking breathtaking in a silver suit. It shimmered under the overhead lights, Polaris guiding me back home. More details emerged as I got closer. The clean cut of his jaw, so smooth I could already imagine how it would feel against my cheek. He'd had a haircut recently, dark waves brushing his ears instead of his chin. I had to clench my fist to stop myself from immediately running my hand through them when I reached the table.

My heart stopped when our eyes met, then restarted in earnest. His smile was small, private. There was no denying the love in his eyes. The urge to kiss him was overwhelming.

The assistant disappeared as Wes stood and helped me into the seat next to him. There was so much I wanted to say to him, I barely knew where to start. I couldn't stop looking at him. I never wanted to stop. He seemed to have the same problem.

"Hi," he said quietly.

"Hi." I was beaming. I leaned in, kissing his cheek in a greeting, and used the opportunity to speak softly to him. "How do you get sexier every time I see you?"

A shiver ran through me when his eyes darkened. "I don't know about that. All I can see is the most incredible woman I've ever met."

I flushed from head to toe. It was killing me not to touch him.

Our table filled up, killing any further conversation and kick-starting the ceremony.

I laughed when everyone else did, smiled when the cameras zeroed in on us, nibbled and sipped as the night went on, but if you'd asked me who the host was or who sat at our table, I couldn't tell you.

All I could see was Wes.

There was no way to talk, not while surrounded by roving cameras and hundreds of other guests. But his warmth at my side and the brush of his arm against mine were familiar and comforting. I'd survived many an interview this way, and knowing I hadn't lost it, hadn't lost him, kicked my heart into overdrive.

———

Sometime after the halfway mark, we were tapped on the shoulders and asked to come backstage to prepare for presenting an award. Another set of hands checked our outfits and hair, someone dusted our faces with powder to reduce shine from the overhead lights, and yet another ran us through the procedure—walk to the neon lectern, say our lines, read the envelope.

We'd been pulled up early. There were at least two awards to hand out before we were needed onstage, including Best Kiss, which we were nominated for.

Wes and I traded secret glances as the community of talent escorts and volunteers worked around us, our attention never straying from each other. I wondered if they could guess what it meant. No doubt someone did. Good. Let them. If I let myself think about how long it had taken me to realize what Wes meant to me, I'd kick myself. But that was why I was determined to not let tonight end without making it clear to Wes that my world orbited around him.

Wes had become everything to me. My favorite thing to do was curl myself around him, his voice soft in my ears, warmth soaking into my skin, his heartbeat steady under my hand. As my friend, he'd become my anchor. My shield.

A log fire and a fuzzy sweater and a spiked hot chocolate. As my lover, he'd become heat and home and a dizzying sweetness that I was already addicted to.

I quickly looked for somewhere we might find some privacy, grabbing his hand before anyone could stop us and tugging him around a corner to a dead end. We weren't far away, and anyone could walk in on us, but it was the best we were going to get, and I couldn't wait another second.

As soon as we were out of view, I crushed my body against his and kissed him.

He wrapped his arms around me instantly, his body heat apparent through his clothes, and the full force of him hit me all at once. His lips against mine, the smell of cologne, hairspray, and a hint of aftershave. The rumble of my heartbeat, heavy against my ribs, beating for him alone.

Our kiss ended, but we stayed wrapped up in each other, foreheads touching, our breathing synced.

"I love you," I whispered, barely audible over the noise that was still going on around us, but I knew he heard it. "So much. I don't ever want you to question how I feel about you. You are the one thing I am absolutely certain of."

He pulled back, looking deeply into my eyes. He brought both hands up, his palms warm against my cheeks, a grounding point. I'd missed this, but I hadn't realized until now how much I'd needed to feel it again.

My eyes fluttered closed at the touch, my hands coming up to hold his in place.

The sound of the crowd faded away. The chaos dimmed, a white noise that I ignored in favor of the feel of Wes' finger stroking the outer curve of my ear. My entire body tingled.

His voice was low. "I've done nothing but love you for

six years. I don't plan to do anything else for the rest of my life. You're the only person I want, and no matter what happens, I'll love you with everything I have."

Tears teased the corners of my eyes when I opened them again.

He continued, "I've spent my whole life keeping myself at a distance from anyone who could hurt me. It's why I never told you how I felt. And you were right; I would have kept that secret if you hadn't kissed me. I didn't want to lose you, but I'm glad that you forced me to stop hiding because it's the best thing that has ever happened to me. You helped me see how far I'd been pushing everyone, and I'm working on letting people in again. I'm sorry for pushing you about Jen. I never want you to think that you aren't capable of making your own choices. You are. You're better at it than I am. I only ever want what's best for you, even if that means we can't—"

"Wes," I cut him off. "I'm not going anywhere, and I'm not letting you go anywhere either." My grip was tight on his wrists; our eyes were locked on each other. "I've already had enough heartbreak for one lifetime. So you'll just have to get used to this being real—and forever—because there will never be anyone else for me. It's only you."

He leaned down as I reached up, our lips finding each other easily. This was where I wanted to be. In his arms, his mouth devouring mine, my every sense filled by him. It was easy to lose time, and I was already wondering how soon we could get out of here and enjoy this for real.

A throat cleared behind us, and I jumped, pulling away from Wes but keeping my hands on him. If it was possible, I'd never let go of him again. Wes looked worried that we'd been caught, but I reached up, wiping my lipstick off his bottom lip, not caring that anyone could see.

"We need you onstage. They're about to announce the BK winners, and it's you." Without waiting, the guy headed for the stage, and Wes started to follow.

"Hey." I pulled at Wes' sleeve, and he stopped, concerned.

The usher looked frantic. I likely had about ten seconds before he dragged us out there or fainted. We didn't have time for this, but I didn't care. "How do you feel about public declarations?"

"What? Liv, we have to go."

"Wes. Look at me."

He did. And I watched the realization occur in real time. He shook his head. "What about the show? Jen? I can't be the reason you do this."

"I fired Jen. And I signed the contract for the spin-off this morning." Wes' eyebrows shot up, but there wasn't time to explain. Right now, I was ready to take a leap, and I needed to know he was with me.

"I'll fill you in later," I said, and his surprise cleared with a smile. "I don't want to be afraid anymore. Whatever happens from here, I want you to know that you're worth the risk. I love you, and in about sixty seconds, 4.2 million people are going to know that."

Dimly, I could hear the presenter announce our names. Cheers erupted, but I kept my focus on Wes.

"Guys," the usher urged, "you need to go. Now."

We'd run out of time. The usher pushed us toward the stage. I was terrified I wouldn't get an answer from Wes. I wanted this more than anything, but I wouldn't do it without him.

Wes stepped out first, stage lights a blinding white. Music played. The crowd clapped. My pulse was racing.

Then, as we walked toward the podium, Wes brushed his hand against mine and nodded.

My heart tumbled and skipped in my chest, leaping over itself at the knowledge of what I—*we*—were about to do. And then I caught Wes' smile and calmed. This was perfect, and right, and no matter what happened next, we had each other. That was all I cared about.

And suddenly, I couldn't get the words out fast enough.

"We can't thank you enough for this. We both love Meira and Ares and their journey together. We can't wait to show you what's in store for them next.

"There's something bugging me, though," I said, no longer following the script on the teleprompter and knowing we now had very little time before the music would play. We'd have to make this good.

"Oh? What's that?" Wes asked, following my lead because he was amazing like that.

"I don't know that it was our very best kiss. I think we could do better."

And then, like the sun exploding over the horizon, his smile took over his face, lighting him up. Without pausing, he cupped my face in both hands. "You're damn right we can."

Our lips met to the sound of excited screaming. This was it. My future, my happiness. Never had a decision been easier.

Choosing Wes wasn't a risk, it was a promise.

EPILOGUE
WES

Six Months Later

"HARDER."

"Yeah?"

"Yeah. I can take it."

"All right," Liv said, with a glint of mischief in her eyes. Damn, that look always did me in. "Lauren Bacall."

It took me ten seconds to stop laughing. "What?"

"You said harder, so go. Six degrees to Kevin Bacon from Lauren Bacall."

"Geez, okay." I hummed, pretending to gaze out the window as I inched my hand slowly toward my phone. Liv lunged forward to grab it first, pulling it out of my reach. "No phones, cheater."

I laughed, wanting nothing more than to kiss the look off her face. "Fine! But give me a minute." I already knew the answer, but I wanted to bask in her loveliness for another minute, staring into her big, beautiful eyes and sending out my gratitude to whatever cosmic forces had let me get so lucky. "Lauren Bacall was in *The Mirror Has Two Faces* with Jeff Bridges. Jeff was in—hey, who would the modern equivalent of this be? Kevin's in his sixties now. The Rock? He's in everything."

Above her bright smile, Liv's eyes narrowed. "Stop stalling."

I couldn't wipe the smile off my face. "Shows what you know. Jeff was in *RIPD* with Kevin Bacon. Next."

"Damn, I thought that would be harder."

I reached out, running a thumb over her cheek. "How are you feeling about tomorrow?"

Liv turned into my palm, pressing a kiss into the skin. "Okay. It's never an easy day, but I'll have you with me. As long as you don't kill us on the drive up."

I laughed. "I'll protect you. I am your knight, after all."

The game forgotten, I crawled over to her, following as she lay back on the couch, hair fanning out on the cushions in a halo.

"It's your turn. You have to pick an actor," Liv said.

I felt her fingers slip under my sweater. Heat blazed in my veins at her touch like it always did.

Resting on my elbows, I hovered above her. "I have a different game in mind."

"Like what?" She asked, breathless.

"Cluedo," I joked, kissing the corner of her mouth.

This house used to be nothing more than a hotel, a temporary stop before I went home. But now I knew home was where Liv was, and I'd make damn well sure to be right by her side.

Liv huffed a half laugh, half sigh. A perfect sound. "I am not playing that with you anymore."

"Because you lose," I murmured. Her neck was bare,

and I ducked my head to press a series of kisses along the skin.

"No, it's because you cheat." Liv's voice was a whisper.

"Maybe I'm lucky like that."

"Yeah, you feeling lucky right now?"

More than lucky. I'd somehow managed to score the love of my life, who not only wanted me back, but had made my entire life better by being in it.

"A little," I said, smiling against her skin before moving the strap of her shirt out of the way so I could kiss lower.

Her hand grazed my cock where it was hard against her thigh. "Feels like more than a little."

"Gonna stroke my ego a bit more or are you going to kiss me?" I said, not waiting as I claimed her lips, parting them and licking into her mouth. Her soft sighs were candy on my tongue, sweet and addictive.

I chased her mouth when she tried to pull away, thumbing the underside of her breast under her shirt and loving the way she arched into me, asking for more.

Eventually, she remembered she'd been trying to say something. Her hand pushed my shoulder, and I had a hard time not diving down for more, her lips red and glistening.

"Please tell me you don't call your dick your ego."

The teasing look morphed into pleasure when I slid a thigh between her legs, giving her just enough friction to tease. "Just a turn of phrase, doll."

Liv hooked a leg over my hip, increasing the pressure. My own body bore down, needing her as much as she needed me.

"Have I told you how amazing you are?" I stroked her cheek, reveling in the softness, memorizing the feeling.

"You've mentioned it once or twice. But maybe tell me again."

"You are incredible." She accepted my kiss eagerly.
"Talented." She tasted of chocolate. "Beautiful."

"You're too much, you know that?"

"Do you want me to stop?"

"Don't you dare."

————

Siri interrupted the music coming from the radio to confirm
the next turn, and I followed the instruction, taking a left
onto the suburban street. Yellowing trees lined the road,
houses sparsely separated by large blocks, their front yards
clean and cared for. Small signs of family life clung to the
edges: a basketball hoop over the garage, kids' bicycles, a
swing set.

Liv had gone quiet in the passenger seat, curled
toward me, her hand in mine. I wanted to offer her
something more, to say something that might help, but I
wasn't sure what the right words would be, and when I'd
asked, she'd told me that just being here was everything
she needed.

Finally, after a three-and-a-half-hour drive, I pulled into
the driveway of a two-story bungalow, parking behind Joe's
sedan. He had either been waiting by the door for us to
arrive or had impeccable hearing, because by the time I
turned the engine off, he was walking down the path
toward us.

I squeezed Liv's hand and felt her squeeze back, then
she slipped out the door, rushing to give her father a hug. I
hung back, giving them a moment alone, understanding the
importance of today.

By the time I exited the car, Joe was waiting for me. I
felt the scrutiny and did my best not to shy away from it.

My face remained calm, but inside, my gut was churning. I really wanted to make a good impression.

"Dad, this is Wes."

Joe didn't bother with a handshake, going straight in for a hug. I could count on one hand how many hugs I'd received from my own father in the last twenty-seven years, and here was Liv's dad, not even hesitating. Suddenly, my eyes were blurry. Shit.

A few blinks, and I'd reined them in, pulling back to clear the lump in my throat. "Good to meet you, sir."

"Sir?" He laughed. "It's Joe, son."

Sheepish, I nodded. "Uh, right. Of course, yeah. Joe."

"Come on, you can grab your things later. Lunch is getting cold." He ushered us inside.

I didn't know what to expect as I walked in—what was the norm on the anniversary of a death? Would they hide Rebekah's pictures or have them out in tribute? I had no idea how to talk about it, either. Liv hadn't ever shied away from talking about her mom, but the last thing I wanted to do was offend Joe.

I shouldn't have worried. Joe's was a perfectly normal home (or as normal as I could imagine a home to be considering how I'd grown up), and while there were photos of Rebekah around, there were also photos of other family members. Grandparents, siblings, cousins, and a whole lot of Olivia.

It was love, plain and simple, as obvious as when I'd been standing at Jackson's wedding. Unlike then, I didn't find myself resentful at the reminder of what my own parents hadn't given me. I was happy that Liv had grown up with parents who cared this much. It was what had made her the compassionate, strong woman she was today.

"Did you get lost?" Joe's voice snapped me out of my

thoughts, and I realized that I'd been standing in the hallway staring at the photos while Joe and Liv had moved into the kitchen.

"Sorry," I started, but he stopped me. "It's fine." His eyes traveled over the same photos I'd been admiring, a proud smile on his face.

Softly enough that Liv couldn't hear, he added, "I put the ring in a drawer for you. If you still want it."

That he was willing to trust me with something as precious as Rebekah's engagement ring was a huge honor. I swallowed back the emotion rising in my chest. "Thank you, Joe, that's …" I choked up. "Thank you.' I finished, finally.

He clapped me on the shoulder, his grip firm and his face serious. "Rebekah always thought you'd make a good match, and I haven't seen my daughter this happy since her mom passed. If they think you're all right, so do I. Just don't hurt her."

"I wouldn't dream of it."

He patted my shoulder twice. Damn, all that gardening gave him some strength. My shoulder ached a little. "Good," he said, then turned.

I followed him into the kitchen, joining Liv at the table.

Joe took a seat across from me. "Eat up, there's plenty."

And there was. A full roast with all the trimmings sat in the center of the table. Far more than we could eat in a single sitting. But more impressive than the spread was the thought that Joe had made it all himself. I could barely be trusted with a sandwich.

Liv pressed a kiss to my cheek when I told him this. "Maybe Dad can show you some tricks while we're here."

"I'd be happy to," Joe said. I felt completely unprepared for his easy acceptance. No, it was more than acceptance.

He had welcomed me into his home, without complaint, on a day that meant a lot to him and Liv. It was his eager offer, given without conditions or judgment, that hammered in the realization that he was a different kind of dad.

I reached for Liv's hand, and she seemed to understand what I was feeling. Affection swelled in my chest. Any time I thought I had reached the limits of my love for her, she found a new way to prove me wrong.

The food smelled incredible, and I dug in.

"Livie mentioned that you have a dog now."

I turned to Joe, nodding. "Temporarily. I'm looking after him while my parents are traveling. It's a bit of an adjustment for him, the apartment isn't as big as he's used to."

"And who is looking after him right now?"

"My younger brother, Lucas. He's staying with me while he looks for a place of his own."

"That's nice of you." I didn't mention that it had naturally worked out that way because I had been spending all of my time at Liv's.

We fell into easy conversation, Joe asking about the last season, which we were halfway through filming, and the spin-off, which was set to start as soon as we finished up on *The Guild*.

Our real-life relationship had done wonders for the press of *The Twelve*. Mike had even said he couldn't have planned it better himself, which definitely made me want to skewer him on the end of my prop staff, but at least he wasn't telling us we couldn't be together. Bare minimum, but okay.

The best part, in my opinion, was the charity that Liv was reaching out to via Sym. She'd toyed with the idea of starting a foundation, then decided that she would rather lend her help to one of the groups that had reached out to her and Joe during Rebekah's last months. It meant a lot to Liv, and I didn't have the words to describe how much seeing her happy meant to me.

————

Liv found me later, alone in her room, halfway between standing and pacing.

After lunch we'd visited Rebekah's grave. It had been difficult not to cry, knowing how much it had meant to Liv to return there. God, she was incredible.

I'd gone back and forth on whether this gift was a good idea and when the best time to give it would be. I'd packed it thinking that being here would help, only now I wasn't so sure.

"Everything okay?" Liv asked, shutting the door behind her.

I smiled but hoped my nerves weren't showing. Wrapping paper crackled under my fingers as I held the gift behind my back. Liv must have caught the sound, her eyes quickly shifting. "What are you hiding?"

I swallowed. *Please let her like this.*

Moving slowly, I held out a white box, roughly the size of a tablet, a gold ribbon tied in a picture-perfect bow on top. "I got you something."

"Wes," Liv whispered, and my chest tightened at the emotion in her voice. "You didn't need to do that."

"Of course I did."

Gently, she reached for the present, and I watched with bated breath. I'd taken a risk, one I'd hope didn't cross a line, but what else could I do? She meant so much to me, and if there was a way to make her happy, I'd do whatever it took. Give her anything.

My eyes didn't leave her face as she lifted the lid. "It's a digital frame with photo and music. I thought you might want to put your mom's voicemails on there with your photos of her."

Liv's eyes shined.

"Do you like it?"

A tear rolled down Liv's cheek. She didn't answer, just stepped forward and threw her arms around me, holding me tight enough that I felt the breath squeezed from my lungs.

"I love it," she said. "And I love you."

There was a second box packed carefully into my bag, one that I knew I'd give her one day. Maybe soon. It was inevitable. I'd get down on one knee, Liv would say yes, and I could spend the rest of my life adoring her.

Perfect.

THE END

THANK YOU!

I can't thank you enough for reading It Has To Be You! I hope you enjoyed reading it as much as I enjoyed writing it.

Want to share the love? Please consider leaving a review on Amazon, Goodreads, or even posting wherever you hang out online (BookTok, Bookstagram, Reddit). Comments and tags feed my romance reading soul.

I absolutely love to hear from my readers.

Dani x

ACKNOWLEDGMENTS

This story was inspired by family, love, and connection. It isn't always easy, and it isn't always where you expect to find it. But those moments, those bright spots in your life when you truly connect with someone, and you feel SEEN and LOVED… those are worth living for.

When I started writing this series, I hadn't actually planned this far ahead. I knew I wanted to tell Audrey's story (of a young divorcee who is struggling to reclaim her independence when finding herself single again), and while I was writing Love & Rum, I fell in love with Tiff (Audrey's BFF) and immediately knew I needed to write her happily ever after. (Ok, I just wanted to spend more time with her, so sue me).

As an author, I'm always on the look out for side characters who have the potential to be MC's (main characters), and even in the first draft of Love & Rum, I knew Wes and Liv had this potential. But it wasn't until a later draft that I started to ship them together, and made some changes to that first book (which were then continued in book two) that planted the seeds for this book and this story.

My dearest Wes. You have become so special to me over the course of three books, more so than I ever anticipated when

I first wrote you into existence. Your fears about trust and opening up have been my own, and I'm not sure whether to apologise for that or not, but know that I will forever cherish you, you dramatic little puppy dog.

I cried multiple times while writing this story. Liv's voicemails, and the story of her cafe chats with her mom, were inspired by my own mum. And that moment at the end of the book where Joe presents Olivia with a stolen spoon? Yeah, that happened. Thanks, Dad. Now I know where my early onset rebellion came from.

To my amazing editor, Beth, you took this book and spun GOLD. Working with you has been an amazing experience, and both I and this book are better for it. I think it helped knowing that we share all the same favourite movies (and Chrises!). I cannot wait to work with you again and again and again.

I also have to thank my good friend, Liia, who bravely shared with me her own story of losing her mom, and the effect it's had on her life. As an author herself, she has also spent many, many hours listening to me talk about this book, has read early drafts and offered help, and is just an all around fantastic person.

To my close family, extended family, best friends, online friends, imaginary friends, and future friends: the love I feel for you cannot be contained in words. I hope you know I'm always here for you.

And lastly, A HUGE THANKS to my lovely critique partners, early readers, reviewers, bookstagrammers, &

fellow romance lovers! Without you I would have no one to talk to about all the things I love about my books, my characters, or romance in general! Anytime I think I might give this up, you keep me going!!

ABOUT THE AUTHOR

Dani McLean is an emerging author of Contemporary Romance stories that feature kickass women who can't quite get their shit together, and the irresistible but confused men who fall in love with them.

Born in Melbourne, she now lives in Perth, Western Australia with two walk in robes and a linen closet that's full of wine.

Dani loves to read, write and travel (in her memories, these days). She loves Hallmark movies because they're unintentionally hilarious, she's been on enough terrible Tinder dates to fuel countless books; and when she isn't conducting unofficial wine tastings in her pyjamas, she's devouring all things romance.

instagram.com/danimcleanwrites

facebook.com/danimcleanfiction

twitter.com/dmc_lean

tiktok.com/danimcleanwrites

amazon.com/author/danimclean

goodreads.com/danimclean

bookbub.com/authors/dani-mclean

www.ingramcontent.com/pod-product-compliance
Lightning Source LLC
Chambersburg PA
CBHW030516120726
47904CB00005B/1493